THE AMBER ARROW
WULF'S SAGA
2

BOOKS by Tony Daniel

Wulf's Saga
The Dragon Hammer
The Amber Arrow
The Dasein Ring (forthcoming)

Guardian of Night
Superluminal
Metaplanetary
The Robot's Twilight Companion
Earthling
Warpath

Star Trek Original Series
Devil's Bargain
Savage Trade

The General Series (with David Drake)
The Heretic
The Savior

THE AMBER ARROW

WULF'S SAGA

2

TONY DANIEL

THE AMBER ARROW

Copyright © 2017 by Tony Daniel

A Baen Books Original

Baen Publishing Enterprises
P.O. Box 1403
Riverdale, NY 10471
www.baen.com

ISBN: 978-1-4814-8253-0

Cover art by Dan Dos Santos

Map by Randy Asplund

First printing, September 2017

Distributed by Simon & Schuster
1230 Avenue of the Americas
New York, NY 10020

Library of Congress Cataloging-in-Publication Data:

Printed in the United States of America

10 9 8 7 6 5 4 3 2 1

Another one for Cokie and Hans

THE AMBER ARROW
WULF'S SAGA
2

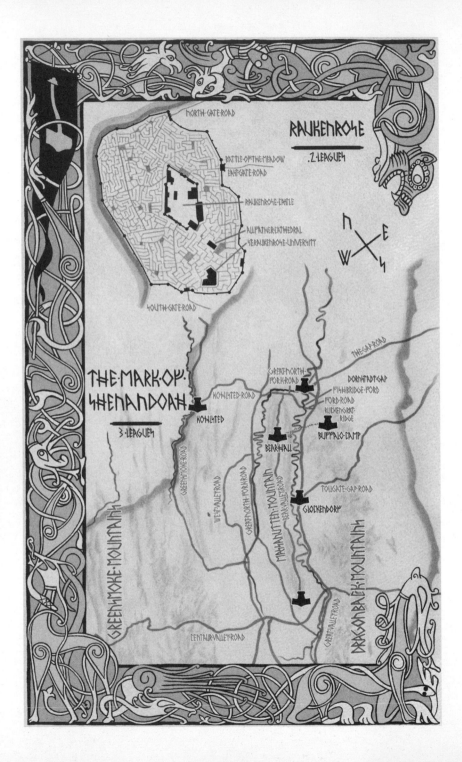

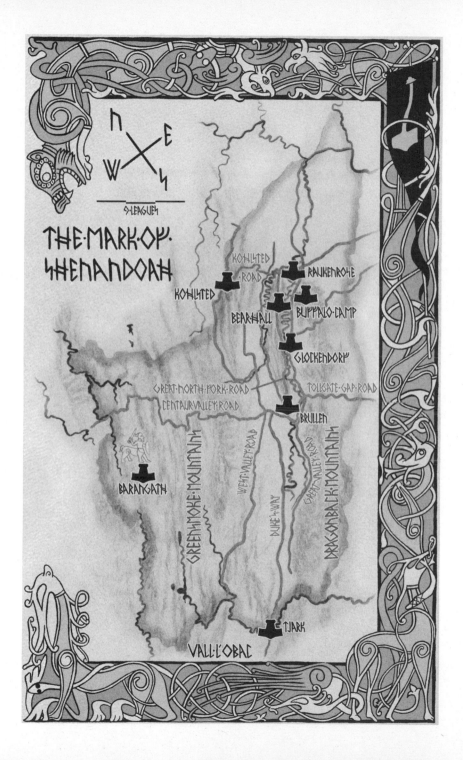

PART ONE

CHAPTER ONE:
THE ARCHER

Ursel Keiler was thinking about him again.

Lord Wulfgang von Dunstig.

Third son of Duke Otto and Duchess Malwin.

Wulf.

Her . . . what? Friend? Maybe not even that.

Acquaintance?

Obsession?

She hoped not. What she felt was real.

Wasn't it?

Ursel prided herself on being the sensible sort, the kind of person who didn't give in to impossible dreams. She'd known when she was young that she would never have the muscles to shoot an arrow three field-lengths. So she'd concentrated on accuracy.

Then just before she'd turned seventeen last year, she'd found she *did* have the strength. And, because of all her hard work, she also had the skill to hit a moving target at that distance.

But persistence could only take you so far in love.

It was either there or it wasn't.

On Wulf von Dunstig's side, it definitely wasn't.

Meanwhile, here she was out in the middle of the Shwartzwald Forest—a forest that was going to *belong to her* one day. She was on a task important to her father, the earl. Important to the entire Mark of Shenandoah if what she suspected was true.

But what was she doing?

Feeling like a lovesick idiot.

Picturing his blue eyes. Intense. That cowlick that wouldn't let his hair fall over them.

His arms. His torso. She'd seen him naked—at least from the waist up. He looked like a guy that had been forced to exercise a quarter-day every day since he was six-years-old was going to look. Wiry. Muscled.

And what was even more attractive, Wulf didn't even care what he looked like. The fact was that he really was more of a scholar than a warrior. He quoted the skalds from memory. He had carried her scarf into battle because the heroes from the sagas did things like that.

He was . . . exactly what she wanted.

And Ursel?

One kiss. That was all they had shared. Or would.

He'd made it clear Ursel wasn't going to be his choice.

Her foolish heart was the last thing she needed to be worrying about at the moment. But she couldn't help it. She'd felt this way for months. It was like she was carrying around a knife in the pit of her stomach. For a while the knife would float there. Then it would twist and stab her with another painful flash.

The pain was one third intense desire.

One third gloom.

One third stupid pointlessness.

I *have* to get over him, she told herself.

But doing it wasn't as easy as saying it. She hadn't seen Wulf for two months, curse it to cold hell. Hadn't seen him since her last visit to Raukenrose. And her feelings had gotten *stronger*, and everything had gotten *worse*.

It wasn't so bad when she was *with* him. Then she could see him with *her*, the beautiful immortal one. Saeunn. In those times, Ursel actually felt *more* at peace.

How could she compete with Lady Saeunn Amberstone, after all?

The yearning died down, and she felt silly for even having this . . . silly lovesickness—or whatever it was.

It was when she was *apart* from him that the knife plunged back in. It twisted inside her at the weirdest moments. Like now, when she might be about to kill a man.

The knife cutting into her soul.

Her heart.

Her destiny.

I'm not going to let that happen. You make your *own* destiny, Ursel thought. Like these idiots who are stalking me are making *theirs.*

Ursel had told everyone she was going hunting, and that's what she was doing—in a way. Strange and dangerous creatures had been reported from the far west woods. She was tracking them. Normally the earl, her father, would have dispatched his trappers to take care of a problem with wolves attacking livestock or a bobcat threatening children in a forest village.

Ursel had decided to act on the reports herself. She suspected that the strange creatures were *not* animals at all. She didn't want them killed, even though they had been feeding on farmers' livestock and making a nuisance of themselves.

They were dangerous. They had to be dealt with. But not destroyed.

So she had decided to find the creatures herself.

She'd been *very* close.

Then the creatures had caught wind of *men.* Ursel's pursuers. They scattered and fled.

Her plan was spoiled.

These men following her, whoever they were, had ruined it. And now she had to deal with whoever had decided following *her* trail was a good idea.

She was in a very bad mood.

Ursel reached for an arrow to nock to her bowstring. She didn't take her eyes from her man-quarry, but trusted her sense of touch to choose the right arrowhead. Her fingertips brushed the goose-feather fletching of an arrow in her quiver. One of the feather vanes had a small notch cut in it. Her fingers instantly reacted to this. The arrowhead was a bodkin.

Could punch through metal. Didn't stick, though.

Not what she wanted here.

She moved to the next arrow. It had smooth fletching.

Swallowtail arrowhead. All-around messenger of death.

Yes.

Her fingers chose this one. It was in between the bow guides in an eyeblink, nocked in another blink.

Her target was a man. She knew he was with a group of six or seven. They were quiet. Probably thought they were completely silent, but she'd spent her life listening to *this* forest. She knew when something didn't sound right.

They believed they were still following her. They were mistaken. She'd doubled back and crossed her own path, while they passed her by and kept going. They were following signs she'd left early in the day—before she'd realized there was someone in the deep forest tracking her.

Now she was stalking *them*.

Him, the leader.

She was sure the others were following one person. It was

what the sign on the ground and bushes told her. A broken twig here, a footprint scuff there. These told her that somebody was taking point position, and the others were following his lead.

They were walking along a game path she often used. She knew they'd stay on it if they could, since it was easier going. She'd trailed them for a watch or so, then taken a shortcut over a ridge and moved ahead of them to a spot where she knew the game trail would lead.

She'd waited for them to come to a clearing beneath a flinty outcrop. There she had both a totally unblocked line of sight on them, and cover for herself. The man moved into the clearing. Then a few eyeblinks later, his companions came from the forest. They were spaced about ten paces apart on either side of him.

Yes, six of them—which made seven including the lead man, her target.

The man was copper skinned, with a broad face and sharp features.

Young. Handsome, if she'd thought about it.

High cheekbones that made him look overly proud.

He was the leader, or at least the person walking in front as they made their way through the forest.

And he was a Skraeling. His ancestors were the first men in Freiland. Some said they'd been there even longer than the elves.

There were quite a few Skraelings who were subjects of

the mark. They lived in the extreme north of Shenandoah. There were also plenty of Skraeling traders who travelled up and down the Shenandoah and Potomac River routes dealing in tobacco, pelts, and cotton. These Skraelings were leagues away from either fork of the river, and thirty leagues from the mark's northern border.

These were not men of the mark. She could tell by their dress, even by their walk.

This was the moment to decide whether she would kill them or not. The man was crossing in front of the old willow stump in the center of the clearing.

Ursel could make most any shot either instinctively or by taking careful aim. She wanted to cut this very fine. She eyed what looked like either a worn spot or a patch on his thrown back cloak. The cloak was flapping slighting in a breeze from the west. She was about twenty paces up the hill from the man. She was firing through a fissure in the outcrop.

Ursel drew the bow.

She used a pinch grip on the bowstring. She was good with all kinds of grips, and could adjust for conditions, but the pinch was the first grip she'd ever learned, and she often used it for accuracy and a hard strike.

Her eye came down to the bowstring. Her pupil aligned with the top of the arrow. Her face contacted the bowstring with a feather-like touch. She used a slight tightening of her cheek to align her shot left to right.

Ursel released.

The arrow sliced through the man's cloak and sank into the old willow stump. The Skraeling man, who was taking a step forward, got yanked back by his own clothing.

He fell on his butt with a *whump*.

CHAPTER TWO:
THE MIDDLE NAME

"*Askwiwan!*" the man shouted. He quickly tried to pull himself up.

Bad move.

The cloak was pinned tight to the trunk. He fell back down again.

"*Makwa ikwe!*" he yelled to those behind him. Then he desperately tried to wriggle around the stump to take cover.

"Stop!" Ursel called out. "The rest of you. Drop your weapons or I'll kill him!"

She spoke in Kaltish, hoping they understood. She didn't speak a word of any Skraeling tongue. She'd hate to have to kill them for that reason.

She'd nocked another arrow without realizing it. She took aim and fired this into the ground next to the pinioned

Skraeling's leg. She must have caught a bit of his skin, because he jerked back from it with a cry of pain.

"I said 'drop your weapons,'" she shouted.

The other men moved into the clearing. They looked to the man by the stump as if they expected to receive orders.

"We don't have any weapons," he shouted back in Kaltish. He sounded more irritated than frightened.

"Sure you do. Drop your bows and quivers," she answered back. "All of you."

"Those are for hunting."

Ursel let fly another arrow. This one thwacked into the stump near the man's head. She knew without looking that she had seven more arrows in her quiver. So that would have to be the last warning shot.

She hoped he'd gotten the idea that she would kill him if she felt threatened.

Because she would.

Evidently he had. The leader nodded toward his men. "Do it," he told them.

They all slowly set down their bows on the leafy ground of the clearing.

"And tomahawks!" she called. "Don't forget your tomahawks."

"Why? Shooting like that, you'd kill us before we could scalp you," the man called back.

"Shut up and throw down the tomahawks."

Five of the men dropped theirs. A sixth, a very tall

Skraeling, suddenly made a twist and launched his tomahawk with a roar of frustration right at Ursel. It clattered off the flinty rock she was behind, shooting out several sparks as it did.

That was one *amazing* throw, Ursel thought.

She instantly had the thrower sighted and could easily have put an arrow through him.

Maybe *should.*

But she let go of her draw.

"Tell your man he almost got himself killed," she shouted.

The pinioned man yelled something at the thrower of the tomahawk. She couldn't see his expression from where she was, but from the way he hung his head, he looked ashamed.

"Now state your business!" she called out. "Why are you tracking me?"

"We are looking for—that is, we have been *sent* to look for—a woman. A red-haired woman."

"Who sent you?"

"The duchess regent of this land."

"Oh yeah? What's her name?"

"Duchess Ulla von Dunstig."

"Wrong answer."

"Ah, that's right. The surname has changed. Not von Dunstig anymore. Ulla *Smead.*"

"Prove it."

"I have a letter of introduction with Lady Ulla's seal, and another letter addressed to the earl. Or actually to the earl's retainer. This red-haired woman who is supposed to receive all messages for Earl Keiler. They call her Ursel. I don't know her surname, if she even has one. She's a commoner, I'm told."

Ursel couldn't help smiling a vicious smile. She *so* wanted to mess with this arrogant outlander.

"I may know her," she called out. "And she *has* a last name. And a middle name."

"All right," the man said with a shrug. "What of it?"

"Her middle name is 'Arrow-to-the-groin.'"

There was a pause as the man considered whether she might be telling the truth. His hand moved down, maybe unconsciously, to cover his privates.

"Very funny," he replied shakily. "You're making me nervous."

"Her last name is Keiler," Ursel said. "*Keiler*, like the earl. She's his daughter by adoption."

"Oh." A pause. "And you? Who are you?"

Ursel didn't bother to reply to him. "You're three leagues away from Bear Hall," she said.

"We *went* to Bear Hall. But this secretary wasn't there. The earl wouldn't receive us without her. They said she handled castle business. So we decided to leave and look for her."

"Without a guide in the Shwartzwald? Unwise."

"We're free men. We do what we want."

"Right. Not in *my* forest."

Ursel sighed. She had a feeling it would be a while before she would be able to get back to her original task. The wild creatures of the western forest would have to stay wild for now.

"We really *need* to speak to this Ursel." The man pulled the arrow from his cloak and stood up. He turned so that she had an easy shot if she'd wanted to spear him through the chest. "My people are dying *right now*," he said. "We've come to plead for help."

He *was* brave. She'd give him that. Or arrogant enough to think she wouldn't shoot.

I ought to put another one through his cloak for that haughty expression, she thought. Or through a shoulder. That would teach him.

But no. She *did* very much want to hear what Ulla Smead had to say. Ulla was the duchess regent, after all, and she was Ursel's liege lord.

And Wulf's sister.

Ursel felt the knife in her stomach twist yet again.

Blood and bones, I have to get that man off my mind.

"All right," she called out. "Come here and show me the letter."

Chapter Three:
The Clash

"Humans? *We're* the shadows, Rainer," Wulf von Dunstig said to his best friend and foster-brother, Rainer Stope. "The Divine Beings are what's real." Wulf and Rainer had spent the early morning out gathering firewood and were headed back to camp, each with an armload of wood. For half that time, they'd also been arguing religion. "Sturmer, Regen, the Allfather, and the others. It's a sacred way of looking at the world. Stuff like the Sun. Storms. Ice. Water. Good luck. Bad luck."

"Tretz isn't just another god, or divine being, or whatever. He's not a swap for your gods of the cathedral," Rainer replied. He adjusted a stick on the top of his bundle that was falling off.

"Not gods. They're *principles*," said Wulf. "Spiritual principles."

"Tretz is a *person*. A dragon. The firstborn dragon."

"I know, I know—a *mandrake*," Wulf replied. "Killed and risen from the dead. Son of the Never and Forever. Firstborn of the land-dragons." Wulf was so intent on making his point, he almost tripped on a root. He managed to step over at the last moment, then continued walking through the layer of newly fallen leaves on the forest floor. There was a chill in the air. Early autumn was settling in. "I *was* paying attention to you all this time."

Rainer smiled crookedly. "You either get it or you don't."

"I *want* to get it."

"It isn't something to prove," Rainer said. He pointed to the star-shaped tattoo on his left forearm. The Aster. The sign of Tretzians. "It just is. *He* just is. Tretz."

"Like Ravenelle and her Dark Angel and Talaia and the rest?" Wulf replied. He slipped a glance over at Rainer. This was bound to irritate his friend.

"No," Rainer replied curtly. "Not like that at all."

"Same roots in history."

"*We* don't dip our bread in human blood," Rainer continued. "And ours is *actual* bread. Not whatever *mold* those Talaia wafers are made from. Makes me nauseous thinking about it."

"Yeah, but somebody might believe that's why you and Ravenelle are so . . . compatible . . ." Wulf let his voice trail off. There was only so far he would push his friend. Kidding him about his frustrated feelings for Ravenelle would be going too far.

Rainer stopped short and turned to Wulf. "Me and Ravenelle are *what*?"

"Forget it. You're both like oil and water," Wulf replied. "Let's get this back to camp so I can check on Saeunn and—"

Clank.

"—shush!" Rainer said, nodding to his right. "You hear that?"

"Yeah," Wulf replied in a low voice.

"Sounds like metal," Rainer said, also speaking quietly now.

Rainer knelt and carefully set the armful of firewood he'd been carrying in the leaves. Then he reached under his cloak and drew his sword.

Wulf set down his firewood bundle and did the same.

Clang.

Definitely metallic, like Rainer said. Then Wulf heard a horse's snort.

The voices of a men.

"*Qui crepitus fecit*?"

"*Erat Remigius!*"

Latin.

"Blood and bones!" Wulf whispered to Rainer.

Romans.

There were Roman soldiers in the woods of the mark.

Not good.

They hunkered down behind one of the granite outcrops that poked out along the ridge they'd been walking along. Wulf carefully look around the edge of the largest of the granite boulders.

Down the slope of the forested hill, a creek glinted as it flowed through a pine-straw-covered glen. From the woods on the left soldiers emerged. Some were riding horses. Some walking.

Scale armor. Red shields. Glinting movement of horses. Horses with armor.

It was Romans, all right. Imperials.

We're lucky they didn't ride down on top of us, Wulf thought.

Wulf and Rainer had been in the glen below only moments before. Rainer had stopped wood gathering long enough to pull out his knife and shave off his morning's scruff. He'd wet his whiskers with creek water, and used the flowing creek to wash away the stubble.

Wulf didn't need to shave. He was blonde, fair, and seventeen. Well, he didn't need to shave often.

Now they had to survive if they wanted to ever shave again.

There was a flutter and what looked like a small snow owl shot down from a tree and settled onto Wulf's right shoulder. Her name was Nagel. She was a talking owl person.

Most *Tier*—animal people—looked as much like humans as animals. Not Nagel. She seemed like a normal owl in every way but one.

Nagel spoke.

"Fifteen horses. Eighteen men," she said in her screeching whisper rasp. "Swords and pikes. Soldiers."

Wulf nodded. "Get back to the others and tell them," he said.

"I want to stay. Blood in the air. I can smell it."

Wulf knew ordering Nagel around wouldn't do any good. He tried to make his whispered reply sound reasonable. "Go get Jager. There'll be blood enough for you later."

"Stupid bobcat. Might swat me," Nagel said.

"Captain Jager knows you're a person."

Another moment of hesitation, then the owl answered. "All right, man. I'll go."

"Thank you. Now hurry!"

Nagel shot away, winging through the trees down the slope of the ridge.

Rainer risked a glance. He quickly ducked back down. "What the cold hell are they doing in the mark?"

Wulf frowned. "I don't know," he said, "but we haven't got time for this kind of distraction."

A voice shouted in surprise about twenty paces to the right side of them. "Hey!"

Wulf turned to see two armed Roman soldiers coming toward them from the right side along the top of the little ridge they'd climbed. They carried armloads of firewood. Both dropped the wood and drew swords.

Iberian blades. Roman short swords.

"Seems like we're about to *make* time for it," Rainer said.

"Blood and bones," Wulf replied, shaking his head.

He glanced at Rainer. His foster-brother smiled wickedly.

"*In inferno quis est?*" one of the soldiers yelled. He spoke in Latin, which Wulf could understand and speak, but Rainer could not. It meant "who in Hades are *you*?"

"I'll take the one on the left," Rainer said.

"Your left or his?"

"Yep," Rainer replied distractedly.

Rainer charged toward them. Wulf's sword was originally forged to be a bear person's short sword. Now it served as a long sword for Wulf.

He followed right behind Rainer.

Rainer feinted toward the Roman soldier on his right. The Imperial instinctively stumbled back. Rainer then took an overhead swing at the other. That Roman managed to get his sword up in time to block the full force of Rainer's blow. But he gripped his sword in one hand only. So the strength of Rainer's strike pushed the tip of the Roman's sword down. It swung like a hinge in his hand, and sliced a gouge across his cheek.

The Roman screamed in pain and fury.

The other Imperial got back his balance. He raised his sword to strike at Rainer from behind.

Uh-oh. Rainer didn't see this.

Wulf put on a burst of speed and levelled his sword at this man.

The soldier Rainer had wounded was facing Wulf. He took a surprised glance at Wulf charging in. He stopped his arm in midswing. Before Rainer could come back with another blow, the Roman turned and ran.

He's going for backup, Wulf thought.

Wulf's focus narrowed to the remaining soldier. The forest was a blur of green and brown as Wulf rushed forward.

Wulf's sword tip rammed into the breast plate of the remaining Roman . . . and deflected to the side. The blow pushed the soldier back, though.

He turned his attention from Rainer to Wulf then. The soldier brought his sword down in a vicious swipe. The blade connected just in front of Wulf's sword guard.

Wulf blocked it.

Wulf's hard-won fighting habits took over. He let the blow of the other's sword push his sword arm into a deadly arch. His run had already carried him inside the Roman's swing. He brought the bear man's sword down from above.

The Roman jerked his own sword up to shield himself.

Too late.

Wulf's blade sank into his left shoulder.

The leather shoulder harness that connected to the Roman's plate armor split, and the armor sagged to one side.

The blow sank into flesh and bone, too. The soldier cried out. He raised his sword again.

Cold hell, he's tough, thought Wulf. Which isn't a surprise—if this guy really is a Roman Legionnaire.

But then the pointed end of a sword pommel slammed into the back of the man's head. The Roman collapsed, unconscious.

Rainer stood behind the fallen Roman.

Wulf heard branches crackle and looked around for more attackers. But this was the soldier running through the forest in the direction from which he'd come from.

"Let's get out of here."

They sheathed their swords—Wulf put his away unwiped and bloody.

Had the Romans been tracking them, or was their meeting just a coincidence?

Doesn't matter, Wulf thought. They've found us.

"The mounted soldiers won't fight with those Iberian swords." Rainer breathed hard as he jogged beside Wulf. "They'll use sabers."

They heard the whinnying of horses behind them.

The clanking of armor.

Wulf risked a glance over his shoulder.

The first of the Roman cavalry was cresting the hill.

"Here they come," he gasped to Rainer. They ran. They leaped over a downed tree. They tore around rocky outcrops.

Now he heard the pounding of horse hooves on the leaf meal of the forest floor. He didn't bother to look back.

"Time to take a stand," he shouted to Rainer.

"No. I see Nagel," Rainer said.

"Where?"

He pointed ahead of them through the trees. "That gulley."

Wulf didn't see the owl, but he trusted Rainer's sharp vision better than his own.

"Head for it," Wulf said. "Down the middle!"

He hoped he was guessing right. If not, he and Rainer were about to die at the end of a Roman sword. In a gulley. In the middle of nowhere.

He would fail. The girl he loved would die.

And the whole trip to Eounnbard would be for nothing.

Chapter Four:
The Gulley

Wulf had always figured that he and Rainer would die together. Probably doing something like this, fighting a bunch of bullies in a ditch. That was the way it went the whole time they were growing up.

They had been the low boys in the castle kid pecking order. The commoner, Rainer. And Wulf—third son, not even spare to the heir.

People who didn't matter.

Both the perfect ones for the castle kids to take out frustrations and resentment on.

Except they had survived the bullies at Raukenrose Castle. The unfair fights. The ambushes.

So he and Rainer swore together, they made a pact.

Never give in.

Go down swinging.

They *had* gone down. A lot. At first.

That was ten years ago. Now he was seventeen and Rainer was eighteen.

Rainer had gotten better, until he was, simply, the best fighter around. Wulf had become, if not a great warrior, at least more durable.

The gulley was formed by what looked like an on-again-off-again stream flowing down the hill. Today it was dry. Its bottom was filled with creek rock. Rainer rattled his way over the stones. Wulf followed close behind, pleading to Sturmer and all the divine beings that he wouldn't twist an ankle.

Sturmer evidently wasn't in a giving mood. Wulf's boots, slicked by the damp leaves he'd been running on, slipped on a smooth creek stone. The pain in his turned ankle was momentarily excruciating. But the ankle wasn't sprained, and after a couple of steps the agony tapered off. He kept going, gritting his teeth against the little sparks of shooting pain that remained.

A javelin flew past him, almost taking him in the side of the head. It clattered on the stones ahead of him.

"They're close!" he called out to Rainer.

There was a slight twist in the gulley. Another javelin embedded itself in the dirt bank where the twist began. They rounded behind the bank. Wulf glanced back. They were out of sight of the Romans for a moment.

Still he heard the sound of nearby horse hooves. Rainer pointed to the side of the gulley.

Blood and bones! No, they hadn't escaped the pursuit at all.

There were four Roman cavaliers on either side of the gulley. Two of the riders had their sabers out. Cavalry sabers were wicked long. These could easily reach down into the gulley and slice into a skull.

The two others were lining up for a spear throw, even as their horses trotted along. The horse was *watching*, in fact, and matched Wulf and Rainer pace for pace.

Cold hell, Wulf thought, Roman horses sure are *well-drilled*.

One of the men drew his arm back to throw his javelin. Wulf couldn't help flinching. He had to fight to keep from raising his arms trying to block the spike—and dying embarrassed.

The man never cast his spear.

Four arrows popped into him, almost at the same moment. One glanced off his plate armor. Another punched its way through the steel and sank deep into the man's chest. The third and fourth caught him below the neck and in his throwing arm.

With a cry, he dropped the javelin. He clutched at the arrow in his chest. Two more arrows struck and sank in as he did so. The man went slack and fell from the horse. He rolled into the gulley, but Wulf and Rainer had already moved past him, and he came to rest somewhere behind them.

Wulf looked up again. The other Roman cavaliers on the gulley sides seemed to run into a wall made of arrows. Two of the horses went down. Another kept running after its rider fell off. The man was filled with arrows like a human pincushion.

Wulf and Rainer still charged down the center of the gulley. It widened as it neared the stream it emptied into.

Rainer stopped, and Wulf slowed and stopped beside him. Rainer bent over gasping. Wulf put a hand on his back, steadying himself while he too sucked in air.

After a moment, Rainer straightened up. "Listen," he said. He pointed to a spot behind them up the gulley.

Hooves clopping on stone. The clatter of armor.

Shouts of anger and shock.

The clopping ceased.

Terrible horse screams.

Men bellowing in agony.

Crashing and clanking of metal striking stones.

Silence.

Then a single white horse in Roman livery dress came galloping down the gulley. Wulf and Rainer dove to the side as it thundered past them. The horse leaped out the end of the gulley and disappeared as it plunged down to the stream. They heard splashing, a great whinny, then more hoofbeats as it charged away into the forest on the other side of the water.

"Let's get out of here," Wulf said. They scrambled up one side of the gulley, then made their way back along its edge.

About a field-march back through the woods, they saw human warriors and Tier lining either side of the gulley. Bear men, buffalo men and, a few other types of animal people. A single very short bobcat man was in charge. Just then, he was ordering a contingent of buffalo men to get down in the gulley and make sure those thrice-cursed, trespassing Romans were finished off with spear thrusts. He ordered the rest of his force to spread out and find any remaining Imperials.

There was a centaur nearby, Ahorn, who carried a sword and buckler. Beside him was a very tall male figure with a bow. His name was Abendar Anderolan. He was an elf. The two exchanged a glance and both charged off into the woods together.

Moments later, there was the sound of crashing through the brush like a running man would make.

Then there was a long, drawn-out scream.

The centaur and elven man returned from the woods, the centaur wiping the blood from his sword on a cloth the tall figure had given him.

I would not like to be a man being hunted by a centaur and an elf warrior, Wulf thought with a shudder.

Wulf gazed down into the gulley at a gruesome sight.

There lay a *pile* of Roman cavalry and their horses. It was hard to pick out individual soldiers and horses. They were all so twisted together. It looked more like a mound with arrows and pikes sprouting all over it.

A few horses still twitched. One kicked out a leg feebly. None of the soldiers moved.

Blood flowed from wounds and pooled in low places among the rocks.

"May Tretz receive their souls," Rainer murmured. Tretz was the dragon-man god that he and his family worshipped. Some of the others would have thought this was blasphemy. But Wulf had been around Rainer most of his life. He had long ago decided to put up with his foster-brother's odd religion.

"You guessed that Jager was setting an ambush?" Wulf asked Rainer.

Rainer shrugged. "Nagel looked like she was signaling us."

The owl flew from a nearby branch and landed on Wulf's shoulder again.

"Blood," she said, sounding satisfied. "I was right."

Nagel was never exactly happy—her emotions seemed to be more those of a bird of prey than a human—but the smell of fresh blood did seem to move her to something like fierce joy. She launched herself back into the air before Wulf could reply.

From the woods they heard the whisper of arrows, the curse of a man struck.

More screams.

Then silence.

"I guess they found one last Roman," Rainer said grimly.

Wulf's eyes adjusted to the candlelight inside the tent.

Near the center of the tent, a female elf lay on a bed. Sitting on a chair beside the bed and holding the elf's hand, was Ravenelle Archambeault, a dark-skinned woman in a black dress trimmed with red silk. Her mass of curly black hair, as usual, seemed about to explode from its hairpins. Ravenelle was a Roman colonial princess. She was also apprentice to a healer.

Nearby was the healer herself, a buffalo wisewoman. She was grinding a pungent mix of dried herbs in a wooden bowl. The smell of sage and something else Wulf couldn't name filled the room.

The buffalo woman's name was Puidenlehdet. She had a human body, over which she wore a coarse wool cloak, but possessed the head of a normal she-buffalo.

She was a wisewoman, gifted in healing. Responding to Wulf's inquiring look, the dark-skinned woman, Ravenelle, shook her head sadly.

Wulf went to the other side of the pallet and kneeled beside the elf woman.

Her name was Saeunn Eberethen, or Saeunn Amberstone in Kaltish, Wulf's language. She wore a white linen dressing gown, but was covered from the breasts down by a buffalo skin robe. She was blonde, with long hair draping over the pillow on which her head lay.

Wulf had been in love with her for as long as he could remember.

Saeunn was awake. She raised her head with difficulty, and looked toward Wulf. Her blue eyes were glazed with tears from the pain he knew she was going through. Sitting up caused her blonde tresses to fall away, revealing her pointed ears.

"Something happened. I heard," Saeunn said. "Are you all right?"

"Roman soldiers. Real Imperials," Wulf replied. "Cavalry scouts, I think."

"This far northwest?"

"Yes. Jager's company took care of them. Don't worry about it."

She lay her head back down and sighed.

"I've put everyone in danger," she said.

"No," Wulf said. "The mark would have had to deal with them one way or another. They are in our territory."

Saeunn lay her head back down on the pillow. She shuddered as a chill ran through her body. This was the way it had been for the past week, alternating high fevers and chills.

"But not *you* personally," she said. "And we'll be over the border soon."

"You're sick. We're going to get help."

A wave of pain appeared to wash over Saeunn. She squeezed her eyes tight.

"It's not too late to turn back," she whispered.

"I won't," Wulf said.

"All right," Saeunn whispered even more faintly.

Wulf's eyes were tearing. He wiped them with a wrist still caked with dirt and sweat from his run.

"Get out of here, von Dunstig," Ravenelle said to him firmly, but with sympathy in her voice. "We have to let her rest. The lady is completely drained from this quite grueling quest that you've seen fit to embark on with her. Not only that, she has to be ready to travel to the inn tomorrow, and that is not an easy ride."

"I know."

"We're really going, aren't we? To *real* beds?"

"So Ahorn tells me."

"You'd better not be lying, von Dunstig," Ravenelle said, "Once we cross into my kingdom you'll have a very cross princess on your hands. One who holds a grudge for a *very* long time." She smiled to let Wulf know she was joking.

Mostly joking, he thought.

He was too tired and worried to say anything funny back to her. "We'll find out tomorrow, Ravenelle."

He stood, turned to leave, but looked back a final time.

Saeunn was an elf. She was supposed to be immortal.

But Saeunn Amberstone was dying.

CHAPTER FIVE:
THE SKRAELINGS

The Skraeling man that Ursel Keiler had stuck with her arrow reached under his deerskin shirt while Ursel kept careful watch. He brought out a cloth bag.

Now that she got a better look at him, she saw that her first impression was correct. He *was* haughty in the way he stuck out his chest and drew in his shoulders.

He was also handsome. He wore buckskin pants and the deerskin shirt was covered with beads. Around his waist was a wampum belt. His hair was cropped short, but three eagle feathers dangled from its rear. In one ear hung a bone earring. Very thin and delicate looking. Bird bone, probably.

The man opened the packet and from inside took a scroll with a wax seal on it. Then he pulled out another scroll bag

and held it up also. "This is the letter of introduction," he
called out. "The other, the unread scroll, is for the earl."

"All right. Bring them."

"*Where* are you? *Who* are you?"

"Just follow my voice," Ursel said. When he reached the
other side of the rock, she told him to throw the scrolls over
to her. He did what she asked.

Ursel quickly picked up the open scroll. There was a
broken wax seal on the outside that had the impression of
the mark on it. On the inside was a wax badge embedded
with trailing ribbons that announced that the bearer of this
certificate had permission to travel within the mark to carry
out his task. The script under the interior wax seal named
the holder of the document.

WANNAS KITTAMAQUAND, SPECIAL ENVOY OF
THE REPUBLIC OF POTOMAK, HIS RETAINERS,
BANNER-MEN, AND ASSORTED RETINUE

"So you're this Wannas Kitta . . . Kitta-something of
Potomak?"

"Kittamaquand is my clan," the man said. "My given
name is Wannas. And you?"

Ursel stepped out of her hiding place. She had lowered
her bow, but still had an arrow nocked.

As she drew closer, the Skraeling captain gazed at her as
if he were a stunned deer.

I know I've been out in the woods for a few days, she thought, but do I look *that* scary?

"Welcome to Shwartzwald Forest," Ursel said. "I'm pleased not to have killed you."

The Skraeling bowed his head slightly. "And I'm glad not to have died," he said. He looked down at his groin. "Or had something worse happen." He turned his gaze back to her, more serious now. "We do come on urgent business, m'lady—"

"Like you said, I am *not* a lady. Just a kind of clerk. A secretary. Very common."

"It's important I speak with the earl."

"We'll see."

The Skraeling stomped a booted foot in obvious impatience and frustration. "Listen, woman, you don't understand! None of you do!" He pursed his lips huffed in exasperation, then calmed himself enough to speak again. "My city is under *siege*—by Sandhaven *and* Romans. Shenandoah *must* come to our aid. We need humans, bear men, buffalo people, anyone. I've even heard your gnomes are warriors. You *have* to help us. The Sandhaveners will be at your gates soon if you don't!"

"We beat them before. We can do it again."

"I heard you lost your duke's castle in the process."

"And got it back."

Ursel remembered the battle for Raukenrose. It had been a very close thing. If not for the gnomes getting there in the nick of time, the capital would still be in the possession of Sandhaven and that evil *thing* that led them. The draugar, they called it.

"This is different. Sandhaven is backed up by a legion from Rome. And they have a new way of fighting. Some new and powerful version of that communion wafer the Romans eat with blood. Their generals control the minds of their troops."

"We faced that."

"Did you face a Roman legion of nearly ten thousand Imperials? Because you *will* if you don't help us."

Ursel nodded. "Okay. You have a point," she said. "But tell me: what did Lady Ulla say when you made demands on her like this?"

Wannas looked embarrassed. "She threw us out. At first."

"Then what? You must have gotten that marquee of travel somehow."

"I came back and . . . apologized for sounding . . . arrogant."

"Right," said Ursel. "Then what?"

"She said I had to ask her brother. He's the heir. He has a direct connection to the land-dragon, whatever that means. She won't send a full levee of troops without asking him."

"So why are you here?"

"Lord Wulf is gone. Traipsing off into the wilderness."

"Yes, I heard. With a hundred men at arms and a herd of cattle to feed them."

"Lady Ulla said maybe the earl would know where to find him."

Ursel shook her head. "No," she said. "He would not."

Wannas looked dejected—and angry. "Then I've come all this way for nothing," he replied.

"The earl wouldn't. But *I* might," Ursel continued. "I have a little skill at tracking. But first let me take a look at the letter from the duchess regent and see what her instructions are."

CHAPTER SIX:
THE LETTER

Ursel broke the wax seal and spread the scrolled letter onto her lap. She allowed Wannas to stand in the sunlight to cut down the glare on the parchment.

"It *is* from Lady Ulla," she said. "This is the handwriting of a castle scribe."

"I told you," Wannas replied.

"Please be quiet and let me read."

The Skraeling started to move away.

"No, keep standing in the sunlight there," Ursel said. "You cast a good shadow. And I can keep an eye on you that way."

"I'll stand here as long as it takes," Wannas said with a snort. Ursel couldn't tell if she'd offended him or amused him. She turned her attention to the letter.

✥ ✥ ✥

My dearest Earl Keiler,

I hope you have identified the respected holder of this letter and have not accidently dispatched him and his men with sword, arrow, or hangman's noose. You bear people can be famously grumpy at times. If identification is needed and has not been provided, then see the accompanying formal letter of introduction and diplomatic passage through the mark. Also enclosed in a separate packet is personal correspondence from myself to Ursel Keiler. I would request that she receive this at your earliest convenience.

The Skraeling man before you, Wannas Kittamaquand, arrived in Raukenrose with an alarming report. He is an emissary from the Republic of Potomak. That city-state is now under siege by Sandhaven's professional military. They have been reinforced, I am sorry to say, with Imperial Roman troops.

Roman troops on Kalte soil, my dear earl!

This has been a reason to go to war many times in the past. It is even worse when the military of an important Kalte kingdom is teamed up with Rome and attacking one of the Skraeling republics, our long-time allies and trading partners.

Potomak sits at the Great Falls of the river. All portage up and down river must pass through the city. For over two centuries, she has guaranteed the mark's route to the sea. She has guarded all trade coming in and out of the Shenandoah Valley.

I am told that this Wannas Kittamaquand, while not of

noble birth—his republic has forbidden royal titles—belongs
to a clan and family of high importance in Potomak. His father
is a senator in the Potomak Assembly. His uncle holds the
executive position of chief of war for the republic.

You may have heard of the Kittamaquand clan in passing.
His family owns and operates Kitty Yards, the largest Potomak
tobacco market.

In order to get to the mark, Wannas and his men had to
break through the siege. It was a dangerous undertaking.
Many were killed and great sacrifice was made while carving
a way through the Sandhaven encirclement. According to the
young man, they fought Roman Imperials as well as
Sandhaveners. I grilled two of his men separately, and their
stories agree. Both also say that Wannas showed great bravery
during the breakout.

I am inclined to believe that the situation is as Wannas
reports it. The city is cut off. People inside are down to their
last food sources.

They are eating horses, my dear earl, horses!

Knowing the respect in which the Skraeling hold their
horses, the people of Potomak must be in a terrible condition,
indeed.

Wannas very forcefully requested military aid from the
mark. I came to see that his agitation, while sharply expressed,
is justified.

I am going to send a limited levee of our people to Potomak
to attempt a diversionary tactic, around five hundred men. I'll

do this so that new supplies might be brought into the city. The alternative is to let the people of Potomak starve. Our centuries-old route to the sea will be cut off.

But I will not send a full force to ally with the Skraelings until I speak with my brother.

I don't need to tell you that most of our trade with the northern sister kingdoms goes out through the Chesapeake Bay. Overland shipment adds one hundred times the transportation cost to our goods. It raises the price of all trade goods coming into the mark, also.

You are no bean-counting scribe, my dear Earl, so if you can't make heads or tails of this, just ask your lovely adopted daughter. Mistress Ursel is quite gifted with numbers. She can put it into a hunter and warrior's terms, as you well know.

My brother Wulf is not in Raukenrose. He is traveling to the Mist Mountains and to Eounnbard, where the elves dwell. We have had no message from him. I can only assume he has been forging on in that direction for the past weeks.

And since he is not here, I cannot seek his advice. I cannot ask his permission to send a full levee of troops to Potomak.

We need Wulf's approval.

Wulf is the only von Dunstig who can hear the land-dragon call. The duke, my father, continues to suffer from the morosis disease, and his reason is fading. Even before the death of our older brothers Otto and Adelbert, Wulf had begun hearing the dragon call.

The gift is said to be passed down to male heirs. I don't know about that, but I can tell you that I myself have not the slightest ability to hear the call. Nor, as far as I can tell, does our ten-year-old sister, Anya.

Wulf is the heir to the dragon call, and so the heir to the Mark of Shenandoah.

He refuses to take on the title of Duke Regent. Instead, he has appointed me Duchess Regent.

I can promise you that I do not want this honor. With him out gallivanting to Eounnbard, I saw little choice but to take it.

For more than a month before Wulf headed south, the dragon-call was strongly on him. Since the Olden Oak, his usual vision-site, was cut down by the Sandhaveners during the invasion, it was obvious that he should return to the spot he'd last communed with the Dragon of Shenandoah. You know the place well. It is Raven Rock, on the northern edge of Shwartzwald County.

Wulf resisted.

He was busy preparing for an expedition to Amberstone Valley. He planned to take our foster-sister Saeunn back to her homeland. Yes, you read correctly. That's a trip of nearly six hundred leagues.

This didn't matter to Wulf.

After her confrontation with the Draugar Wuten, Saeunn was left wounded. During the summer, she became deathly ill. As you know, elves do not get sick often. There are very few diseases which can kill an elf. They are born immortal after all, with a strong constitution meant to last them for centuries.

But Saeunn died in that battle, then got brought back to life. She wears a star-stone—an artifact that seemed to revive her after the final fight with Draugar Wuten.

Wulf is convinced that the star-stone is failing.

He thinks Saeunn will die if he can't get her to help. So his plan was to take the Elf Road west with her.

That didn't work out.

Wannas is not the only strange visitor we have had to Raukenrose lately.

About a week before Wulf's planned departure, an elf warrior stumbled into the mark. He'd been on what sounded like an impossibly hard journey from Amberstone Valley— which was where Wulf was planning to go.

The elf's name is Abendar Anderolan. Abendar reported that the Wild Kingdoms between the mark and the Great Mississippi River were in an uproar, and that the Elf Road to Amberstone Valley was closed.

He claimed to have set out in a traveling caravan of over one hundred elves, complete with wagons full of trade goods from his valley. Only five elves survived. Once they reached relative safety, they decided to separate to warn the Kaltelands that taking the Elf Road is a march of death at the moment.

Abendar convinced Wulf that only a full battalion of warriors might punch its way through. Wulf almost ordered up the general levee to raise such a force.

At that point, our friend and Wulf's advisor at the university, Master Albrec Tolas, stepped in. He convinced Wulf this was a terrible idea. It was. It would have left the mark defenseless. Even Wulf, in his desperation to help Saeunn, could not justify doing that.

I don't really need to explain why Wulf is so determined to help Saeunn Amberstone, do I? They haven't agreed to a marriage—I don't think that will ever happen, given the nature of men and elves. But they've made no secret of the fact that their friendship has grown into something more for both of them.

They are a couple. In love.

At this point, Ursel's hands began to shake as she held the scroll.

To hear it so plainly stated . . .

A couple. In love.

She knew she must be flushing, and she blinked water from her eyes. She didn't look up at Wannas. She didn't want to have to explain what was affecting her so much.

Then Ursel got a hold on herself and continued reading.

Now there is turmoil to the west. There is grave danger in the east if Potomak falls. And the divine ones only know what is happening in Vall l'Obac. We've had no word from the south in over a year. Our rangers report that trade at the border towns has slowed to a trickle.

This is worrisome to me because of our other castle

fosterling, Princess Ravenelle Archambeault—yes, the one-year-old child you took as a hostage after the Little War. Princess Ravenelle is now seventeen and, per the agreement with Queen Valentine, is free to return to her native country. As you and my father may have foreseen when you made the fostering arrangement, my family has grown to love Ravenelle—I think Wulf may feel closer to her as a sister than he does to me, to tell the truth.

This is not a surprise, since they are the same age. They grew up as something like outcasts among the castle children. Wulf as third son, and Ravenelle the living symbol of what we've been taught to believe are Roman vampires, down to drinking the blood of her servants to gain control of their minds.

Ravenelle has always been a devoted practitioner of the Talaia faith. Her freedom to do this was also part of your arrangement with her mother.

The mark has never been so threatened in a thousand years, and all our young heir can think of is saving his girlfriend, even with the dragon-call knocking at his mind.

Something had to be done, and Abendar stepped forward with an alternate plan. He was headed to the south himself to find refuge among his relatives, the Mist Elves of Eounn Anderolan, the Mountains of Mist. He considers them as something like poor relatives to his own folk, the Smoke Elves of Amberstone Valley. But their king is extremely old. It is possible he knows some way a starless elf might be saved.

It was a long shot, but it was a chance for Wulf to do something about Saeunn.

Please understand, I love Lady Saeunn as a sister. I would gladly have gone with Saeunn to anywhere we might find hope.

I offered. But my brother wouldn't have it.

I must confide that I am afraid that he may be running from his responsibilities as heir and regent as much as toward help for our foster-sister, Saeunn.

Again, this is not a secret opinion. Half of Raukenrose thinks the same thing. In fact, mobs who claim to be either pro- or anti–Wulf von Dunstig have taken to the streets in our beloved capital. They are practically at each other's throats. Sometimes it seems all I can do is to keep the peace, much less prepare for war.

But I do prepare.

War is coming. And despite what my brother may think, it doesn't give a fig about love.

CHAPTER SEVEN:
THE NECKLACE

"Bring me Marchioness Valentine," said a tall, somber man. He looked to be about thirty years old. He had a close-shaven face and wavy hair that fell to his shoulders. His hair was dark brown. So were his eyes. He had the olive skin color of a Tiberian. Here in the Roman colonies, he stood out. Most of the inhabitants of Vall l'Obac were much darker in complexion. They were of Afrique and Aegyptian ancestry.

The young man wore the jet-black tunic of a Talaia priest. His red collar showed his clerical order.

The Talaia faith called this order the *Fratelli di Sangue*, the Brothers of the Blood.

Two guards in Roman scale armor near the door to the room left to execute the command of the man in the black tunic.

The man's name was Quintos Rossofore. His official title was Continental Magister Praelatus of the Inquisition Suprema and Vice Abbot of the Fratelli di Sangue Order of Talaia.

Although vice abbot of an order was a higher title, Rossofore liked people to address him as "Magister."

While he was waiting for the marchioness, Rossofore gazed down at the lovely necklace of amber beads in his hands. Yellow-golden beauty. He let it swing freely and shifted it this way and that to catch the afternoon light streaming through a citadel window.

Dragon amber.

So much concentrated *dasein*, he thought. Magic. That was what dragon amber *was*. Dasein that brought the world to life and sustained it.

And now he held that power in his hand.

Life.

Dominance.

If dasein was the essence of life, then the dragons were life's greatest enemies. They fed on the dasein in the Earth. They took its magic for themselves, only allowing tiny amounts to escape their horrible appetites.

So said the articles of the faith of Talaia.

Rossofore knew the teachings of Talaia. Oh yes, he knew them well.

He'd spent his younger days in a special orphanage in Rome having them beaten into him.

No matter. That was years ago. Now he was a very powerful man.

Because of amber. Because of dasein.

If the free amber in the world could be collected . . . concentrated . . .

He took the beaded necklace in both of his hands. Each golden amber droplet was the size of a robin's egg.

He was admiring it when his guards returned with Valentine Archambeault, Queen of the Colonial Kingdom of Vall l'Obac, and Marchioness of the Holy Roman Empire.

"You wish to present yourself to me?" Valentine asked. Her voice was low for a woman, a rich alto. Some might call it edged with iron, but Rossofore thought it ridiculously prideful coming from a colonial.

"Yes, Marchioness," Rossofore replied with a bow. "Thank you for coming."

Valentine hesitated. She was obviously miffed. All in Vall l'Obac called her "Your Majesty," Rossofore knew. Even though it was officially correct, calling her marchioness was an insult. What Valentine didn't know, and never needed to know, was that he called her by a lesser title for his *own* sake as well as hers.

She reminded him of his mother.

His *imaginary* mother.

He had never known his true mother or his father. Instead there had only been old Brother Luigi who had drummed the books of wisdom and the Testament of the Covenant into all the children at the orphanage.

Brother Luigi and his knotted whip.

And when memorization didn't work, the children were *sold*.

Sold away. Gone.

Rossofore later learned that these were sent to the mines or indentured as chimney sweeps and night-soil collectors. But when he was a small boy all he knew was that children who didn't learn what Brother Luigi wanted . . . disappeared.

He'd been constantly worried that it might be *him* next. He'd had to come up with something to keep himself from digging his nails into his palms and grinding his teeth every night.

So he'd secretly imagined having parents.

He thought they might be a rich couple, possibly noble, who had to hide him from jealous relatives who wanted to kill him for his inheritance.

He was a smart boy. A boy of quality. Why shouldn't he be of the nobility? After all, nobody *knew* where he'd come from. He'd just appeared in a dirty basket on Brother Luigi's doorstep one night.

He *might've* been brought from a manor house.

Rossofore fantasized that his mother would one day show up. She would claim him from the orphanage.

She would hug him, and tell him what a good boy he was.

Then she would take him home to her big house and feed him everything he ever wanted to eat. She would have him sit next to her by the fire. She would stroke his hair.

Rossofore hadn't been touched often in the orphanage, and when he was it was usually by the back of Brother Luigi's hand.

His mother would never spank him. He would be a good boy. In his fantasy, he would get his own room, a really nice one. But sometimes when he had nightmares—which was *all the time* at the orphanage—she would let him crawl into bed between her and his father.

He would fall asleep between them, warm and safe.

He would know that nobody was going to send him to the mines.

His parents would never allow *that.*

Rossofore had grown older and learned that such daydreams were foolish. Idiotic, even.

Many orphans had them. They couldn't all be the secret sons and daughters of nobility could they?

In fact, none of them were.

Such fantasy was a weakness and had to be stamped out.

Rossofore tried.

But he never could *quite* stamp out the memory of his imaginary mother.

Marchioness Valentine Archambeault reminded him very much of that daydream mother. She looked almost exactly as he'd pictured her. He'd been struck almost speechless when he'd first met her. Now whenever he was around her, he had to make extra sure that he didn't give her any special privilege because of some childish delusion that he hadn't succeeded in wiping out.

She was *not* his mother.

No one was his mother.

Valentine Archambeault was a heretic. She deserved punishment. He knew it. He just had to prove it.

And she never came for me! She just left me there for Brother Luigi to torment!

Stop it. That was nonsense.

The marchioness was merely of professional interest to him. After all, he was an inquisitor of the Holy Roman Empire, and she was a heretic. Most colonials *were* in one way or another.

After a moment off balance, Valentine regained her proud bearing and nodded to Rossofore, acknowledging that he didn't have to address her as he would a queen.

Then she saw the necklace he was fingering, and let out an involuntary gasp.

Rossofore raised his hands and let the sunlight from the open window of the tower hit the amber beads. His office in the castle had once belonged to the marchioness's lord high counselor.

That was before the same high counselor had been burned at the stake for heresy.

On Rossofore's orders.

They were in a towering turret that was part of Pierre du Corbeau Castle, residence of the queen. The window looked out over the western regions of Montserrat, the capital city of Vall l'Obac.

"Do you recognize the jewelry?" Rossofore asked.

"Of course I do. It's the Golden Rose of Lerocher. It belongs to the countess. I have no idea what *you* are doing with it."

"It *was* owned by the Lerochers," Rossofore replied. "By the old count and his young countess. She's twenty years younger than the count, you know."

Count Lerocher had disgusted Rossofore. He could still picture the wrinkled old man's claw of a hand grasping the lovely, smooth hand of the countess.

He'd brought the man and his young wife to Montserrat. He'd told them it was for a special duty to the Brothers of the Blood. And it was, in a way. He'd immediately seen the count's seemingly devout nature was merely a cover for deep heresy.

"In actual fact, the necklace was only in the *possession* of the countess. It *belonged* to the count. It has been in the Lerocher family for generations. When he confessed his heresy, naturally he forfeited his family's earthly possessions. So now the Golden Rose belongs to the faith."

"You mean, to *you*, Magister Rossofore."

"As Rome's highest representative in the kingdom at present, I am the Hand of the Bishops, so yes, I am in charge of its fate."

"Poor Count Lerocher," the queen murmured.

"Your sympathy is misguided. He *was* a heretic."

"You would know, Magister."

"Marchioness, the man confessed to sacrilege and crimes against the Colonial Dispensation. He allowed his bloodservants Roman *surnames*. He made midnight sacrifices to the Kalte gods to beg for good tobacco crops."

"And you got him to confess this after only a *little* prodding with red-hot pokers?" the marchioness said. "Amazing."

"The Resonance of the Faith demanded his confession, not me. But it is my task as a master inquisitor to bring the heretic into harmony."

"With the use of the whip and rack, I'm sure," Valentine said. Rossofore detected the marchioness's obvious sarcasm, but decided to ignore it. He had more important matters to attend to.

"Sometimes the body must suffer so that the soul can be saved."

He'd thought the young Countess Lerocher a self-serving coquette. It had turned out that the young girl loved the old man after all. How disgusting and unnatural!

She came to Rossofore and pled with him to keep her husband from burning at the stake. She offered him nearly everything, even—he thought with disgust—herself as a mistress.

Then Rossofore had named the price he'd intended to demand all along.

"The Golden Rose of Lerocher would be suitable atonement for what Count Lerocher has done," Rossofore had said.

The little countess's hand had gone to her mouth in shock.

"Please don't ask that of us," she pleaded. "It's the foundation of the family fortune. If you take it, we'll be ruined. My husband would rather burn than give it up."

"Do you care nothing for your husband's *soul*, Countess? Would *you* rather he never resonated with the Emptiness?" Rossofore asked. "I remind you that the souls of the excommunicated are doomed to walk in the underworld forever."

"Yes, I know it."

"The Golden Rose stands between your husband and the Blessed Void. With its weight upon his conscience, he will never ascend from this world of suffering."

Even then, she had wavered. So he'd ordered the stakes erected and the wood piled high for burning. There were ten heretics currently held in the Montserrat dungeon.

He sent a messenger to the countess saying that one of those stakes was for Lerocher.

The messenger came back bearing the Golden Rose in a strongbox.

"The count confessed," Rossofore told Valentine. "And the faith was merciful. He did not burn."

"You had the old man hanged in his cell," the marchioness replied dryly.

"Yes, but we released the body to the widow to be buried in consecrated ground with a wafer of blessed celestis on his tongue. This is the foundation for passage to eternity, as you know, Marchioness."

Rossofore looked from Valentine down to the necklace again and smiled.

Mine.

There is nothing that this old woman can do about it, either.

He took one of the amber beads in his hands and gave the metal that enclosed it a powerful twist.

"No!" Valentine gasped.

He gave it another twist. The bead popped from its casing and into Rossofore's hand.

"That is a priceless relic from the first days of the colony," Valentine said, her voice trembling with dismay.

Well I certainly wiped that arrogant smile from her face, Rossofore thought. Good.

One by one, as the queen watched, horrified, he twisted the other amber stones out in the same way. He threw aside the rest of the necklace. It was gold, and worth a small fortune, but was useless to him. He held the amber beads before his eyes.

Lovely. Perfect. Concentrated *dasein*. The power that had made the world, and that could unmake it.

He stepped over to his writing desk near the window where a wine pitcher and glasses sat.

He smiled at Valentine. "Join me in glass of wine, Marchioness?"

Rossofore poured himself a glass. He began to pour one for Valentine, but she shook her head and put a hand over the top of the glass.

The obsidian Raven Ring of l'Ange Noir glinted on her right hand. The Montserrat rivulet topaz sparkled in a bracelet on her wrist. She wore a subtle and no doubt expensive perfume, a mixture of jasmine, vanilla, and musk. Rossofore felt for a moment that he was in the presence of a creature who maybe *was* a little more than merely human.

A true queen.

Mother of a kingdom.

He quickly shook the feeling off, however. No time to be foolish.

Rossofore raised the wine glass, then put one of the amber beads into his mouth. He rolled it around on his tongue.

Valentine whimpered at the sight.

"Don't!" she gasped.

The bead was warm. There was no taste to it. This always disappointed him. Pure power ought to have a taste.

"Blood and marrow!" the marchioness exclaimed. "Are you crazy?"

Rossofore smiled. He took a sip of wine.

He swallowed.

"No!" Valentine cried.

She lunged at him, but the guards were nearby to hold her back. There was no need. She controlled herself at the last moment.

At least she has *some* self-dignity and good breeding, Rossofore thought. For a colonial.

One after another, he swallowed five more of the dragon amber beads. He washed each down with another sip of wine.

Each swallow drew another whine of agony from the marchioness.

It took only a moment for the power to blossom. He felt the warmth flow through his body. His skin began to shine, the dasein inside him producing its own light. His mind raced with a thousand thoughts and plans. If he gazed into a looking glass, which he'd done before when the amber flush was upon him, he knew he would see his eyes glowing like reddish-yellow orbs of fire.

He stretched out his hands. They were crinkling. No, they were *scaling*, like a fish. A reptile.

He was becoming a dragon.

A man-dragon. A mandrake. A creature of pure dasein.

"Dark Angel protect us!" the marchioness shouted. She backed across the room at the sight of Rossofore. She would have fled entirely, but the guards would not let her pass.

He walked to the citadel window and looked out over the stronghold of Montserrat, his base in this cursed colonial land.

"Come here!" he commanded Valentine. He saw her try to resist, but with the amber power behind it, his voice was compelling. Its dasein was irresistible. She turned and stumbled toward him.

"Stand beside me at the window," he continued. Valentine did as he said. He smiled. "Watch this, Marchioness."

Rossofore raised his now scaly hands and stuck them out the open window. He clapped them.

A great peal of thunder boomed through the city.

Lightning forked across the sky, then crashed somewhere near the horizon.

The people looked like bugs from here in the tower.

Roaches, Rossofore thought. Like those cursed colonial Palmetto bugs. Ugh.

And like roaches, they scurried in all directions, startled and frightened, but not knowing which way to go.

He clapped his hands again. This time the thunder was louder. It shook the ground. A blast of wind flowed through the town and the people below were blown from their feet.

Then the wind stopped. The people slowly picked themselves back up. After a moment, they went back on their ways.

"*I* did that," Rossofore said. "Me!"

"This is sacrilege," Valentine whispered.

Rossofore chuckled. "How can it be, Marchioness? *I'm* the one who decides what sacrilege *is* in these cursed colonies. That is my appointed task."

He reached over and pulled Valentine closer to himself.

The old daydream returned.

She did smell *so* good. Rich. From some other world.

A beautiful world beyond the filthy orphanage and Brother Luigi's leather straps and knotted rope whips.

Rossofore shook his head to clear it.

No, no, no. She *isn't* my mother. She may not be *anyone's* mother soon.

But he would have to find out the name of whatever perfume she was using. He might recommend it to the true ladies of Rome.

Later. There would be plenty of time.

"What you are seeing is dasein," he said. "Pure power. You colonials have had it for generations. But you're ignorant. You didn't know how to unlock it."

Rossofore took another bead, put it in his mouth. Swallowed.

"But I do."

Chapter Eight:
The Couronne de Huit Tours

Magister Rossofore managed to suppress a wild laugh, but he couldn't help chuckling in delight.

"Who . . . what have you turned into?" Valentine whispered.

"Something more than human, Marchioness. A mandrake," Rossofore said. "I am destruction personified. Let me show you."

Then he picked out a rooftop toward the city's great wall. He'd been bothered by that rooftop since he'd taken up these chambers in the Pierre du Corbeau Castle.

Green tiles.

All the other roofs were red.

The green *offended* him.

It was wrong.

The houses and shops of Montserrat should be the same.

Who did they think they were, these people under the green roof? Special?

Probably blasphemers. Most colonials were.

He concentrated on the house, then slowly reached toward it with an open palm.

He clenched the palm into a fist.

The roof, and the house under it, imploded in a puff of dust. The green tiles collapsed—then shattered in a thousand pieces. Along with the house and everything in it, they disintegrated when they hit the ground. A large cloud of dust rose from the spot, roiling outward into the streets and alleyways.

Rossofore heard distant shouts of alarm and horror.

Beside him the marchioness cried out again. Bloody tears rolled down her face. "What have you done? You've killed my people. *Innocent* people."

Rossofore felt a twinge of regret.

"The faith doesn't kill for killing's sake," he said. "But this was sadly necessary."

"*Necessary*? Why, in the name of the Bishops and all that's holy?"

"Can't you see?" Rossofore said. "Now the roofs are the *same*."

Valentine was trembling. Her voice shook as she spoke. "You're a monster."

"Yes," Rossofore replied. He smiled. "A mandrake."

There was so much more to do. He needed more amber, lots of it, if he were to accomplish the great things he was meant to do. Most of the Roman Empire had been picked over for every scrap of dragon amber. Aegypt and the Afrique had no more to give. The mines of Roman territories on the continents of Meridianus and Austrinalis were worked out. The Freiland Roman colonies had some, but it was not near the surface. So far very little had been produced, almost none of it for export. Beyond Rome, Sarmatia and the Eastern empires of the great continent had been mined bare.

Rome's control was based on the Talaia faith, and the faith's power came from celestis, the holy herb of Talaia. Celestis was grown on dragon amber, consuming it in the process.

"Rome needs—"

He turned to the marchioness, but she had stepped back from the window. She was sitting in a chair on the other side of room. She dabbed her tears with a handkerchief already stained blood red.

He walked over, looked down upon her.

"Marchioness Valentine, you see the power of amber now. It is not meant to be worn as pretty baubles. Dragon amber is pure power. It must be *used*."

Valentine didn't answer or look up at him. He could only see her coiled black hair held in place by pure silver clips. Her black and red dress left her tawny shoulders exposed. They quivered in her distress.

"Where is amber to be found? In the colonies, yes. But

the Kaltelands and Wild Kingdoms of Freiland—they have amber, and lots of it."

The heathens didn't even mine it. They left it be while they worshipped their false gods and cringed in awe of the dragon parasites feeding beneath the land.

"They leave their amber in the *ground*!" Rossofore found himself shouting. He tried to control his voice, but his agitation was too strong. "Rome needs that amber. *I* need it! Don't you understand, Marchioness? I could be the conquistador Rome *needs*. We could finally take the north lands. Avenge *your* humiliating defeat. Make the heathens suffer for what they've done."

Rossofore opened the hand with which he'd crushed the house with the green roof. Five more beads of the Golden Rose of Lerocher still lay within it. Their tawny glow was spellbinding.

"You saw what a few beads can do in the hands of a true priest of the faith," he said. "I need more. If I'm going to conquer the north for Rome, I *have* to have more, much more. And at the moment, there is only one place I can get that much."

Rossofore could see that Valentine understood immediately what he was saying. She looked up at him. Red streaks ran down her face, but her gaze was fierce, defiant.

"You cannot have the Couronne de Huit Tours to aid you in this craziness!" she said. "The royal crown is the symbol of my kingdom."

"It is made of pure dragon amber."

"I *know* that. It's the crown *because* it's made of amber."

Rossofore nodded. "You believe you cannot give it to me. But I have to tell you, the deficiencies I noticed in Count Lerocher, I have perhaps seen in your home. Could it be that heathen ways have infected your household, as well? After all, your daughter, the heir to your crown, has been given to the barbarians to raise."

"For peace. The Little War ravaged both our lands. We were . . . defeated. Shenandoah was exhausted, nearly ruined."

"There are no excuses before the Emptiness. What is true is true. What is right is right. So say the bishops."

"You wouldn't dare accuse *me* of heresy."

"No one is above the Inquisition, Marchioness," Rossofore said darkly. "Not even you."

"It doesn't matter."

"What do you mean?"

"You can't have the crown."

"But I *will* have it. And you will hand it over to me. For the glory of Rome."

A sly smile began to spread over the marchioness's face. Rossofore did not like this one bit.

"You cannot have it," Valentine said, "because it isn't *here* anymore."

It was Rossofore's turn to feel shock and dismay. "What have you done with the crown, woman?"

"Do you think I didn't notice what you did to Lerocher? I even knew *why* you did it. Do you think I'm ignorant and powerless in my own castle? In my own kingdom? I am the queen of this land, and my people have not forgotten this."

Rossofore gripped both arms of the chair Valentine was sitting in. He leaned close and loomed over her. She turned her face up and met his gaze with a defiant stare.

"Where is the crown?"

"Far away."

"If you do not tell me, I promise you that I will wring the truth from you in the most brutal way imaginable. Then I will burn your bones until they crumble to dust."

Valentine laughed.

She *laughs* at me!

Rossofore backhanded her across the face. Her head twisted. He hit her again. Blood flowed from her nose and lips.

"Drag her back to her chambers!" he bellowed at the guards. "Lock her in. I'll decide what to do with her later."

His men obeyed instantly.

Rossofore stood for a long time, shaking with rage.

Dragon-rage, he thought. Righteous fire within. Dasein flowing through him. Pure power.

Something in his palm?

Ah yes. The remaining beads from the Golden Rose of Lerocher.

I could save them for later, Rossofore thought. But why? I need one now.

I will use it to look far and wide. I will use it to locate the thief in the night who has stolen the Couronne de Huit Tours.

The crown was pure dragon amber. It contained the dasein he would need to fully transform into the dragon he knew was inside him.

It held the amber he would need to consume for the triumph of the faith in the north.

My crown.

In Rossofore's wildest dreams he dared to hope he might *become* one of those heads of the faith, those bishops sitting so serenely in the Basilica of St. Judas on their huge block of amber, pronouncing the fate of Rome. They were the rulers of the world.

He was young yet. That would be later. For now, his task was to bring Shenandoah under Roman control.

And once I devour the crown . . .

Rossofore imagined all the dragon amber that was waiting in the Kaltelands.

A feast.

But I need power to get at it. More dasein.

He plopped another amber bead into his mouth, took a sip of wine, and gulped it down. The flush of power was immediate, intense, and incredibly pleasurable.

A man might become a slave to sensations like this,

Rossofore reflected. Might want more and more until the desire drove him crazy.

But not me.

I'm a master inquisitor, with training in self-abnegation to fall back on. With knowledge of what it takes to sacrifice for the greater good.

And besides, I do have *more* beads before I need to feast on the crown.

Which reminded him . . .

As soon as he had the crown in hand, Marchioness Valentine Archambeault, the so-called Queen of Vall l'Obac, must *burn*.

The fulgin didn't know why it travelled north, only that it must. This drive wasn't a compulsion exactly. More like a purpose. In the same way that water wasn't compelled to be wet, it just *existed to be* wet.

So the fulgin existed to go north.

Seeking a girl.

A young woman.

It had taken an image from the Dark Angel Queen's mind. In fact, it had been *molded* around that image, so that its every thought involved her. The girl.

The Dark Angel Princess.

She was darker of skin than the pale people of the north. Her hair was raven black. Her locks twisted into cascading curls. Her lips were full. Her features were fine boned.

The Queen Mother remembered.

Loved.

Longed to shelter and get to know the daughter better.

The fulgin *felt* this. It had been formed in the queen's mind, after all. But it couldn't understand any of it.

The fulgin couldn't love.

But it did know that the girl's skin was as smooth and soft as a toadstool cap. That would help in identifying her.

The creature was naked except for a bag strung around its back. In the bag was the crown. The creature did not know beauty except for the crown. The beautiful crown. The amber crown. The Crown of the Eight Towers. Eight amber towers carved in one strong amber band. The Couronne de Huit Tours.

The *crown* was beauty.

It was every purpose the fulgin had.

The creature must protect it. Deliver it to the princess. For the most beautiful thing in the world would be the crown in the girl's hands.

The crown on the girl's head.

Then the creature could cease. Dissolve. It couldn't die because it wasn't really alive. But it would have finished its task. In complete happiness. Its purpose fulfilled.

There was a long way to go still.

The fulgin could feel the princess to the north, but she was not near. It must struggle on.

Travel by night.

Hide in shadows during the day.

No matter what, avoid pursuers.

For there *were* pursuers. Many of them.

Romans. The red-collared priest who burned people for fun. The priest that wanted to eat the crown.

Wanted to eat it almost as badly as the fulgin wanted to take the crown to the girl.

The fulgin could sense the priest's greedy desire for the crown.

To be captured would be agony. All would be lost. And it could never die, but would live forever in the shadows, seeking a crown and a girl that were dead and gone.

It must *not* be captured. It must cross fields, forests, slink through villages. It must find the girl.

It must give her the crown.

Her mother, the Dark Angel Queen, had made the fulgin . . . made it not wise, but *clever*.

Good at hiding.

And *very* good at sneaking.

Chapter Nine:
The Inn

Wulf's company had spent a morning burying the Romans and their horses in the gully as best they could. It was enough to keep the ravens away for a day or so, which was the real purpose. Romans did not like pyres. And Wulf didn't want to attract the attention a giant fire for bodies might draw, anyway.

Captain Max Jager had overseen the grisly task until midmorning. Then he'd called it done. They'd moved out.

Wulf would never forget the tangle of dead Roman cavalry and their horses. It wasn't that he felt guilty. The Romans had invaded. They were spies. They had tried to kill him.

But he was beginning to realize that the more he fought, the bigger the toll it took on his memories. Those dead Romans were something you couldn't forget

He was afraid that images like that might one day push a lot of the good memories that were more fragile from his mind.

By the late afternoon, Wulf's band arrived in the village of Tjark. It was the southernmost outpost of the Mark of Shenandoah. Tjark was a crossroads for travelers, but Wulf wondered if the town were prepared for his company of one hundred soldiers to march in and want food and lodging.

And not just *any* one hundred, but one hundred soldiers wearing the insignia of the Mark of Shenandoah.

This badge was a red buffalo *passant* on a green field with a silver moon behind it.

The men-at-arms carried small shields—bucklers—that marked them as sworn to Wulf's family. They were painted with a black-and-gold hammer on a red field. The hammer was the Dragon Hammer of Tjark, the symbol of the von Dunstigs, the rulers of the Mark of Shenandoah.

The soldiers rode the intelligent valley horse breed called kalters. There was also a small herd of cattle along with them. These were handled by buffalo people as cattle drovers, both male and female. Behind that was a train of mules carrying tents, food, and supplies. Of course, this was the mark, so many of the "men-at-arms" of the company weren't humans, but a wide range of Tier. There were buffalo men, bear men, raccoon men, and centaurs. The mule drivers were mostly goat men, the fauns.

Near the middle of this band was Saeunn Amberstone.

She rode bareback on a graceful white kalter mare named Kreide. Much of the time Saeunn was slumped over the neck of the horse, clinging to her mane. Even half-unconscious, Saeunn could stay on a horse. She had grown up riding on a huge ranch in the Amberstone Valley out in the Great West. Ravenelle kept a watch, but nobody was worried Saeunn would fall off.

Wulf knew this didn't mean Saeunn was well. She wasn't.

That was one reason he'd diverted southeast to the inn at Tjark, instead of crossing into the Wild Kingdoms many leagues to the west as he'd planned.

For the past week of traveling, Saeunn had been getting weaker each day. She was fading. Sleeping in tents and riding a horse were wearing her down even faster. She had to rest for a little while. In a real bed.

Wulf rode beside her. On his other side was Captain Max Jager. Jager was the leader of the armed company. He was a bobcat man. At first glance, he looked like a child on the horse he rode. Wulf knew from firsthand experience Jager's courage, his grittiness, and his intelligence.

If an enemy underestimated Jager, they would wind up dead fast.

Wulf had seen it happen.

Ravenelle Archambeault rode on the other side of Saeunn. They were off the woodland path they'd been following for days and were on a wagon road called the Duke's Highway.

Rainer rode to the side and a little behind Ravenelle. To the rear of this lead group were Ravenelle's three servants. Then, on one of the massive draft horses the buffalo people rode—horses that dwarfed the kalters—sat the wisewoman, Puidenlehdet.

Several other buffalo women were with her. Buffalo women traveled with their men on long journeys—and to war. They were experts at pitching tents and setting up camp quickly in any kind of weather. And, like Puidenlehdet, at treating wounds.

We won't need tents tonight, Wulf thought, breathing a sigh of relief. We're staying at the best inn in the land. Or so they say.

It was called the Apfelwein auf der Therme in Kaltish.

The Applewine at the Hot Spring.

They'd been on the trail for three and a half weeks. They'd made their way west from Raukenrose, the capital of the mark. The seat of Wulf's family was at Raukenrose Castle. Then they'd turned south and wound through the ridges and valleys of the Greensmoke Mountains. Tjark was the largest settlement they'd seen in many days.

It was a town of about one thousand. There were men and other Tier, but the original settlers, who still made up more than half of the population, were *centaurs*. And because it was a town run by centaurs, the Apfelwein wasn't just *any* wayside inn, with a rough tavern and rickety stables attached.

The Apfelwein was special.

"Real beds for the ladies tonight, m'lord," the centaur Ahorn told Wulf. "New hay in a clean stable for my Puidenlehdet."

Ahorn was in love with the buffalo wisewoman who was looking after Saeunn. Wulf didn't understand all the ins and outs of the relationship, but he did know that the kinfolks on both sides were uneasy about it.

"Sounds good," Wulf said. The day had started rough, but improved the closer they got to Tjark. Riding on a road, even if it was rustic and barely wider than a cart track, was much easier than tramping through the woods. Near sunset, the tired people and livestock plodded into Tjark.

Ahorn, in his excitement to see some of his own people, rode ahead. He'd made sure there was a corral for the cattle and that everyone had a place to stay. The Tier soldiers were put up each according to his kind in the outbuildings of the inn. By doubling and tripling up on rooms, making use of the stables, servant quarters, and barns, all of Jager's company could have either a bed or at least a warm and clean place under a roof to sleep. Officers, gentry, and their servants had rooms in the main inn.

The centaur had ridden ahead happily to make arrangements. But when he returned to the group, he seemed upset. He stamped his forelegs in the dust of the trail and frowned furiously. Wulf was about to ask Ahorn what was bothering him, but the centaur seemed to shake off whatever mood had come over him. He smiled broadly.

Then he proudly reported that his kinsmen and the other people of Tjark extended their wholehearted hospitality to Lord Wulf and company.

For a very nice price, Wulf thought.

Ahorn had arranged a "discount" of nine hundred thalers, which would have to come straight out of Wulf's traveling funds.

They don't know it, but I'd pay them triple that for a bed to sleep in tonight, even though it is blackmail, Wolf thought.

The Apfelwein was made of logs on the outside—huge logs brought from deep in the mountains. It was finished with beautifully carved wood on the inside. There was a large hall with a fireplace almost as large as the one in Raukenrose Castle. In that fireplace, entire tree trunks were used as fire logs. There were dining tables and a sitting area in front of the fireplace. The sitting area was filled with rocking chairs for humans. There were curious contraptions that a centaur could step over and be supported by. Hallways led off to guest rooms.

Wulf wished he could appreciate the place more, but he was worried about getting Saeunn settled. Wulf called up his personal servant, a faun named Bleak. He and Bleak helped Saeunn down from the kalter when they arrived. They placed her on a pallet Ravenelle's bloodservants brought up. Then these two servants carried her to her room in the Apfelwein. Ravenelle followed.

Wulf stood in the entrance of the inn watching them disappear down a candlelit hall within.

"We're going to save her," he murmured to himself, not for the first time that day. "They'll know what to do in Eounnbard."

Rainer clapped him on the shoulder and startled him out of his thoughts.

"You look like somebody rolled you around in the practice yard dirt," Rainer said.

Wulf grimaced, took off a glove, and wiped his forehead. Rainer was right. The back of his hand came away with a stripe of trail dust.

Rainer pointed to some rocking chairs in front of the huge fireplace. "I'll go check on the women," he said. "You take first watch by the fire."

Wulf grinned. Rainer knew how to get him to do things.

Call it a "watch." Make it sound like a challenge, Wulf thought. Even if it is just taking a load off for a while.

Ravenelle will deal with making *Rainer* rest, he thought. She had her own way of getting to him.

Mostly by direct order, colorful and extended commentary on the state Rainer was in, and endless razzing. It had been that way between them for practically seventeen years.

Rainer was as much in love with Ravenelle as Wulf was with Saeunn.

And his love was *just* as doomed.

Ravenelle was going to be a queen.

Rainer was going to run a coal mine and arrow factory in Kohlstad.

Queens did not marry men who made their living in trade.

"Get out of here, Stope," Ravenelle said. "You are *looming*. Looming like a raven. A raven ready to eat the eyeballs of the battle-fallen dead once the living have passed from view."

"If you don't want me to loom," Rainer replied, "let me do *something*."

Ravenelle shook her head. Her hair bounced. It was barely contained as usual. She raised a finger to push back a curl that had escaped.

"Go and get some food for yourself." She gently pushed Rainer toward the door.

Rainer allowed her to, but turned before she could get him all the way out of the room.

"What about you, m'lady?" he asked. "Venison stew? Lord Ahorn claims it's the best in the south."

"Completely barbaric," Ravenelle said. "Do they actually cook it, or just mix the meat up in a bucket of warm blood?"

She took a long look at Rainer. His chin was drooping and his eyes had dark circles under them.

Oh no. He's too tired to tease, Ravenelle thought, feeling disappointed. Trying to get a rise out of Rainer was one of her favorite ways to end a day.

No, she thought, why deny myself? There's *never* a reason not to poke Rainer for a little fun. I'll do it anyway!

"And you appear to be the next thing to a dirty urchin off the street, Stope," she said. She raised a hand and patted his cheek. "So adorable." She sniffed. "And *so* ripe with the perfume of the trail."

Rainer gave her a tired smile. "You've smelled better yourself, Princess."

Ravenelle raised an eyebrow and faked a scowl. *That's* my Rainer, she thought.

"Get some rest, Stope. I'll have Jakka bring a meal. Harrald and Alvis will get my things delivered to a room."

The Torsson brothers were Ravenelle's bloodservants and bodyguards. Jakka, her lady's maid, was a woman of the mark. She was not bound to Ravenelle by the blood ceremony of Talaia. Ravenelle's original lady's maid had died a year and a half ago while defending Ravenelle from an attack by Sandhavener horsemen. Ravenelle had felt every moment of her agony.

Ravenelle hadn't had the heart to replace her with another bloodservant.

Ravenelle leaned toward Rainer. He was a half elb taller than she was, so she had to stand on tiptoe to brush her lips against his ear. "Will you still go with me?" she whispered. "To Montserrat? To Pierre du Corbeau?"

Rainer looked at her for a moment before answering.

"I swore to do it, Ravenelle," he said.

"Yes," she replied. "I know *that*." She blinked. A red tear flowed from the corner of her eye. That was the way of Roman princesses. Their tears were blood.

Rainer wiped it away and rubbed it gently between his fingers until it dried on his fingertips.

"And you know the *other* reason," Rainer answered. "The *real* reason I'm going. I'm not hiding it anymore."

Ravenelle came down from her tiptoes, and stepped back. "I'm sure I don't know *what* you're talking about, Mr. Stope," she said. She tried to say it lightly, but it came out callous. It always did.

So be it.

I can't be with a barbarian. A commoner.

An enemy.

No matter how much I want him.

Rainer stood a moment longer, then abruptly turned and went into the hall. Her eyes trailed him as he closed the oak door. The heavy latch fell into place with a clunk.

CHAPTER TEN:
THE SERVANT GIRL

The fulgin paused on the outskirts of a large plantation. This farm grew a mixture of cotton and tobacco, with some wheat and corn mixed in to feed the bloodservants. The creature didn't know anything about this. It only understood that here, at this place, were others who had a master, just as it did. A master who answered to the Dark Angel Queen.

And it could sense that the master of this place did *not* belong to the red-collared priest and the soldiers who were chasing it. Who wanted to steal the crown from it.

Here the master's master was the creature's own mistress. The fulgin could smell it in the air. Here it could hide away from the Romans for a little while.

✛ ✛ ✛

Marguerite was six years old. People told her she had far too much imagination for a servant girl.

For instance, right now she could see something in the shadows that none of the other adults could. It looked like a shadow in some ways, but this thing was darker.

It's the kind of shadow a *shadow* would make, Madeleine thought.

She had spent the morning at chores around the bloodservant quarters while most of the adults were away in the fields. She fed the chickens. She spent time grinding corn for the pone that all the bloodservants would eat come supper. Everybody had to take a turn at that.

In the afternoon she went to the mansion to get the waste food and table scraps that she would use to slop the hogs. Of course she would also pick the good pieces out, especially the meat. Then she gave the rest to the hogs.

She was very proud that whatever she could find in the slop would be extra for everyone to eat, and how good she was at picking it out. After supper, if she had found something special, Mamma and Papa, or one of the uncles or aunts, would pat her on the head and tell her she was a good girl and that she done a very good job.

They would also be sure to remind her that she was never to mention to the master's family, or the servants in the house, that she picked through the slop and kept things from the pigs. She was also to keep it out of her *mind* as much as possible. But that was easy, because the master and his family seldom got into the mind of a six-year-old bloodservant even though they could. They could get into everybody's minds if they concentrated hard enough.

It was during her chores that she noticed the shadow thing lurking about. It didn't seem particularly dangerous to her. It seemed more afraid than anything. So now and again she would throw it a scrap, or a handful of chicken feed. She would walk away and when she came back the food was gone. On the first day, she had tried to tell Papa about it, but he had looked at her like she was crazy and told her never to mention this again.

It was well-known that sometimes children who weren't right in the head were sold away to work in the amber mines. She had to fit in and never give anyone a suspicion that she was different—or she might end up at the bottom of a pit and never see the sun again.

This was enough to scare Marguerite into staying quiet about the shadow thing. But she knew what her eyes were seeing. It wasn't made up, it wasn't like an imaginary friend to talk or sing a song to.

The shadow thing was *real*.

Then something bad happened. On the second day after seeing the shadow thing, she leaned over a little too far while slopping the hogs and fell into the hog pen. Mamma had told her to be careful and she knew better, but the rails were so rickety and the hogs so hungry.

This was very bad.

Hogs could kill you, especially if you were little. A man could kick them away, but even a man couldn't kick a dozen pigs away if they thought he had some kind of food. You could get trampled, then eaten yourself.

Hogs would eat anything.

Hogs would most certainly eat little girls.

As soon as she fell in, some of the meanest of the boars came right for her. She tried to scramble up the split-rail fence. She almost made it, too, but then she gave in to temptation and looked back at all those hungry hogs. Her hands trembled so much that she couldn't make herself climb anymore. She wasn't going to get out in time. Those hogs were going to bite her and pull her back into the pen.

Then the shadow thing appeared.

It just *showed up* right where she had been standing in the dirt of the pen. The hogs couldn't see it. No more than the adults could, she reckoned. But then the shadow thing started twisting. It started turning around and around like it was dancing or happy and twirling. And there was proof that it was real right here, because the *dirt of the pen started kicking up*. It started swirling up in a dust devil that the shadow thing was making by all of its twirling and whirling.

The hogs didn't like this at all.

The dust scared them.

Where had that wind come from? What did it mean?

Pigs were pretty smart but they weren't smart enough to figure *that* out. The big boar who scared Marguerite so much started squealing in fright. He ran away. The other hogs followed. She finally felt the strength come back into her hands, and she could climb out of the pen.

Before she jumped down on the other side she turned around and looked straight at the shadow thing.

"Thank you," she said to it. "I don't know what you are, but I know now that you are *good*."

She was about to get back to her chores, when she heard a small voice coming from the shadow thing. It sounded almost like a little bone flute, like the ones Grandpa made from chicken legs.

"Can I *please* have something more to eat?" the shadow thing asked.

"Why sure," Marguerite replied. "I'm going to set the rest of the slop bucket down right here. Why don't you eat everything that's in there, okay?"

She put the bucket on the ground and then backed away. The shadow thing seemed to melt through an opening in the split-rail fence. It approached the bucket. It didn't have a head or a mouth, really. Instead, it put something like a funnel or a beak like a hummingbird had down into the slop and started sucking the slop up. It made sounds like "Hmm hmm hmm" and "yum yum" that got Marguerite to giggle.

When it was done, the beak went back into the shadow thing's form. Even though it didn't have a head, the shadow thing did seem to have legs and arms.

Not so scary.

Its legs kind of came to a point and didn't have feet, but it could still walk.

"Thank you," it bone-whistled. "That was good."

"What are you doing here?" Marguerite asked. "Where'd you come from? What kind of thing *are* you?"

The shadow seemed to look around and check to make sure no one else was listening except Marguerite.

"The Magnificent Dark Angel Queen made me," it said. "I'm a special messenger. I've got her crown in a sack, and I'm taking it to her daughter, the Dark Angel Princess."

"You mean Queen Valentine?" Marguerite knew that the queen made special devotion to the Dark Angel. All of the kingdom did. "She has a daughter that lives up in the Kalte lands."

Marguerite knew about this because sometimes Mamma put her to sleep with stories about what it was like to be lovely Princess Ravenelle among the barbarians. Barbarians were rough folks who didn't properly appreciate the princess and were always scratching themselves because they had fleas and lice. Sometimes Marguerite imagined herself being the special bloodservant to the princess. She would get to eat all the treats at Montserrat Castle. One day when the princess returned, that's where she would live.

"Yes," said the shadow thing. "Bad ones come after me. Have to hide. That's why I'm here."

"Are they chasing you? Are they after the crown?"

"Yes," said the shadow thing. "Had to hide the crown in

a nest in the chicken coop. You get eggs there. Please leave it where I put it."

"I will," said Marguerite. "I'll try to get you some more to eat tonight after supper or maybe in the morning."

"Thank you, little daughter," said the shadow thing.

"My name is Marguerite," the girl answered. "I belong to Master and Mistress Robecheau."

"This one does not have a name," the shadow thing said. "Do you want to name me?"

"Okay," Marguerite said. "But I'll have to think about it."

"Goodbye, Marguerite," the shadow thing said. It walked to a nearby cabin on its pointy legs. Then it melted into the shadows under the porch crawlspace and was gone.

Marguerite spent all night trying to think of a name for the shadow thing. The next morning after everyone else had gone to the fields of tobacco and cotton to work for the master, she set out some food scraps and chicken feed for it. When it came, she told it that she had thought of a name.

The shadow thing waited expectantly. It seemed eager to learn its new name.

"Windy," she finally said after drawing out the suspense a little. "Because you made that whirlwind that got the pigs to go away."

"Windy," it said. "Good." Then it gobbled up the food she had set out and disappeared again.

The next day, the Romans came.

This was scary. The soldiers from across the sea marched

right up to the master's house and banged on the door. When he came to greet them, one of the soldiers grabbed him and dragged him out to the mansion's big front yard.

Marguerite drew closer so she could hear. Nobody noticed her. The Roman soldiers said that something precious had been stolen from the queen, and that they were there to find it and bring it back. They said that they absolutely knew it was somewhere on this plantation.

The master didn't know anything, of course, so he couldn't tell them where the precious thing was.

Marguerite guessed that they were talking about the crown. She was probably the only person on the whole plantation who actually *did* know where it was. Even though she didn't know exactly *which* chicken nest it was under.

When the master didn't answer the way the Romans liked, they waited. Soon, a tall man in a black robe rode up. He got off his horse, which was a big black horse, too. Then he told the soldiers to tie the master to the sycamore tree in front of the plantation house.

Once they did this, he asked the same questions of the master that the soldiers had, only every time he asked a question and the master didn't answer the way he wanted, he whipped him across the back with a cat-o'-nine-tails.

The master's son had once hit Marguerite with a whip, and it had hurt really, really bad. That cat-o'-nine-tails looked like it had metal in the leather, too.

When they cut the master down he looked like he had a

puddle of gooey red mud and flesh on his back. A puddle all chuffed up by cows walking through it.

Then the man in the black robe and red collar held up his hand. He sniffed. Was there something in the air?

Oh, no, Marguerite thought. He might smell Windy! Or even the crown!

The man in the black robe walked toward the blood-servant quarters, sniffing, sniffing. The soldiers followed him. He looked confused, like he couldn't believe that whatever he was looking for could be in this rundown place.

Marguerite hid a smile. Windy had been right to hide it here. It was the last place people would look for treasure.

The man in the red collar stood in the middle of the servant quarters and gazed around. Finally his eyes alighted on Marguerite. He motioned for her to come over to him. He knelt and spoke to her face to face when she got there.

"Do you know anything about this precious thing that we seek?" he asked her. "Do you know what an orange is?"

"I saw my master eat one once," Marguerite mumbled.

"This thing I seek. It is a smoky orange color. Have you seen it anywhere, girl? If anybody here is hiding it, I would have to hurt them very badly. That is, unless you tell me. You saw what I did to your master didn't you?"

"Yes," said Marguerite. "But I don't know where any jewels or crowns are."

The black-robed man stood there for a long moment staring at Marguerite. He looked as if he sensed something was not right in her answer. For an eyeblink, Marguerite felt him in her mind, the way the master could get in your mind and dominate your will. But she was not linked to this man, and he hadn't bothered to dominate Master Robecheau, just beat him.

The black-robed man was not *her* master.

He might get into the edges of her thoughts, but she would not let him into the deep parts. She got to work. She made it so whenever she thought about chickens and nesting, she thought about an egg. And whenever she thought about the crown, she thought about an egg.

She thought *really hard* about eggs.

Finally the man turned his head and faced away.

"It's not here," he said. "We'll have to search the road to the Whitmore plantation. Two more leagues today. Let's go."

Marguerite sighed with relief. And deep within a nearby shadow, so did something else.

CHAPTER ELEVEN:
THE ADVICE

Ravenelle Archambeault finished reading aloud the last chapter of *The Pierced and Bleeding Heart of Julia Silves* and closed the codex with a sigh and a shudder. *Such* a bittersweet ending. All of the stories she read tended to finish that way, true, but that never really bothered Ravenelle. She could will herself to forget when parts of a story were repetitions (and sometimes outright stealing) of the many dark romances she'd read before.

She sat, knees drawn up, in a chair at the side of Saeunn Amberstone's bed in the Apfelwein Inn.

After tossing and turning for at least three watches, suddenly burning with fever, then just as quickly shivering with chills, Saeunn had finally fallen into a fitful sleep. Ravenelle considered going back to her own room to rest.

Yes, she really ought to do that because she expected to be needed again soon.

Ravenelle moved her perception into the minds of her bloodservants, her retainers Harrald and Alvis Torsson. These were men who had once been commanders in a Sandhavener elite legion, fighting under the names Rask and Steel.

They had kept guard outside for as long as she'd been tending to Saeunn. She hadn't compelled them to guard her, although she could have. They'd done it of their own will.

So strange that she even let them *have* a will. But things had changed a lot in the past year—including her attitude toward her religious faith, Talaia.

Ravenelle could feel her men's weariness. Literally. She could share their viewpoints, their senses, their very thoughts if she liked. She could also force them to obey her will any time she wished. They were her bloodservants and she was their dominator.

Harrald, tell Jakka to turn back my bed and open the windows in my room to let the stale air out.

Yes, m'lady.

They communicated in Talaia thought-speak—which they could do for up to a half-league distance—with no spoken words being exchanged.

And both of you go to bed. I'm perfectly safe here.

It isn't that, Harrald explained. *It's just that we want to be near when you need us.*

Well, I need *you to get some rest now. If Saeunn can be moved, we will reach the border soon. And I will enter my kingdom.*

Yes, m'lady.

Harrald's hearing and touch sensations were acute. She could see nothing through his eyes, however. This was because he was blind. She was the one who gave him sight. She used her eyes and her thought-link with his brother Alvis. Harrald had adapted to these weird, displaced perspectives, and had learned to function very well. He even claimed to *like* having a bigger field of vision, from multiple perspectives. All the better to protect his lady, the one who had saved him and Alvis from mental domination by a terrible evil thing.

The Draugar Wuten.

Now dead. Dead and crumbled to dust.

He'd memorized the layout of this wing of the inn, and was able to find Ravenelle's lady's maid by touch and sound alone.

Before Harrald left to do so, he shook Alvis awake and grunted for him to take his place by the door. For a moment, his disobedience infuriated Ravenelle. She'd told them *both* to go. She would *never* have allowed even well-meant insubordination like this from her bloodservants before. But those bloodservants were all dead—killed defending her from attacking horsemen. And now this unlikely pair was all she had left under her domination. That is, if you didn't count Father Calceatus. He was one of the dominates of her will and a bloodservant, true. But he had a special place and specific duties as a Talaia priest. Besides, he was back in Raukenrose.

She moved into the mind of Alvis. She felt him come awake and rub his eyes. He sat up from his slump, and looked through the hallway window of the inn, out at the town of Tjark. The town was a sea of neatly thatched and slated roofs. Its spread was broken only by a river-rock chimney here and there trailing smoke.

The town bell tower rose in the distance. Just then, the elder bell at the top of the tower began to toll. Beyond the tower to the north and west was the Shwartzwald Forest, where the leaves of the trees were just beginning to show their colors. It was late in the month of Anker, as the Northern barbarians, the Kaltemen, called it. It was named after the first anchorage of Leif Ericsson. He was the Northman, the Kalteman, who had left the Old Countries and crossed the sea to settle on the continent of Freiland.

For a moment she couldn't think of the Roman name for the month of Anker. She *hated* when that happened. There was so much about being Roman that she knew she was just guessing at. She should be good at the things she had control over, at least.

Then she remembered.

"*Septembres*," she whispered to herself.

Still in Alvis's viewpoint, she counted three strikes of the village bell. That mean it was Melkin bell, the beginning of the morning watch.

She had promised herself to be on her way home by the month of Gilbfast.

Octobris.

She'd meant to leave earlier, but her foster-sister had begun to have her bouts of sickness, and she'd stayed to tend her.

I'll have to leave soon, Ravenelle thought. Even though I'm terrified of what I'll find when I get there.

There had been no word, not a letter or report, from her mother the queen in over a year now.

At least Rainer will be with me, she thought.

Rainer had promised to accompany her to Montserrat. They'd grown up together and he knew how to handle her worries and fears. Just being around Rainer had a calming effect on her.

What she was going to do about *his* feelings for *her*, she tried not to think about. She had decided to worry about that after they both arrived in Montserrat.

And Harrald and I, m'lady, came the thought-speech of Alvis Torsson. *We, too, will be there to protect you always.*

She was embarrassed to have allowed her thoughts about Rainer to leak over to the bloodservant. She abruptly pulled out of his mind and back into her own single point of awareness.

Tjark was a lovely town, she had to admit, filled with the kind of order a Roman could appreciate. At least, she *thought* so. She'd not been outside of Shenandoah since she was a year old. She had been sent from Vall l'Obac as royal hostage to enter the family of Duke Otto at Raukenrose castle.

Her secret fear was that she was as much a barbarian as any Kalte woman—and maybe her mother had *finally* realized this. That Ravenelle would never fit in down south.

Would *never* make a good queen.

No. She wouldn't let herself think this way.

She was staying at an inn famous for its hospitality and comfort, but she hadn't been to her room yet. Instead, she'd been sitting at the bedside of Saeunn during her latest spell of sickness. The spells had begun to come over Saeunn about three months before. They had grown steadily worse. They were also lasting longer.

"You should go," Saeunn said. Ravenelle saw that she was awake.

"I'm not tired."

"Go to Montserrat, I mean," said Saeunn.

"I'm worried about my mother. About what's happening there."

"Yes, but that's not why you should go now."

"Okay, why then?"

Saeunn sat up wearily and looked Ravenelle in the eyes. "It's time for you to decide what to do about Rainer. When you get there, you finally will."

Then Saeunn collapsed into her pillows and fell back to sleep.

CHAPTER TWELVE:
THE SITUATION

Even though she was surrounded by possibly dangerous Skraelings, Ursel Keiler continued reading the letter from Duchess Regent Ulla Smead.

And Wannas Kittamaquand kept looking intently at her as she read.

Have I got a bug in my hair or something? Why does he keep *doing* that?

Never mind.

She needed to get to the bottom of this, and decide *what* to do.

The letter was addressed to her father, Earl Keiler, but Ursel knew Duchess Regent Ulla well. Just as Ulla knew that, aside from matters of war, Ursel ran Shwartzwald County for her father. The letter from Ulla was really meant for her.

✤ ✤ ✤

The thing is, Lady Saeunn agrees with me about Wulf's so-called quest. I'm sure of it. Wulf should answer the dragon-call, not set out into the wilderness on a wild hope. But Saeunn had been so ill, only awake a half-watch or less each day for weeks now, that she had not been able to put up any resistance to Wulf's determination.

After Wulf heard Abendar's suggestion to go to Eounnbard, he grabbed at it. Abendar had offered it very cautiously. But off Wulf went three weeks ago—it will likely be a month when you receive this.

He took with him a company of the Bear Valley levee commanded by that young bobcat man, Captain Jager, who Wulf met. He came to admire Captain Jager during the battle to retake Raukenrose.

Also along are Abendar Anderolan, the elf, and—at my request—Ahorn the centaur, a lore master and star gazer, who I ordered to act as my private agent and surrogate.

And there is yet another complication. Princess Ravenelle was determined to go to Vall l'Obac and find out the fate of her mother's kingdom. She has also been studying healing under a renowned buffalo wisewoman. Both of them have been nursing Lady Saeunn.

So the princess decided to travel with this company to the mark's border with Vall l'Obac. Once there, she plans to separate from the group, and head southeast to Montserrat. My foster-brother—Rainer Stope—and Princess Ravenelle's bloodservant bodyguards will accompany her the rest of the way.

That is the state of things at present. And so we—you and I—are left in a quandary. I will not send thousands of men and Tier to battle and grave danger until Wulf answers the dragon-call.

What if there is another way?

What if the dragon has been trying to reveal this to Wulf?

I know the dragon trance doesn't necessarily work in such a way, but I am haunted by the prospect of ordering those men to their deaths—and then it turning out to all be a mistake that could have been avoided.

So I have sent Wannas Kittamaquand, this young Skraeling envoy, to you for two reasons. First, I think that if anybody can get through to my stubborn brother, Wannas, with his eyewitness account of the siege of Potomak, can. But Wannas will need help finding Wulf.

I know Wulf intended to cross the west valley and travel south through the Greensmokes. From the southern border, he planned to make his way through the wilderness trading paths to Eounnbard.

Without a native guide, there is little chance that Wannas will be able to catch up to Wulf. Your daughter, Ursel Keiler, would make an excellent guide.

The second is to deliver a personal postscript, appended to this letter, to my dear friend Ursel.

Your servant, etc.,

Ulla Smead, Duchess Regent of the Mark of Shenandoah

Ursel closed her eyes for a moment, trying to imagine Ulla sitting at her small desk in the Great Hall side room she used as an office. She'd converted her father's old map room into her work space, although the maps still remained.

Ulla had dictated this letter. The script was too professional, even for Ulla, who had an artist's hand for calligraphy.

And there it was. The postscript. It was a private letter, rolled up and sealed inside the outer scroll.

Imagining Ulla at Raukenrose brought back a flood of other memories. Memories she'd spent the past few weeks trying to get away from. They had dulled for the most part. All except one. The final one.

The last time she'd seen Wulf von Dunstig.

Chapter Thirteen:
The Garden

They were walking in the Castle Garden. The name was a misnomer, because the garden wasn't actually inside the castle keep. It was at the bottom of the hill Raukenrose Castle perched on. The garden also wasn't just a garden, either. It was as much a place for trees as flowers. The Sandhaveners had cut most of the older trees down for firewood when they'd invaded. Wulf had ordered it replanted, but the new trees were only saplings now.

Wulf wore a light-blue tabard, with only a dagger stuck in his belt. Ursel had on her favorite green dress, trimmed in red. It was the start of summer, a hot, sunny day, so there was no need for cloaks or hoods.

"I'm wondering about your trip to the west, Lord Wulf," Ursel said. "Considering the state of things over in

Sandhaven. The problems with the Romans in the south. I mean, it's a dangerous time to be going."

"You've been talking to Ulla."

"She and I have gotten to be good friends, I think."

Ursel and Wulf walked through last year's leaves. Over the winter they had turned to a soft meal. It looked and felt almost like ground coffee.

She planned to return to Bear Hall within the week. Her father needed her. She'd heard in a letter from her youngest brother that the house was in complete disorder without her around to keep it up. Also that the earl was holding off making major Shwartzwald County decisions until she got back and he could consult her. This included permission to marry for a dozen villagers up and down Bear Valley.

She wasn't one to surrender easily. After all, she'd stayed on the archery competition circuit until she'd won the Mayfield Championships against the best bowmen of the Shwartzwald when she was fifteen.

But she had to admit defeat when faced with a problem like Saeunn Amberstone. And of course she had come to really *like* Saeunn during the months she'd spent in Raukenrose. Who wouldn't?

Wulf von Dunstig wasn't going to fall in love with Ursel Keiler.

With me.

But, curse it to cold hell, Ursel Keiler hadn't fallen the slightest bit *out* of love with *him* during all that time.

She was leaving Raukenrose. And so, apparently, was Wulf.

"I'm being stubborn. I don't care," Wulf said. "I believe in loyalty. You stick with your friends. You stick with family. You don't do anything for the principle of the thing if it interferes with loyalty. Because it won't be a real principle if it *does*."

"Doesn't being, well, the heir get in the way of that attitude?" Ursel asked. "I kind of thought that you'd put the mark above anything."

"I have to put the land-dragon above everything else. It makes me sick—I mean, sick in my body and my mind—if I don't. I guess the sickness might even kill me if I didn't pay attention to the call long enough."

"What if the dragon tells you to do something different?"

"It's not *like* that. The dragon doesn't tell me what to do. It doesn't think like you and I do. It *dreams* about things. It's old, but still a sort of baby. I feel the dragon-call and see the dragon-visions, but I still have to make the choice, whatever it is, myself."

"And you choose Saeunn?"

Wulf's eyes clouded over. He turned from her, picked a beech leaf from one of the saplings in the garden.

"I really feel bad about hurting you, Ursel," Wulf finally said. He stripped a side from the veined leaf. He let it go and watched it slowly drift to the path. It spun as it fell.

Then he turned back to her. "You've told me more than once how you feel."

Ursel smiled. "Forget about that. I wouldn't ask now if I didn't want to understand."

"All right," Wulf said. "Then yes. I choose Saeunn."

"Out of loyalty?" Ursel knew she sounded pitiful. She got mad at herself immediately. "Partly, I mean?"

Wulf nodded. "That's some of it. I'm all about loyalty with Rainer. He's my best friend. We have each other's backs. I even feel that way about Ravenelle. And that's how it is with Saeunn.

"And she sacrificed her star to kill the draugar," Ursel said.

"To an elf, her star is her life. There would've been no way for me and Rainer to take that thing on if Saeunn hadn't done what she did. We owe her. Everybody in this realm owes her."

"But that's not all," Ursel said. She sighed. "Is it?"

"She was always there for me when I was growing up." Wulf paused. He glanced ruefully at Ursel. "You sure you want to hear this?"

"Yes."

"All right, then," Wulf said. He rubbed his forehead, glanced back at her again. "I've been in love with her since I can remember, Ursel. So saving her is an easy choice."

"I get it," Ursel replied. "Even if I don't want to, I do. It's just—"

"Just what?"

"If there wasn't any Saeunn. I mean not that she died or anything horrible like that. But if she'd never come to the castle—"

"Would I have fallen in love with you when we met?"

"Would you?"

Wulf didn't hesitate. "Instantly," he said. "How could I not?"

How could you not? Ursel thought. Pretty easily, it turns out. When the other woman is elf royalty.

"So I hope you understand," Ursel said. "That's what happened to *me*. I fell in love."

Wulf faced Ursel and looked her in the eye.

We're both even the same height, Ursel thought. Perfect fit. Saeunn is a half-hand *taller* than Wulf. Not fair.

"You have the greenest eyes I've ever seen," Wulf said. "You're smart. The best pure archer I've ever seen, and I've seen some good ones." He glanced down. "You're also beautiful," he said bashfully. "And you saved my life."

"But she's the one."

"Yes."

Wulf looked back up. He leaned over, pulled her to himself. Kissed her on the cheek. She put her arms around him. A final squeeze. She was just wicked enough to make sure he could feel her breasts pressing up against him as she did.

"Take care of her, Wulf," Ursel whispered.

"You'll be all right?"

More of a wish than a question.

"Sure," Ursel replied. "I'm going home."

Chapter Fourteen:
The Postscript

Ursel paused a moment to force herself completely back to the present.

The scroll. The postscript from Ulla.

Wannas Kittamaquand standing against the sun, giving her shade to read in. Unaware of the reason she was tearing up.

Ursel sniffed, wipe away another tear, and made herself look back down at the unopened scroll.

She could do something about *that*, at least.

She took her knife from its sheath on her belt, and cut the seal. She rolled this scroll out on top of the first. Ursel recognized Ulla's personal, flowing script. She'd written this bit herself. She began to read.

✣ ✣ ✣

Dearest Ursel,

I don't know if I can forgive Wulf for his selfishness. All right, I know I will, but really he's gone too far. I understand how he feels. I love Saeunn, too. The thought that she might be fading before our eyes twists my stomach into knots.

But we all have our duty. And the mark seems to be in its greatest peril in a generation. He's needed here. He needs to talk to the dragon under our feet. He needs to make a decision on war.

My heart warns me that a terrible trial may await my brother before he is done traveling this road he has chosen. Of course I may be giving in to my own fears. But if my worries prove to be true, I want to have done something. I want to have set some plan in motion that has a chance of keeping the disaster into which I suspect my brother is headed from leading to his death and the end of our freedom.

My, I sound melodramatic, even to myself. I'm sure that my fears are mostly phantasms because I'm worried about Wulf.

Nevertheless, what I would like most is to have you there to look out for him. I say this, first of all, because I know how you feel about Wulf.

Second of all, speaking as your regent, I have a job for you. Think of it as an unpaid government appointment.

Ursel, I know you are extremely competent in ways both physical and mental. It's a rare combination, and frankly, you're the only person I know in the mark who has a chance at succeeding at this assignment.

What assignment?

Find Wulf.

Stop him from doing something idiotic.

Well, more *idiotic.*

If you can't stop him, then I want you to help him out of whatever bog he throws himself into.

I think you understand duty better than most. I also know that you are someone I can depend on. You saved my brother's life once—and did it in style, with an arrow shot worthy of mention in a saga, from what I've heard.

From what I've been told, you are not merely your father's recording secretary, you are at this point running both the household and the county.

Your brothers are fine folk—I went to university with Hans and Frederic, you know—but it's also clear they trust you with the big decisions. Your father talks openly about having settled an incredible dowry upon you. He made this very clear to Wulf.

Some may doubt he'll follow through when it comes down to it. Bear folk with bear folk, some people say. Humans with humans.

I know he will.

And since I understand how you feel about my brother, I have had a few trusted advisers do some poking around in the Shwartzwald concerning just who you are.

Most interesting.

The story goes that you were found in the woods by the earl while he was out hunting one day. It is a very striking tale.

Deep in the forest, there is a thick grove of beech saplings that has been carefully cultivated by the woodsmen of the western valley. Iron nails are driven into the trunks of each beech sapling. The tree is then left to grow around the metal. When it's done properly, the nail heads are fixed in place. You have the makings of a war club as deadly as any mace or morning star.

When the beeches are big enough, dangerous enough with their embedded nails, they are harvested. Cut to lengths. And made into deadly striking weapons for peasants who can't afford swords.

So picture that. A grove of war-club beeches, nails driven into every tree, impassable even for most forest animals, especially the dangerous ones. And in the middle of this impregnable thicket? A little baby girl.

The story goes that a poor family who could not afford another mouth to feed put you there, a babe in the woods. But they couldn't leave you to be eaten by wolves, bears, or any other terrible creature. So they put you in the safest place for a baby in the forest.

The middle of this specially cultivated war-club beech grove.

For all practical purpose, nothing can get into a beech war-club grove. It is like a little nest of nails. There you were safe from the bear and the wolf.

But, of course, left to starve to death.

So the story goes the bear man earl heard your hungry

cries from the middle of this little grove. And, not caring a bit about himself, waded into that thicket. He was willing to cut and tear his own hide on the war-club beech trees to get you out.

And still Earl Keiler couldn't reach you. The nails were too sharp, the thicket too dense.

I can see it now.

Still you cry.

The soft heart of the earl melts.

He orders axes brought up by his servants. He directs them to chop down those beeches so he can rescue the baby from within.

The war clubs must be sacrificed!

The question never answered in all the reports I have heard: how did you get in there in the first place?

If no one could get to you, how did your poor parents put you there?

Well, let us set that question aside for the moment.

Back to Earl Keiler.

So the earl has the beeches chopped down. He steps over the stumps to find the little babe. He plucks you up, babe, blanket, and basket—yes, I hear that you were found in a basket of woven oak strips, according to this legend, wrapped in a woolen red riding cape.

The great bear man is entranced with your sweetness. He loves your little cries, which sound very much like a cub's cries for its mother. So he takes you back to Bear Hall. Lady Hilda, his wife, doesn't like you at first. After all, you are a mewling human girl.

But you smile at her, and soon she warms to you. She raises you as the daughter she never had.

You grow up the enchanted foundling, the good luck charm of House Keiler.

It's a wonderful story your family tells.

But that isn't how it went at all, is it?

What I am saying to you is that, even knowing what I know about who you really *are, what* you really *are, if there was ever a chance you might join my family, I, for one, would welcome you with open arms.*

Wulf cannot marry Saeunn. Someday, after he realizes this in his heart of hearts, he may learn to love another.

I would not mind in the slightest if that other were you, *Ursel Keiler. Daughter to bears.*

Your sincere friend,

Ulla Smead

Ursel found herself blushing. She was thankful that Wannas had finally ceased staring at her. He had gone to confer with his men and was not watching her.

So.

Ulla was asking *her*, Ursel, to guide Wannas Kittamaquand to find Wulf.

Ursel didn't for a moment think she would be able to win Wulf from Saeunn.

Ulla was dreaming when it came to that.

But there was no reason to avoid him.

It wasn't like being away had gotten her heart to grow less fond of him.

After all, whether Wulf wanted to or not, he was going to be duke of the mark one day, probably soon. His father, Duke Otto, with his mental wasting disease, was fading. Everyone knew it. And whether Ursel wanted it or not, she was a true child of House Keiler, the most powerful Tier family in the land.

She and Wulf would be seeing a *lot* of each other over the coming years.

That is if the Romans and Sandhaveners don't overrun us all first, Ursel thought. And in that case, I'll be dead.

She knew she would defend her family and her land until her last breath—and go down fighting.

But right now she needed to do all she could to make sure it didn't come to that.

She carefully rolled up the correspondence from Ulla and tucked both under her bedroll. This was in a satchel she always carried on hunts.

Inside the satchel also was her small looking glass.

On a whim, she took it out. For a moment, she gave in and allowed herself to gaze into it.

What is wrong *with him?*

I'm not so bad. Not so bad at all.

Cold hell.

What is wrong with *me*?

For a moment, a red-brown glow came into her eyes.

A "dasein ring," some called this. It was a telltale marker for her kind.

My kind, Ursel thought. What I *am*.

She raised a finger and touched a sharp tooth.

So Ulla knew.

One day her deepest secret may be out to all, Ursel thought. She was now old enough to deal with the bigotry this would arouse. It was prejudice the Keiler family had been shielding her from for years.

For now, though, she would keep it to herself.

She would remain just Ursel. Commoner. Foundling.

Instead of what she really was.

Sister to bears.

CHAPTER FIFTEEN:
THE STAR-STONE

"Don't tell me what to do," Ravenelle Archambeault said.

"All right, sister," Saeunn whispered. "Don't be mad at me."

She struggled to sit up, but couldn't. A wisp of blonde hair fell across her eyes. Ravenelle reached down and brushed it away.

"I'm not," Ravenelle said. "I'm mad because I can't help you."

"You're a great help," Saeunn replied with sigh. "Will you read some more of your romance to me?"

"We finished it," Ravenelle said.

"Oh." Saeunn blinked. "I guess I drifted off."

"The prince finally tells Julia Silves he loves her and hands her a rose. But she pricks her finger on a thorn on the stem and—well, you know she has that noble bleeding sickness where it won't stop?"

"Yes. I think so."

"She's sure she's going to bleed to death, and it's going to be long and drawn out and painful, so she asks the prince to plunge his dagger into her heart. He won't do it, so she does it for him. She dies in his arms. But at least they get to kiss."

"Gruesome," Saeunn said. "But pretty." She smiled wanly up at Ravenelle. "It makes you shudder."

"That's kind of the point," Ravenelle replied.

Saeunn nodded. She tried to shift and sit up, but the strength went out of her and her head fell back on the pillow. Suddenly her eyes grew bright and hard, like little blue flints. Her smile turned to an expression of sadness. "The elfling loses more of her soul-roots," she said—to no one in particular.

"Brennan?" There were allegedly two beings within Saeunn. One was Saeunn. The other was the elf whose star fell from the sky. It was Brennan Temeldar whose star-stone meteorite Saeunn wore on a chain around her neck.

"Yes, dark girl."

Ravenelle hoped Brennan was only talking about the color of her hair and skin, which came from her Afrique and Aegyptian ancestors. But sometimes she was afraid that Brennan was seeing some other kind of darkness *inside* her.

Brennan Temeldar was an elf woman who allegedly

shared Saeunn's body now. She was supposed to be beyond ancient. Ravenelle didn't know the sagas like Wulf—learning Kalte sagas had absolutely *not* been the part of her education she paid much attention to—but she did know that Brennan was *in* the oldest sagas. The sagas said she had done something terrible to herself—what that was, the saga was a bit vague on—and given up her soul. That was when her star had fallen from the sky. But a small part of her lived on in some way in the star-stone necklace. At least that was what everybody around Saeunn believed.

Ravenelle figured it was all some barbarian myth. But it was clear that Saeunn believed that part of her was Brennan Temeldar, and that had somehow helped her recover from what she'd done against the draugar. She had made him vulnerable to weapons. If it was good for Saeunn to believe in Brennan Temeldar, then Ravenelle would play along.

"What are soul-roots?" she asked.

"The places where the mind and body are together so closely you can hardly tell them apart," Saeunn/Brennan answered. "She and I, we are . . . separating."

"What can we do?"

"I do not know. So little remains of me. Just this ash, this cinder." She fingered the star-stone at her breast. She let it go and sighed. "I've forgotten so much."

"What I can see is that Saeunn has a fever and chills, and gets as weak as a baby. Then she recovers for a while. Today she seemed almost back to her old self."

"No," Brennan said. "She will *never* be back to her old self. The star that she was is gone. Fallen."

"I don't believe that. She can still laugh and cry like always. She still makes little Anya giggle when she plays with her." Anya was Wulf's youngest sister. She adored Saeunn and Saeunn returned the adoration. "She's even kissed Wulf. A lot."

"She burns brightly before night falls."

"You are really depressing me, Brennan Temeldar," Ravenelle replied. "Saeunn would never do that."

"And are you angry, Ravenelle Archambeault?"

"I'm worried," she answered truthfully. "There's still no message from my mother. Nothing for over a year."

"Then you must go and find out what has happened. You are of age now. Childhood is fast fading, and it is time to become a woman."

Ravenelle looked down at her breasts. When she was twelve they had started growing. And growing. Even though she'd willed them over and over again to stop. She envied Saeunn her small, perfect breasts.

"I think I've been becoming a woman for a *while*," she said dryly. "Listen, Brennan, please, please do something to help my sister."

Saeunn/Brennan looked at her and shook her head in wonder. "You are so young," she said. "You think you can stomp your feet and make the world obey."

"I've gotten over thinking that."

"You will always be young to me," Brennan said. Her voice seemed to be fading. Saeunn/Brennan closed her eyes. "I will do what I can for now."

Saeunn was sixty-three and a half years old—which meant she was an elf teenager. She would live on and on. Elves did not die of old age. Humans did. Even Roman nobles.

But elves *could* die of other causes, Ravenelle thought. It'll be so *wrong* if Saeunn dies before me.

It wasn't fair. Saeunn should always stay her wonderful older sister. Kind, quirky, laughing *with* you and not *at* you like so many others did. She also tended to fall into rhapsodies when standing in moonlight—then let you make fun of her about them when she came out of her trance. Ravenelle had teased her a lot about that when they were young. Looking back, she realized her younger self must've been quite a trial sometimes, even for Saeunn, who hardly ever got ruffled.

She loved her sister. She would do anything for her. Even stay in the Kaltelands for as long as she was needed, even though she had spent years thinking about finally being set free to go home.

"Your hair is a mess," said Saeunn. "You'd better let Jakka fix it."

"You're back," Ravenelle said.

"Was I gone?" Saeunn asked.

"Brennan Temeldar was here," said Ravenelle.

"Oh."

Ravenelle reached up and put a hand to her crazy, curly hair. No matter how she pinned it, it seemed to spring free. It was never long before it was as tangled as a bramble bush again.

"I feel much better, actually," Saeunn finally said.

"I think Brennan did something to help."

Saeunn reached for the star-stone and wrapped her fingers around it. "It's cold," she said.

Ravenelle bent over and touched the stone. It wasn't just cold. It was freezing. A thin white layer of ice was on its surface.

Saeunn tucked the stone back under her nightdress. She sat up.

"I think I'll get dressed," she said. "I'm hungry."

Ravenelle nodded. "If you're feeling that well, I'm going to get some sleep. I'll send Jakka to look after you for a while." Saeunn had never wanted a lady's maid during her years in Raukenrose castle, but now she nodded.

"That would probably be a good idea," she said. "We don't know how long this will last. Where are Wulf and Rainer?"

As if in answer, there was a soft knock on the door.

Ravenelle glanced outside through the eyes of Alvis.

It was Wulf, of course.

"Come," said Ravenelle. She stood.

The door opened and Wulf stepped in. When he saw Saeunn sitting, his eyes lit up. "You're better!" he said.

"For now," Saeunn replied.

He went to her side and, before he could settle in, Saeunn pulled him down. She kissed him passionately for a long moment.

When she let him go, Wulf looked stunned. And very happy.

"Oh Wulf, it's good to have *now*," Saeunn said.

Wulf sat down in Ravenelle's chair. He took Saeunn's hand and kissed it. Tears were in his eyes.

And that cursed von Dunstig determination.

He'll never give up, Ravenelle thought. And if he loses her, he'll love her till the end of his days.

It would be nice to be loved so completely, she thought.

And then she realized that she probably was.

Don't go there, Ravenelle thought. You are not a barbarian. Act like a Roman. *Think* like a Roman.

Ravenelle quietly left the room. In the hallway, she put a hand to her hair. Saeunn had been right. It *was* a continuing explosion of a briar patch. She would finally take the half-watch the task required, and have Jakka brush it out, wash it, and pin it back up properly.

Then she would check back in on Saeunn.

If she's still strong, Ravenelle thought. If I think she's better . . .

Then Rainer and I will head for Montserrat.

Chapter Sixteen:
The Hunt

Ursel was brooding on the dream again. She'd had the same, or nearly the same, dream for the past three nights. She'd been sleeping on her wool ground cloth as usual. In the dream she even knew where she was. Asleep on the forest floor.

But the sky above felt like it was *reaching down* to her. *Calling* to her.

She'd never felt anything like this before. So real. The *realness* took her over completely.

Maybe this was the way Wulf felt when the dragon-call came to him.

At first the dream was confusing. She was gazing up into the sky and the stars were growing brighter and brighter. What was strange and wrong and terrible was the fact that she was lying in a pool of *her own blood* in the dream.

In the dream she had been shot through and through.

Pierced by an arrow.

She had bled out.

She was *dead*.

Not dying, not near death.

Dead.

This was the part that set her heart racing during the dream. And the part that set her mind in turmoil after she woke up.

She was dead.

It seemed so real.

And the sky was calling her.

What could it mean? She wanted to know before she let go and slipped away.

Ursel had always been faithful to the divine beings. She had a special devotion to Scathi, the divine mother of the hunt. She hadn't been particularly religious, but she had expected to end up in Valhalla at the end of things. She was a warrior at heart, after all—even if only with the bow. But this vision was not of Valhalla. Not of the afterlife.

What was going on? What was she supposed to *do*?

Then she heard a song. Something lovely beyond any beautiful music she had ever heard before. It took her a moment to realize that it was a lullaby. It was a song the stars were singing to the dragons.

The dragons slept, and the song was in their dreams. It calmed them and nurtured them.

She understood.

This was what the stars were *for*.

But the song . . . she felt a lack in the sky. There was a star missing. There was a special note that was not sounding, that was meant to be part of the song and was not there.

Was it *her*? Was she somehow going to join the stars? Was that what dying *really* was?

If so, maybe it wouldn't be so bad.

But she didn't think that was it.

No. Something else.

The dragons did not know that a star was missing. They didn't know anything. They *felt*.

And they felt that the song was not as comforting as it should be. Or could be.

That star needed to return. The note should sound. The sky-song was not right without it.

Ursel lay gazing up at the stars and felt this longing and lack. She felt that she would do anything to be able to restore peace to the dragons. To *her* dragon, the child dragon that lay under Shenandoah and needed to be cared for.

If only *I* could make a star, Ursel thought.

But it must take incomprehensible magic to do that. Beyond any she had at her command.

Then she understood the note that was missing in the lullaby. She felt the shape of its absence. In the dream-logic, that shape became a word.

An understandable word.

It was part of the last name of an elf that she knew.

Eberethen.

Amber. Stone.

Saeunn's last name, Amberstone.

That was when she woke up. Each night. Three times now. It was infuriating. Now *she* was obsessing about saving Saeunn Amberstone.

I don't even know if I *want* to save her, Ursel thought. Although maybe she would if it came down to it.

It *wouldn't* come down to it.

And what is the other stuff.

About me being *dead.* I don't like that one bit.

Am I seeing the future? Some vision?

Or just a lot of mixed-up nonsense bubbling up from my mixed-up heart?

There was a crackling in the brush to the northwest.

"Do you hear that?" the Powhatan named Manteos said.

Ursel put her finger to her lips, motioning him silent. She held up her other hand to signal the group to stop moving. It took a moment for everyone to obey. They were strung out in staggered fashion in the woods.

She'd heard the sound of the woods rustling several moments before, even while she'd been brooding on her dream. She hadn't said anything because it could have just been an animal. But the leaf crackling got louder and closer. It wasn't just one animal. What it sounded like was a traveling wolf pack. She'd run across wolves several times in the forest. They were one of the most dangerous of all predators. When they were nearby, she hid carefully. Usually she did this by climbing a tree after masking her scent as best she could.

At the moment they were walking through a little grove of saplings that was growing where a huge old tree had fallen down and left a small clearing. There wasn't anything to climb here. But it was a much different thing to face a wolf pack with eight people than one person. Because humans were *the* most dangerous predator when they hunted in packs.

Then there was a scream from the forest in the direction the rustling had come from. It sounded almost as if some child were being torn apart. There were more whines and screams, a big chorus of them after that. The saplings began to shake on the other side of the clearing.

She had already fitted an arrow into her bow. She gazed around and saw that the others had too, except for big Ottaniak, who was deadly with his tomahawk. He had it ready.

From the trees charged—

Not wolves.

Too little.

Coyotes.

Yipping, screaming, sounding like a cross between a barn owl and a squeaky door hinge. Coyotes in a pack, headed for her. As if their lives depended on reaching her.

Looking over their surging backs, Ursel saw that this was true.

They were being *chased* by wolves.

"Don't shoot the little ones!" Ursel called out. She turned to Wannas. "Tell your men in Algonquin. Don't shoot the coyotes." She took aim over the coyote shoulders. "*Do* shoot the wolves."

Wannas translated what she said in a commanding voice.

Ursel let fly her arrow. It sank into the chest of the closest wolf, and the animal collapsed, rolling around and whimpering in pain.

She didn't wait to see if it died. She nocked an arrow, took aim at another. This one didn't give her an easy shot at its vitals. So instead she shot it through the eye. It collapsed as if it had run into an invisible tree trunk.

The other Skraelings were letting their first arrows go. Most found their mark and at least distracted a wolf. Ottaniak's tomahawk neatly split one through the skull. Ursel had her third arrow nocked. But the wolves were turning to retreat. They scampered for the forest. She almost released a shot after them, but she didn't want to waste arrows. They were going.

The coyotes collapsed on the ground nearby panting. There were ten of then. One was bleeding from a mauled rear leg. It tried to lick the blood away, but the flow was too fast. Ursel saw that it was a male. He was a little more muscular than the others.

Maybe he was injured so badly because he had stayed behind to fight and drive away the wolves, Ursel thought.

"Let's make sure those wolves are dead," she said. She nodded toward the carcasses of the downed wolves, which they could see through the saplings. She took a step toward the bodies. When she did the coyotes all got up and moved with her. Even the one with the badly hurt leg. She turned back to look at them.

They were all arranged in a semicircle behind her. She spun around and took a few more steps. The coyotes matched her pace staying just behind her. She turned again.

"I'm just going to make sure we are safe from the wolves," she said to them. But the coyote pack kept following her. She stopped. They stopped. She moved, they moved.

Ursel sighed. "All right. I don't want you going over there. I'll just stay here." She turned to Wannas who was a few paces away. "Can you see to the wolves while I try to figure out what is going on here?"

Wannas nodded. There was a curious smile on his face as he looked at Ursel. "They seem to think you're their mother," he said.

"Well, I'm not," Ursel replied. She turned her gaze to the coyotes. "I'm not!" she said again, this time to the coyotes.

When they saw that she was not going to move anymore, they lay down again. Ursel went to tend to the coyote with the bleeding leg. There wasn't much to do except to wrap it in a strip of muslin cloth with enough pressure to stop the blood flow. The little coyote limped, but it was able to stand up on its four feet after being bandaged.

Ursel looked over the pack. Their panting was dying down, and they didn't seem to be whimpering and whining as much. Then the muscular leader started to growl. He hunched up and backed away. For a moment Ursel thought he was about to attack her. But then she realized he was gazing at something over her shoulder.

She didn't think. Didn't look, just reacted.

Ursel swung her bow around with two hands. It was good that she didn't wait a moment longer. The wood of the bow connected with the skull of a wolf lunging toward her throat. Its teeth were bared and she could actually see the saliva strands in the wolf's mouth, a hand away from her neck. She'd swung hard, and the bow knocked the wolf to the side. It already had an arrow in its side. When it hit the ground, it tried to get up, but the arrow stopped it from being able to roll over.

Then the coyotes were on the wolf.

They attacked with fierceness. And they were led by Bandage-leg. The wolf was already wounded to the point of death. It couldn't withstand ten coyotes pouncing on it. Biting. Tearing

Ripping fur. Skin. Meat.

The coyotes took the wolf apart. Then, almost as if they'd gotten a signal, they went back to sit near Ursel. They stared up at her.

She looked into Bandage-leg's eyes.

And she understood.

Around the pupil was a shining purple iris. Even in the daylight, the iris seemed to spark slightly. It was an eye color that no true coyote ever possessed, nor a coyote man. Ursel had no doubt that at night, the edge of the irises would glow.

This was called a "dasein ring."

It was a sign that Tier and humans had mated across species.

These were were-coyotes.

Changelings.

"All right," Ursel said to them. "Why don't you transform? Then we can talk about what you are doing on my land."

Wannas had come to stand beside her.

"What are you talking about?" he asked her.

Before she could answer, the coyotes started to whine. Several of them fell over and rolled around, yipping. All of them contorted in some way. Then they writhed about.

Then they contorted again, in ways no animal could.

They seemed almost to be turning themselves *inside out*.

Hair disappeared. Claws retracted. Snouts shortened.

When it was all done, they were not ten coyotes.

They were ten humans.

Small, naked humans.

Boys and girls.

Children.

Chapter Seventeen:
The Changelings

Several of the half-breed children were sharing blankets that the Skraelings had rolled out from their bedrolls.

"They done run us out of the West," said the little boy who had been Bandage-leg. His leg looked even more hurt than before. Changing form definitely did not mean that wounds were healed.

There was a gash down his calf that split the muscle in two. The gash was at least a half-finger-length deep. Nootaw, one of the Skraelings, had taken a look at it. Without asking, he'd sat down next to Bandage-leg and produced an iron needle and thread.

The boy looked warily at the man, but continued talking with Ursel.

"Who ran you out? How long have you been traveling?" Ursel asked.

"Days and days," said the boy. "Our folks set us to running when the bad ones came in to burn the camp."

"You're from the Cantuck?"

"I reckon you call it that over here. We just call it the Happy Hunting Ground. It's supposed to be ruled by old King Gil Yarmo, but he's more of a bandit. Least that's what folks say." He glanced at Nootaw, who had finished threading his needle. "What's he going to do with that?" he asked nervously.

"He's going to help you. He's going to sew up that wound," Ursel replied.

"I don't like that."

"If you don't let him, you're going to bleed to death," Ursel said. "So is this king the one who attacked your camp?"

"Naw, it wasn't him. There's been a bunch of bad ones pushin' in from the south and out west toward the Mississipp. Men. Trolls. A few Tier with 'em. The Romans put a bounty out on us, they said, and they aimed to collect. Bring in a were-skin and get a hogshead of tobacky. Float it down the river to Orleans and make your stake for a year."

"Why would the Romans do that? They've left the Wild Kingdoms in peace for a hundred years."

"Don't rightly know. Paw and Maw didn't say. So we ran a long way and I been showing them others how to cross the mountains on account of I've been over to Shenandoah before once or twice. We got into the valley okay and we were living off a sick heifer now and then. Then you was following us, I think."

"I was."

"Didn't know that for sure. You're crafty."

"Thanks."

"And you didn't seem to mean us no harm."

"I don't."

"Anyhow, then these here men rustled and bustled up, and we took off. But that pack of wolves picked up our trail and they been running us since yesterday. We was about to just lay down and die when we come across your sign again. I figured you *might* help. Don't know why. But I did. We'd just about give up."

"I *was* looking for you before. I knew you couldn't be wolves, because you weren't being a danger to any people, or dragging down healthy cattle."

"We was hungry," the boy said. "And we have to eat to get enough strength to change back, you know. So we needed to do that so we could talk about where we was going and whether or not to go back now and see if we can find our folks, or if they're all dead. Last we saw them they was fighting the bounty hunters so's we could get away."

"You've had a really hard trip," Ursel said. "I wish I could take you back to my father's hall and feed you. But we have to be pressing on. Do you want to go with us?"

The boy seemed to think about it. He started to speak then hesitated. He looked to the others. The bedraggled children gazed at him. None of them spoke. They all seemed very tired and scared. "I reckon we'll stay here," the boy said. "There's a lot of food now." He nodded toward the dead wolves.

He means to eat them, Ursel thought. Well, turnabout is fair play, I suppose.

"We'll get that meat up, and then I reckon we'll head on back to see what become of our folks."

"I want to give you something," Ursel said. "I can write you out a note of passage through the mark. You could maybe wear it on a little bottle around your neck or something to keep it safe. If anybody tries to stop you, you pull that out and show them my signature. Everyone in these parts knows who I am. I'll even tell them to feed you if they have any extra food."

The boy gazed at Ursel for a moment. Tears came to his eyes. "Thank you, Mistress," he said. "We didn't know there was any kin in these parts no more."

"Now you have to let this man sew up your wound," Ursel said. "You've got to be brave and let him do it, okay?"

"Does he have to?"

"He has too."

The boy clenched his hands and scrunched up his face. "Then let's get it over with."

Ursel walked a few paces away while Nootaw put several stitches in the whimpering, but obedient, boy.

"What's he talking about?" Wannas asked. "These are not

coyote people. These are were-creatures. Human-Tier changelings. They would just as soon rip your throat out as look at you, I've always heard."

"These kids aren't going to rip anyone's throats out," Ursel said.

She went back to the children. The wound was pulled shut on Bandage-leg. It was seeping blood, but the major flow had stopped.

"If you go back and find that your parents are not there, I want you to come back to me," Ursel told the whole group. "Come to Bear Hall. You can bring anyone you pick up along the way, too. There shouldn't be any children wandering around in the wild. That's the way changelings got the bad reputation they have in the first place. You go see about your parents, then come to me if you need to."

"What do we call you? You have the bear look, and there's no mistaking it."

"My name is Ursel. Ursel Keiler. Everybody in this forest knows who I am, and they will be able to show you how to get to me."

"Okay," the boy said. "But I guess we'd better be eatin' if we want to keep our strength up."

"Are you *sure* you want to go back?"

"Wouldn't *you* want to go back if it was *your* folks?"

Ursel nodded. "I understand. My offer stays open. Come to me if you need to. You won't be harmed in my forest."

"Thank you, Mistress."

The boy raised a hand to signal the others and soon the writhing and growling came back. This time they were transforming from human into coyotes. The only thing that marked them as different from regular coyotes was the purple glowing ring in their eyes around the iris.

They picked themselves up and went over to the wolves. Soon they were yapping and playfully fighting each other for a chance to feed on the carcasses.

"We'll rest here tonight," Ursel said to Wannas. "I want to make sure that those wolves don't come back to bother the children. They ought to get at least one night of safety."

"I don't get it, Ursel," Wannas said. "I understand that they are just children, but they are interlopers on your father's land. You don't really know whether you can take them at their word or not. We'll have to set a guard to make sure they don't rip our throats out in the night."

"I'll take the first watch," she said. "I'm not worried about getting my throat ripped out. I'm worried about what is happening in the Wild Kingdoms to send kids as refugees here. Anyway, I have a special interest in weres."

"Really, why?"

"Because nobody else does," Ursel replied. "Everybody thinks they are evil. I've always thought they are just ignorant. And they never get a chance to learn any different, because they are always being chased like animals."

"Maybe there's a reason they get chased," said Wannas.

"Maybe there's a reason that people think Tier hybrids and human changelings should be stamped out."

Ursel smiled slyly. "These puppies?" she said. She shook her head. "These cute little puppies? Come on, Wannas. Really?"

"They could grow up to be killers and cutthroats. They likely will."

Ursel pointed over toward the coyotes tearing into the wolves.

"They get a bad reputation." She stood up and cinched up her belt holding a quiver of arrows. She unstrung her bow. Then she wiped the blood from the wolf off its end. Finally, she looked around and found a place to set up her guard over the changelings.

Chapter Eighteen:
The Mistake

Wannas found Ursel at the end of the first watch. "I will spell you," he said. "Are you sure this is the right thing to do? We have such pressing business but there are children wandering around in the woods here."

"I know more about them than I let on," Ursel said. "I was out here looking for *them* when I came upon *you*. They aren't the first changelings to come over the mountains. Something is happening in the Wild Kingdoms and it's bad. Whole families of were-creatures and changelings are being slaughtered. I didn't want them to know that their parents are probably dead."

"Then you will send them to a place where these refugees are being kept?"

"If and when they come back."

"Why let them go at all?"

Ursel shook her head. "You know why. They need to *know* there's nothing they can do to save their parents and kinfolk. Then they can live in some kind of peace with us."

"You'll take them in?"

"Yes, we have a spot on the western side of Massanutten Mountain where we are keeping them until we can sort them out. There's a lot of bad feelings against changelings in Shenandoah. It comes from the early days when werewolves had teamed up with some death-cult Skraelings. We called them the Wutenluty. It was six hundred years ago, but people still remember. Old Duke Tjark led the first settlers to take them on and defeat them. He had a magical weapon called the Dragon Hammer. All of this is part of the founding story of the Mark of Shenandoah."

"Does your father know about this camp?"

"Yes, he's the one that suggested it. He's always had a soft spot in his heart for changelings."

She considered saying more to him, but they already had so much on their minds trying to find Wulf and deliver a message that Potomak needed help. There was no reason to bring up details that didn't have anything to do with the mission she'd taken on to help them.

Ursel stood up from the rock she'd been leaning against and stretched. Then she crouched back down. She counted her arrows. Wannas leaned over and gently touched her arm. She turned to face him.

"Mistress Keiler. Ursel," Wannas said in a low voice. "I've been watching you the past few days and I've never met a woman who was so sure of herself. You're the best shot I've ever seen with a bow. Your form is beautiful."

"Even with muddy boots and a face covered with scratches?" Ursel said, trying to lighten up where she feared this conversation was going.

"I meant your archery," Wannas replied.

"Oh," Ursel answered, embarrassed.

Wannas smiled. "Your face looks fine, too," he said. "Lovely."

So much for keeping things lighthearted, Ursel thought.

"I wonder if . . . are you supposed to remain a spinster so you can take care of your father into his old age? Is that why they adopted you?"

Ursel could feel the flush coming to her face and she was glad it was night so that Wannas couldn't see her. Both of them were squatting. Ursel reached over and quickly pushed him back over his haunches. He fell splaying into the leaves.

"You shouldn't talk about things that you don't know anything about," Ursel said.

"I didn't mean to offend you," Wannas said. He sounded shocked that she had taken his words the wrong way.

But how could I not, Ursel thought. He practically called me a *spinster-in-the-making*!

I'll bet he's used to everyone making allowances for him being disrespectfully candid. He's definitely a rich kid who thinks that people admire his always being truthful no matter what. But actually they are probably just afraid of losing trader status with his big, rich family.

Ursel knew the type.

Raukenrose, the capital, was crawling with men like that.

That was one of the reasons she felt relieved when she'd left.

"To answer your nosey question," Ursel said. "No. I am *not* expected to stay unmarried. The *opposite* is true. My father is going to give me a dowry. At first, it was in silver thalers. But I told him I didn't want that. So it's going to be land instead. And it *isn't* a dowry, despite what people call it. I get the land either way, whether I get married or not."

"That must be nice," Wannas said. "I'm supposed to become a factor at Kitty Yards. That's my father's tobacco market in Potomak. He hopes I'll take over the business one day. I don't know if that's what I want. I wanted to go to Raukenrose University. Well, before the Romans decided to take over my city and box me in."

"Well, you got *to* Raukenrose, at least," Ursel said with a laugh.

"Yes, I guess I did. I even met the head of the university. He is a very little man."

"He's a gnome."

Wannas nodded. "Yes. I told him I wanted to study the history of my people, the Powhatan. He was excited about that. He said he was looking forward to meeting me again in more peaceful times."

"I'll probably go. Women study at Raukenrose University, too, not like in Sandhaven," Ursel said. "University *colleges* are for male and Tier. The sections called 'houses' are reserved for women. But everybody mixes when they are taking classes." Ursel smiled. She reached out a hand and helped Wannas to sit back up. "Maybe you'll meet a girl at the university. Somebody right for you."

Wannas touched her arm gently again. "Maybe I already have," he said softly. He leaned over toward Ursel, moving in for a kiss.

But she couldn't have this. Not here and not now. She moved her head away and said gently, "No."

Wannas took a moment and withdrew. "I'm sorry. That was stupid."

"Don't worry about it," Ursel replied.

"Is there already somebody?"

Ursel considered for a moment then smiled mischievously. "What makes you think I have to be in a relationship with someone *else* to reject *you*?"

"I guess . . . you don't."

"Listen, I know what it's like to make a fool of yourself in front of somebody else because you feel something that they don't."

"Is that what just happened?" Wannas replied, bitterness in his voice.

"I'm just saying that there's no reason to be embarrassed. You and I are from completely different worlds. We're on the same path for a while, but soon the path will fork and we'll probably never see each other again. I don't take you for a one-night sort of man. Are you?"

Wannas puffed out his shoulders. "No," he said. "I am not."

"I know *I'm* not a one-night sort of woman. So this just can't work."

Wannas hunched silently for a moment. In the darkness she couldn't tell whether he was angry or not. Finally he spoke. "You're probably right," he said. "But I *do* think there's somebody else. Got to be. I won't ask you any more about it, though."

"Please don't." Ursel put the arrow quiver around her shoulder and stood up.

"Probably some noble guy, right? I never have understood you monarchists, with your rules about firstborn and second-born inheritance. In a democracy like I come from, the father can decide to give his children whatever he wants, or nothing. Land, huh? What would the adopted daughter of a bear person get set up with? Some fields near the ancestral hall? Maybe the yearly lord's share from a village or two? That land around Bear Hall is prosperous. Some prime tobacco land would make a pretty good lure for a man." He chuckled at his own wit.

Just when I thought you might be not a donkey's ass,

Ursel thought, something like that comes out of your mouth.

"No villages," Ursel replied. "Not even any farmland. Just some woods."

Wannas nodded. "I'm sure that's very generous. I didn't mean to hurt your feelings again. So where are those woods of yours going to be?"

"You've been traveling through my woods for the past five days," Ursel replied dryly. She reached down and patted him on the shoulder.

"*All* of this forest?"

"Just the western Shwartzwald," she said. "My brothers will have the farmlands and the eastern woodlands. But it's all a family kind of arrangement. Bears are like that."

"That's . . . a lot," Wannas said.

She took several steps away, then turned back to Wannas. She spoke with a more serious tone in her voice. "Please keep a watch over these children tonight. Who knows what kind of mischief they could get into out here. I feel kind of responsible."

"We saved them from wolves."

"They're just children. Orphans, probably."

"I will. Nootaw says he will take third watch."

"All right," Ursel said. She lay down within the saplings. She'd given her bedroll to some of the children, so she just rested on her back in leaves. Overhead, the stars were burning brightly. The temperature was pleasant enough, and it wasn't going to rain. With her bow and arrows tucked under a shoulder, Ursel was asleep within moments.

When the morning dawned, Nootaw had fallen asleep at his watch.

The coyote pups were gone.

CHAPTER NINETEEN:
THE COMPETITION

The mead hall of the Apfelwein Inn was filled with Jager's men and with many locals, too. It was now the third night of staying in one place.

In the inn were centaurs, Tier, and humans. By the fire, Wulf saw Abendar sitting in a rocking chair. He was smoking a long-stemmed clay pipe provided by the inn. Beside him stood Ahorn, who was smoking his own personal pipe, a hollowed briarwood root that looked extremely well used.

Wulf did not smoke, but he was overcome with the desire to take in the odor of good pipe tobacco. Pipe smoke reminded him of his old tutor Albrec Tolas.

Tolas was a gnome less than six hands in height, but he would always loom as a giant in Wulf's regard.

When he'd left, Tolas was mad at him.

His old tutor had told Wulf that his expedition to Eounnbard was reckless. He'd said Wulf could send Lady Saeunn there with others if he had to, but that the *heir* needed to stay in Shenandoah.

Besides, Tolas knew that the dragon was calling again. He said he could see it in Wulf's worried expression. Wulf was the heir. It was his duty to answer.

To cold hell with the dragon and with Tolas's attitude, Wulf thought.

He was tired of feeling bitter about it. He just wished he could talk to Tolas now when he had many doubts about the way forward. Saeunn had gotten so sick on the way.

Now she seemed to be getting stronger, but could he trust it?

Tolas would have given good advice. He always did, even if it was often something you didn't necessarily want to hear, at least at first.

The least Wulf could do to bring Tolas to mind was to take in a little pipe smoke.

Wulf told Rainer he'd eat later, and went to join Abendar and Ahorn where they seemed to have set up shop near the fire.

The elf bowed his head toward Wulf, but did not get up. Ahorn bent a knee, and said, "My lord."

I'm never going to get used to being treated like I already have Father's position, he thought.

They shouldn't do this bowing. The duke was still alive. But he didn't have the energy to scold them. Instead, he sank into the deerskin-covered rocker next to Abendar and sighed.

"Maybe tomorrow we take to the woods again," he said.

Ahorn nodded. "It may also be the day the princess leaves us. Ahorn here tells me that the road south leads to a border crossing less than a league from here. After that, the way goes onward into the Vall l'Obac piedmont."

"Yes."

Ravenelle was going home after sixteen years as a hostage fosterling in Raukenrose.

And when Ravenelle turned south, that meant that Rainer would leave, too. He had promised to take her to Montserrat.

What Rainer would do when he got there, Wulf did not know. Probably turn around and head back. Rainer did not talk about his feelings much, even to Wulf. But Wulf knew how conflicted he was. Rainer was all about loyalty.

Even though he is walking straight toward a broken heart, Wolf thought. Ravenelle wanted him to take her to Montserrat, so Rainer was going to take her.

It seemed to Wulf as if all the safety and certainty of his childhood had come apart in the past year and a half. His two older brothers were dead. Now his foster-siblings were intentionally splitting apart. All of them seemed to be moving on a path Wulf could not follow even if he wanted to.

"Your face is clouded with worry, m'lord," said Abendar. He took a puff on his pipe and looked a Wulf quizzically.

"Almost stormy," Ahorn agreed with a wink and a nod.

"Is there anything I can do to help?" Abendar continued.

Turn back time and return Saeunn to health and happiness, Wulf thought.

"No," Wulf replied. He sighed. "It was another long day."

"It was," Abendar said. "I spent it tending to the horses. I am skilled at it. That wonderful mare Kreide does not like to show it, but I could tell that even she was tired from the ride. On the way here, she was careful to step lightly with Lady Saeunn on her back."

"Kreide is a good horse," Wulf said. "That's why I picked her out for Saeunn."

"I would be very happy to have her among my brood mares one day," Abendar put in. "I suppose I'll go back to raising and selling horses once I settle in Eounnbard."

"I didn't realize you had a *job*."

"It is my main occupation. It's an Amberstone and Anderolan specialty. Saeunn's family owns Amberstone Ranch, where she grew up. They have always been horse breeders. They turn out the best travelling horses for the Elf Road."

"I never heard about breeding horses," Wulf said. "I knew she grew up on a ranch of some kind."

"I remember Lady Saeunn when she was a toddler,"

Abendar said. "Very happy. But she had her own mind even when she was very young."

"Like in what way?" Wulf asked.

"She loved animals, especially the big ones. She loved buffalo, even the ones that might have trampled her. I saw her once running beside a big heifer buffalo when I was visiting her father. Saeunn must've been about three or four years old. She was running along a meadow lane holding a handful of daisies, trying to get the heifer to follow her. Which it did. I was scared for her. I was about to go and get her, but the buffalo seemed to know it was a game, too, and was being very careful."

"What happened?"

"Finally her mother thought she'd teased the heifer long enough. She went and scooped Saeunn up."

Wulf smiled. "I'd liked to have seen that," he said. "Seen Saeunn when she was little, I mean."

Abendar nodded. "I suppose that was about, oh, sixty years ago," he said, and took another draw on his pipe. He puffed out a smoke ring. "Elves do not have many children. Even for us, she was special. That's why her family sent her to the Old Countries after she was star-melded. They wanted the best education for her."

"She learned to be a healer there," Wulf said.

"And many other things," said Abendar.

"I wish we could take her home to Amberstone Valley," Wulf said. "That was the original plan."

Abendar took his pipe from his mouth, looked at the stem. It was getting blackened. When the taste got bitter, it was time to break a small piece of the clay stem off. The elf carefully snapped off a section and dropped the broken bit onto the wooden floor beside his rocking chair. This was the custom at the Apfelwein. It would be swept away in the morning.

Taking time with the stem caused the elf's pipe bowl to go out, however. Beside him, Ahorn took out a wax-coated punk stick from a pouch he wore about his flank. He dipped it in his own pipe bowl. The centaur took a couple of deep draws, and the tobacco in his pipe crackled with building heat. This ignited the punk stick. Ahorn then handed this to Abendar to relight his own pipe with.

The elf did this, then blew out another cloud of smoke. From the odor, Wulf guessed it was Valley Orinoco, which was the more popular tobacco brand. Ahorn's brand was Perique, which had a stronger odor with more bite. This was also the type of tobacco Albrec Tolas smoked, so Wulf knew the odor well.

Finally Abendar spoke.

"I would gladly have taken her home," he said.

"We were *going* to," Wulf put in. "*We.*"

Abendar smiled playfully. "Yes, I understand, Lord Wulf," he said. "You're not the only one to have ever felt Saeunn's allure, though."

Sounds like *you're* one of those, Abendar Anderolan,

Wulf thought, a twinge of jealousy passing through him. Everyone seemed to want to kid him about his feelings for Saeunn. Well, let them.

"I'm *sure* I'm not the only one," Wulf replied curtly.

"I meant no offense, m'lord" Abendar said.

"I know, Friend Abendar. I'm just . . . worried."

"Neither one of us can take her back to her homeland. The Elf Road is impassable. My traveling band was attacked over and over on the way here. Brothers and friends were killed. When our sulfur wagons burned, all the profits went up in smoke. The ones like me who fought through to the east are lucky to be alive."

"I *get* that the way west is closed," Wulf said, irritated by having to hear yet again why his first plan had been a bad one. "That's why we're going to Eounnbard. To the Mist Elves. To find help there."

"If there is help."

Wulf stared at the fire. He rocked back and forth. Finally he spoke.

"This can't be for nothing," he said. "There has to be."

Chapter Twenty:
The Brush

The Skraelings could move quickly through the forest. Not as quickly as *she* could. They were basically townies, even if they had grown up hunting. At least Wannas had. It was pretty clear that he'd not only been raised rich, he'd always been treated as the golden boy of his family. She could also see he was constantly striving to live up to it.

There may not be any royal titles allowed in the Skraeling city-states, but Wannas behaved like he was some kind of merchant prince. He also pounded on the fact that nothing was more important than his mission to Wulf. Ursel was getting tired of the repetition. Even if they found Wulf, even if Shenandoah sent an army, could it really defend Potomak from *Sandhaven*? Plus, according to Wannas, there were Romans, too.

And now there had been that aborted attempt to kiss *her*.

Wannas was handsome enough, she had to give him that. Raven-black hair. His face bronze with high, angular cheeks. His eyes light brown, almost clear.

And he was *very* intense. Every day. All the time.

But whenever she found herself softening to him, he tried to order her to go faster, or asked whether she'd lost the trail. He *really* didn't like it when she took time near sunset to hunt up a rabbit or squirrel for their dinner—all of their dinners. Because she was good at it, she'd found herself feeding the whole group for many nights in a row. They all now acted as if they expected her to do it, too, which was *very* annoying.

I'm not some paid hunting guide, Ursel thought. And I'm sure as cold hell not your mother.

But it wasn't courteous to eat fresh meat in front of them while they gnawed on their pitiful dried pemmican. Ursel believed in courtesy. In courtliness.

Unlike Potomak, Shenandoah had a duke. And her father was an earl, even if she herself was a commoner.

So she put up with the attitude from the Skraeling men as a lady would.

Which didn't mean she was going along with their plans.

She'd heard at Bear Hall that Wulf had finally left on his quest to save Saeunn Amberstone. In fact, she'd half decided to go in search of the changelings partly in order to get away from everyone at Bear Hall talking about the "foolishness" the young heir was up to.

It wasn't foolishness.

It was love.

It just wasn't love for *her.*

Not again! Blood and bones, I'm more pathetic than those men chewing and spitting tobacco by the fire.

It was late in the evening. Wannas had set a watch, and the rest of his band was settling down to sleep around the small fire Ursel had started. Every night the Powhatans went through the same ritual.

A cup of yaupon tea.

A long chew on a knot of tobacco they placed in one cheek until it bulged.

Another cup of tea, then to bed.

They each carried a woolen point blanket—white wool with blue, red, and yellow stripes. The blanket was to wrap up in, and to sleep under when it rained.

She herself liked to sleep on the outskirts of her fires, usually with her back to a tree or rock. Fire drew too many curious visitors in the night, and it ruined night vision. Besides, she was hardly ever cold, even in the dead of winter. It was a trait she'd been born with.

When traveling, she carried a satchel over her shoulder with a wax wool rain jacket in it and her own bedroll blanket. Also inside the pouch was her fire-making kit, her bow repair tools, a small looking glass, some cake soap, a tiny tin of cheek rouge—she had to admit she was vain about having rosy cheeks to match her red hair—and a brush for that red hair. Most nights, she built a one-person shelter with her bow stave and the rain jacket. She covered this with leaves.

Her ritual at night by the fire was brushing her hair. It was long and thick. It could get oily between washings, too. To keep it from becoming a tangled mess while camping, she gave it one hundred strokes every night. Then she would plait it up for sleeping and brush it out with fifty more strokes every morning.

Wannas seemed fascinated by this. He had watched her make every stroke for many nights.

Tonight his stare was starting to irritate her as much as his other behavior.

"Are you not allowed to look at women brushing their hair back home?"

Wannas seemed to start out of a daydream.

"No," he answered. "I mean . . . yes. Men can watch women brush their hair. Put on makeup. Whatever." He placed a hand to his chin, and kept gazing at her. Then his eyes seemed to grow troubled as a thought occurred to him. "Is it wrong here? Have I offended you?"

"No. Not at all."

"Good."

"What I'm wondering is, why do you keep staring at me like you've never seen a girl brush her hair before?"

"I've never seen . . . there are not many red-haired women in Potomak. I've hardly ever seen it. And none with hair as red as *yours*. Or eyes so green."

"So I'm a curiosity to you?"

"Just your hair," he said. "I mean, yes, I find you interesting in other ways. But—"

"But it's mainly the hair," she said, cutting him off before he said something even more awkward.

"Do you . . . are you going to remain in your father's service for your whole life?"

"We've been over that."

"No," he replied. "I mean . . . Could you leave Bear Valley? Marry and live elsewhere?"

"Not your business really," Ursel said sharply.

"But with your dowry, where could you find a good enough match?"

Ursel hesitated with her stroke. "Oh, there might be a boy or two around," she answered.

"And I was wondering if you . . . wanted to finally tell me about *him*? About whoever it is who is constantly on your mind?"

"I do not."

"But there *is* somebody?"

"You have to stop this, Wannas."

"Yes. You're right, of course."

Where was I? Oh yes, sixty-three.

She resumed brushing.

Sixty-four.

"All right. Even though it's really none of your business, the truth is that I probably *won't* get married."

Wannas looked surprise. "Why not?"

"Because, I can't marry the one I'm *expected* to marry."

Because I was raised to think of myself as a little princess by my father. I was raised with the expectation that I would one day meet one of the duke's sons, it didn't matter which, and that he would fall helplessly in love with me—or at least with the fact I'm inheriting a large chunk of the western Shwartzwald Forest. I would be the final, bodily union between the Keilers and the von Dunstigs, the two greatest families in the land.

Then Wulf von Dunstig came along and I fell in love with him. *Not just who he was, but him.*

I even saved his life.

Not enough.

She's still immortal. And beautiful. And with hair like sunlight. And eyes the color of the sky. And cute pointy ears that stick out a little.

And she's filled with elven magic.

And she's kind. And thoughtful.

And loves him.

And I am apparently somehow supposed to help her.

The dreams of the star-song and dying had not stopped. They'd gotten more intense.

"Let's just say that I've won a lot of competitions in my

life," Ursel said. "But I'm not going to win *this* one. I'm outclassed."

"I doubt that."

Ursel considered. Should I tell him? Share my misery? Give him a glimpse at the pathetic love-fool I *really* am?

Blood and bones, no!

"It doesn't matter," Ursel said. "Now where was I?"

"Sixty-five," Wannas replied softly. "I count along with you."

"*Why*, for Scathi's sake?"

"Because it helps me to get to sleep, Mistress," he said. He shrugged. "Nothing more."

Wannas smiled wanly in his infuriating, arrogant way. At least she *supposed* it was arrogance. Maybe he was just uncomfortable with this sort of conversation.

Marriage. Dowries.

She knew very little about Skraeling manners. They were democrats. In Potomak, anybody could marry, well . . . *anybody*. This all must seem strange to him. Confusing.

For the first time, she actually felt the smallest bit *sorry* for him.

"Mr. Kittamaquand, you have my leave to count away," Ursel said. She smiled her own pale smile. She pulled the brush through her hair.

Sixty-five.

And again.

"Sixty-six," he whispered.

CHAPTER TWENTY-ONE:
THE COUSIN TRAP

The fire in the Apfelwein common room had burned down to coals. Wulf had thought about going to bed, but the rockers were so comfortable. And the company was good. Besides, they had been talking about Saeunn.

"I have never heard of an elf living long who has lost her star," Abendar said. "Death is usually quick. Instant. But the lady lives on."

He gazed upward, and Wulf suspected he was in communion with his own star. As Saeunn and the sagas had always told him, "Elves are stars and stars are elves." Each elf had a star for a soul. When the elf died, the star went out.

"She has the star-stone."

"A fragment of Brennan Temeldar," Abendar said, shaking his head in wonder. "It's a tale that's old even to elves." He turned his gaze back to the fire. "But for Saeunn Eberethen to have given her star so that Wuten of the Draug could be killed—well, she helped put to rights one of the greatest troubles my people ever let loose on the world." He bowed to Wulf again. "And so did you, Lord Wulf. And Mr. Stope, also."

"We had to. No choice. The draugar was going to kill us. Rainer and I had to fight him. And we couldn't have gotten rid of him without Ravenelle either. Or, really, all of Shenandoah."

"It's a very good thing you've done and my folk will never forget it," said Abendar. "*I'll* never forget it."

Wulf didn't want to *like* Abendar. Abendar had as much as admitted he'd considered courting Saeunn once she was old enough. Which was now. But the elf was hard not to respect.

"I appreciate that," Wulf replied. "I ought to go see her, I think."

He started to get up from the rocker.

"You've looked in on her twice already. She should settle in and rest, m'lord," said Ahorn. He put a soft hand on Wulf's shoulder. "The princess is with her. And so is Puidenlehdet."

"I guess you're right," Wulf replied. "But I'm *going* to check on her later."

Ahorn nodded. "Yes, you should. And spell my dear wisewoman. Puidenlehdet has to sleep, even if she does think she's indestructible."

"I'll make sure that she gets some rest," Wulf said. "We're going to need her more than ever."

Ahorn didn't seem to be listening to Wulf's reply. He shook his head and stamped a forefoot down hard. It resounded against the floor, causing several people to glance in their direction.

"And that cursed cousin of mine had the gall to tell me she couldn't have a pallet in my stable," Ahorn said. He gave a dismissive snort. "He doesn't *approve* of our relationship."

"Lots of people don't approve of a centaur and a buffalo person match. You know that. People say that's where were-beasts come from."

"It *is* where were-beasts come from," Ahorn said. "If the child is unloved and treated like an outcast. Which we would never do."

"I'm sure you wouldn't, my friend," Wulf said with a smile. "But you two aren't married yet. Are you?"

"No," the centaur said. "That's not the point, m'lord. You don't understand the family politics that can go on with my kind. And hers."

"There aren't a lot of centaurs in Raukenrose," Wulf admitted.

"Tawdry, sordid stuff," Ahorn replied. "Stupid stuff."

"Okay, now you *have* to explain," Wulf said. He nodded toward Abendar, peacefully smoking. "He wants to know, too."

"It's always amusing to find that somebody else's family

is as peculiar as your own," Abendar said with a chuckle. "But, Lord Ahorn—your people listen to the stars and use crystal vibrations to sense the movement of the dragons. Are you telling me that you don't spend all your time gazing at the sky and talking about deep philosophical things?"

Ahorn huffed a dry laugh. "I wish." He took his pipe from his mouth and knocked the tobacco onto the floor. There were a few bits of burning weed left. These he stamped out with his foot. He held the pipe in one hand, using it like a baton to emphasize his points. "Cassis, the innkeeper, is the son of my mother's sister, Cyrene. So, he is not my cousin, but my brother."

"But that makes him *exactly* your cousin," Wulf said. "Doesn't it?"

"In the human way of reckoning, yes. In our way, no," Ahorn went on. "The brother or sister of a parent is not always an aunt or an uncle. In fact, they are only *half* the time."

"What?"

"The sister of our mother, we also call 'mother.' But her brother we call 'uncle.' The brother of a father we also call 'father,' but his sister we call 'aunt.'"

"That is . . . incredibly confusing."

"Not to us, m'lord. The rule is simple," Ahorn said. "The same-sex sibling of a parent is a blood relative. The different-sex sibling is considered a more distant relative. The same with the children. The children of my father's brother, I call 'brother' and 'sister.' The children of my mother's sister, I also call 'brother' and 'sister.' But the children of my father's sister or my mother's brother I call 'cousin.'"

"I know some about centaur ways, but I've never understood this," Abendar put in. "Frankly, it seems . . . pointless."

"It has to do with how our bloodlines work and how traits are passed down. We are insular, so we have to keep these things mixed."

"If you say so."

"Here's the thing: you can marry your cousin. But you can't marry a sister or a brother."

"A sister or brother who is really a cousin," Wulf said.

"Right, m'lord," said Ahorn, gesturing at Wulf with his pipe as if he was an apt student who had answered correctly. "Or they might be your *actual* brother and sister, in which case you can't marry them either."

"I hope not."

"But *cousins*—now cousins you *want* to marry. That is the tradition."

"Why, for Sturmer's sake?"

"Because they are *distant* enough relatives to keep the bloodline sturdy, but *close* enough to keep the family wealth together."

"So Cassis is your brother? That is, your cousin?"

"Yes," Ahorn says. "But he is married to Flaum, my mother's brother's daughter."

"So she's an actual cousin, the way *I* would think of it," Wulf said.

"Cross-cousin, yes. Cassis and Flaum have a daughter. Her name is Syrinks. That's her over there." Ahorn nodded toward a young centaur woman holding a serving tray. She was delivering mugs of mead and wine to the diners.

"She's pretty," Wulf said.

The centaur woman noticed them looking at her. Particularly, Wulf guessed, Ahorn. She shook her long brown hair and threw back her head slightly.

As usual, centaurs only wore functional clothing, such as satchels for carrying items. The centaur woman's human-looking upper half was bare naked, including her breasts.

"She seems like she's got a lot of personality, too," Wulf added lamely.

As swiftly as she'd reacted to the male glances, Syrinks turned up her nose and looked away. She went back to waiting on the guests.

"Yes, she does," Ahorn replied with a doleful look. "I like her. I just do not want to *marry* her. I don't really think she wants to marry me, either."

"Why should you?"

"Because I don't have any other cousins to marry. And neither does Syrinks."

"I don't get it . . . you mean centaurs *have* to marry their cousins?"

"When you think about it, m'lord," Ahorn said with a smile, "it does make a lot of horse sense. Just not for me."

CHAPTER TWENTY-TWO:
THE LOVERS

"Tradition is *very* important to us," Ahorn continued. "I even agree with it, most of the time."

"There's got to be someone else Syrinks can marry."

"I have only sisters. My cousin has only brothers. I could take you through all of it. She and I are the only cousins who can mate."

"And if you were to marry her—"

"Her parents are rich. She has a large dowry," Ahorn said. "Cassis and Flaum have gotten wealthy running the Apfelwein. They'll settle twenty thousand thalers on her. He told me that this afternoon. Upping the price because of my stubbornness, he calls it."

"So you'd be rich."

"Yes, and it would help the Krisselwissers in Barangath."

"Krisselwissers?"

"Krisselwisser is my surname, m'lord. We don't use them much, but *everyone* knows them. We Krisselwissers are gentry. Ancient nobility going back to the first migration. That's how I have my title. But I'm earl of nothing much, let me tell you. Over the years, the family fortune has gone downhill, especially in my grandfather and his father's time. And we have more and more mouths to feed."

"But no eligible cousins to marry Syrinks."

"Except for me."

"So the fact that you are actually in love with Puidenlehdet really messes with everyone's plans."

"They don't understand it. They think I'm trying to deliberately sabotage the family."

"Of course you wouldn't. But love is love."

"Try telling that to my cousin. He practically challenged me to a duel today. He is offended for his daughter. For the family name—part of the reason he moved to Tjark and worked so hard to build this grand inn is to be able to give it back to the family. Restore our fortune. By not marrying his daughter, he says I'm spitting on his dreams."

"Wow. Those are fighting words."

"I am a one-hundred-and-seven-year-old centaur. I know my own heart. I will spit on more than his dreams if he says one more word about Puidenlehdet rooming with me tonight," Ahorn said, grinding his tobacco ash deeper into the floorboard.

"But how is it going to work with you two? Puidenlehdet already has sons, right? I've met Dirty Coat."

"She's a widow," Ahorn said. "Her husband Metsanhoitaja was one of the few buffalo people who ever came to the university. Metsan, we called him. He was a good friend to me and to Albrec Tolas when we were students there. The three of us were very close. I was best man at Metsan and Puidenlehdet's wedding. She was so lovely that day. I was jealous, even then."

Wulf had given up trying to understand the attraction between the centaur and the buffalo woman. But that it was strong and mutual, he had no doubt.

"She was apprenticed to be a wisewoman, and she became one—and a great one. She is sought by people from all over."

"She saved my father."

"Yes. So you see why Metsan was attracted. She understood the ways of nature, the body. Metsan was interested in living things. His family members are mostly foresters. They tend the land, clear ground when more grazing pasture or fodder fields are needed. They barter the wood to river traders for the clan. Metsan's specialty was the diseases of trees."

"I didn't even know they could *get* diseases."

"Oh yes. They do," said Abendar. "Mold, mildew, root wilt, heart-rot, canker, leaf plague. Not to mention the different sorts of bore bug infestation. And the tree people get all the same illnesses as trees themselves. So he was a physician to them."

"After Metsan died, Puidenlehdet was left in a terrible way. Five sons to raise, and people needing her skills constantly. So I came to help."

"Wait," put in Wulf. "You skipped something. When did Metsan die?"

"About twenty years ago," Ahorn said.

"And *how* did he die?"

"A tree fell on him. A regular tree."

"Oh."

"At first I was only there to help her. It was hard for a centaur to make a living as a loremaster among the buffalo people, which was what I was trained for. So I collected crystals from the Dragonbacks. I sold them to traders in Barangath to earn my keep. My people prize crystals of all kinds for soothsaying, healing, stargazing. Lots of other things. I unearthed some really good ones, too. Cassis has a couple of my finds on display over by the entrance, if you get a chance to look."

"How long did you stay?"

"Five years I lived with her. Like I said, at first there was only friendship between us, and our shared love for Metsan's memory. But it became something deeper."

"So why didn't you get married then?"

"We would have. But my father died, and I had to go home. I was the heir, after all. And like I said, the

Krisselwissers are poor. Poor but proud gentry, that's us. It was true that they needed me. I've managed to make us a little better off in the past few years, to pay off some of our debts. Not much, but a little. I eventually became Master of Lore at the Barangath Library. The position comes with an annuity." He shook his head sadly "But 'Earl Ahorn Krisselwisser.' Every time I hear that title, it makes me depressed."

"Puidenlehdet stayed with her people?"

"She had her sons to look after, and many sick people to help. She still does. But the time is coming when we can finally be together permanently. I feel it. We'll find a way."

"I truly hope so, Friend Ahorn," Abendar said.

"Me, too," said Wulf. "Do you want me to talk to the innkeeper? Tell him I need you at court or something so you can't take on the inn? I do. You and Tolas—you're two of the wisest people I know."

"Thank you, Lord Wulf. But it wouldn't do any good. After all, he'll say I could just as well marry Syrinks and take her to court with me but spend her money building up House Krisselwisser in Barangath."

"All right, I give up for now," Wulf said. "I hope you work it out. And *no dueling*. That's an order." Wulf got up from the rocker. "I really am going to look in on Saeunn now."

Abendar also rose. "There is a lovely half-moon, and it is a clear night," he said. "I think I will take a walk in the moonlight. Would you like join me, Friend Ahorn?"

"Rather than stew in my own juices and scratch up Cassis's floor? Yes. Yes, I'll come along with you, Abendar."

"Good."

"Well, goodnight, gentlemen," Wulf said, bowing tightly, his back still stiff from the days of riding.

"Goodnight, m'lord," said Ahorn.

Abendar bowed more deeply. "Lord Wulf," he said.

The centaur and elf headed for the entrance. Wulf realized he had confused which hallway held Saeunn's room. He must have looked as if he were wandering aimlessly, because Syrinks the centaur came up to him and asked if she could help.

Up close she was even more lovely. And her naked breasts also tended to rivet his attention.

There *are* human and centaur pairings mentioned in the sagas of *Heilin's* and *Brotinn's*, Wulf thought. Then he aimed his eyes upward and shook the idea from his head.

"I'm looking for the room where Lady Saeunn Amberstone rests," he said.

"I will show you there, m'lord," Syrinks said. She bowed slightly to Wulf, then clopped past him and he followed after. He watched her swaying horse's hips and swishing tail.

Yep. Pretty in a *disturbing* way.

CHAPTER TWENTY-THREE:
THE STALL

After a stroll with Abendar, Ahorn retired to the stall he'd demanded of his cousin to find his lover waiting. The stall was four sided, but open to the half moon shining above. Puidenlehdet was sitting calmly in a corner playing a flute made from a buffalo leg bone. It sent a soft and eerie melody up to the Moon.

She finished the tune, then looked at Ahorn with her gorgeous brown eyes.

"Done all I could for the Lady Saeunn tonight," she said.

"How is she?"

"The star-stone sparked up, maybe for the last time," Puidenlehdet replied. "For the time being, she is much better. Won't last long, I fear."

Ahorn went to stand beside her. He gazed up at the stars.

Something was . . . *off* . . . in the heavens. He couldn't quite say what. The stars were in their usual positions, but the brightness and flickering were varying.

"My dear, the stars are unsettled tonight. I can feel . . . something," Ahorn said.

Puidenlehdet put down her flute and took a curry comb from a leather packet she'd stowed nearby.

"Can you say *what*?"

"The dragons sleep fitfully," Ahorn said. "The stars sing to calm them."

"Sounds like centaur affectedness when you speak in such a manner, my lover," Puidenlehdet replied. "Now kneel down and let me take a brush to those brambles in your tail."

He did. The buffalo woman pulled the curry brush down his tail hair.

"Ouch!"

"We have to get them out, you old fool," Puidenlehdet said evenly. "Else your tail will cut stripes across your hindquarters every time you flick a fly."

She pulled the curry brush further through the hair of Ahorn's tail. After it had collected a handful of brambles, she took it out, cleaned the bristles, then started again at the top.

"Blood and bones! That hurts, woman!"

"For the best," the buffalo wisewoman said in a low voice, as calm as a slow river at night.

"I suppose."

"You stick to your high centaur matters and let me deal with the real problems of life," Puidenlehdet murmured.

"I'm happy to let you deal with anything you want to, my dear," Ahorn said. He closed his eyes and a resigned look came over his face. "Go on. Finish it, woman."

Puidenlehdet didn't waste any time. She yanked the brush the rest of the way through Ahorn's tail hair, collecting brambles and stickle balls along the way.

Ahorn clenched his teeth and held in another yelp.

Five more passes and Puidenlehdet was done.

"There you go, brave one," she said. "You clean up nice."

"So do you."

"That hot bath did these old bones wonders," Puidenlehdet said. "Would have been better if all your relatives weren't standing around giving me the Evil Eye when I got out."

"They're jealous of you."

"I'm sure they are."

"You know why."

"I'd rather strangle myself than try to figure out centaur family goings-on," Puidenlehdet answered.

"None of it matters," Ahorn said. "I'm yours."

"Tell that to your cousins."

"Oh, I have," Ahorn said. "Repeatedly."

"I say we forget about that tonight," Puidenlehdet. "We both have worries enough as it is. My boys are holding the eastern passes. The Lady Saeunn is fading, and I don't have the art to save her."

"Nobody does," Ahorn replied. "It's a metaphysical problem."

"Regen's tears, that's the most foolish thing I've heard come out of you," Puidenlehdet said. "And I've heard some dillies."

"Then what?"

"Her blood is thinning out. It's not feeding the muscles. Her lungs don't work, her heart don't pump right—though Regen knows what is the right beat for an elf heart. I'm just guessing at that. Still, the problem is exactly *not* metaphysical. She's physically breaking down like an old wagon. Only she's young and shouldn't be."

"She has the star-stone."

"She's about drained that thing of whatever glamor it had. It's growing cold. I'm afraid of what that means."

"Then we have to hurry and get her to Eounnbard."

"No assurances there," Puidenlehdet said darkly. "I'm frightened that the only thing we'll find when we get there is an end to Lord Wulf's hopes."

"Do you really think so?"

"I learned a long time ago not to make pronouncements unless I'm sure as rain and night."

"*I'm* sure about *us.*"

"As am I."

"Do you want to . . . it's been days since we've been alone."

"You sure your relatives ain't got looky holes punched in this stall?"

"Let them look," Ahorn said.

"Why, Ahorn Krisselwisser," Puidenlehdet said. "I never knowed you were an exhibitionist."

"I am not. I do enjoy a dramatic gesture now and again, however."

"That you do."

"So, want to make some drama?"

"That ain't all we're going to make, lover," Puidenlehdet replied. She pointed to the other side of the stall. "Let's go over yonder to the fresh straw."

CHAPTER TWENTY-FOUR:
THE SPRING

Come to the springhouse.

The dragon-call had hit him while he was walking toward Saeunn's sick room.

Come.

Wulf had a room and bed ready to fall into. In fact, he had thought about it for days while sleeping on a blanket roll in the Greensmoke forest. He should go there, if not to Saeunn.

But now here he was in the middle of the night trembling and feeling feverish, with flashes of alternating hot and cold.

Come to the springhouse.

Many times before he'd tried to resist the call and gotten sick. Nauseous. Light-headed. Completely out of it.

That was the thing about the dragon-call he'd felt recently

back at Raukenrose. It *hadn't* been urgent. Hadn't been nauseating and disorienting.

He'd tried to explain this to Ulla, but she hadn't really understood. After all, a dragon-call was a dragon-call. If you were a von Dunstig, you dropped everything. You answered.

But it hadn't seemed like the dragon had *wanted* to communicate. Not then. It seemed more like it was having a troubled sleep, and this was spilling over.

So he had decided to ignore it and take Saeunn to Eounnbard.

But tonight was like old times. The dragon-call was *intense*. It surged through him. It would not, *could* not, be ignored.

Before, the call had grown stronger and stronger and at times he had found himself crawling through castle corpse doors and coal chutes to answer it. Of course, he'd been trying to hide that he heard it back then.

With the dragon-call came the ability to commune with the huge beast curled below the Shenandoah Valley—the beast whose backbone made up one mountain chain, and its front leg another.

It had been an ability passed down in the von Dunstig family for six hundred years, since old Duke Tjark had joined with the good Tier to fight and defeat the dark coalition of were-creatures and marauding Wutenluty Skraelings and bring peace to the valley.

As third in line, Wulf was not supposed to have it, or to

only have a touch of it. But even *before* his brothers had been killed, Wulf had felt the call.

Back then, there was no way to fight it, and in the end no way to deny it. It had prepared him to use the Dragon Hammer, an artifact from the depths of time that had finally unmade a terrible enemy that no other weapon could touch.

What was he supposed to do about the dragon-call now? He was *going* to get Saeunn to Eounnbard. He was going to find a way to save her. He was very near the border of his own land, and so near the edge of the dragon's influence. Or at least that was the belief.

He'd taken a few trips partly down the Potomak River, and had seen the sea—or at least the Chesapeake Bay—on a visit to see Adelbert when his brother was studying sailing at Krehennest. So he *had* been out of the mark before. But that had been before the dragon-call had gotten so strong inside him. It had nearly taken over his life and blasted his sanity in Raukenrose last year.

He didn't need to hide it now. He was the heir to the mark, whether he wanted to be or not. His sister Ulla was older, but she didn't hear the dragon. He had tried his best to get her to take the role from him, but she'd refused.

He stood up, half thinking he might continue down the hall, go check on Saeunn before answering the call. That was foolish, of course.

Come to the spring.

The call was not really words so much as an image, and

an overriding urge. But even if that hadn't been there, it wouldn't be hard to figure out which spring he was supposed to go to.

The Therme of the Apfelwein. It was why the inn was originally built here.

The spring was a pool about three paces across. It was covered by an open-air shelter with living wood for posts. These were planted and tended by the family of tree people who lived in the nearby woods. A huge muscadine vine grew up one post and its leaves, now browning in autumn, covered the upper timbers and roof of the shed.

The spring rose from an underground heat source. It steamed and smelled faintly of sulfur. The odor wasn't strong enough to smell like rotten eggs or farts. In fact, it wasn't too unpleasant an aroma at all when mixed with the scents of a nearby grassy field and the huge tended garden behind the Apfelwein.

As Wulf walked along, the time-smearing of the dragon-vision began. At first it was smells. The sulfur odor of the spring became the blossom-filled fresh air of a meadow, then a heated-steaming sulfurous smoke surrounded him. He saw the formation of the spring, centuries ago, as a bubble of hot rock-melt from a league below rose to the surface and flowed over the ground.

At the same time, he saw groundwater below the earth collect. It was pushed upward by the heart from below. The spring level rose. At the same moment, he saw the centaurs carving out the natural hot spring further, lining it with smooth stones. The gazebo went up.

Smeared over that, a fire.

The gazebo burning. A dead soldier next to the water, his blood trickling in to mix with the water and flow away.

Then the spring only a dry hole. It had become a gaping maw in a landscape of burned tree trunks and ruin.

Was he seeing the future?

Was this the way it was destined to end?

Wulf didn't know how to interpret the future parts of his visions. Could he *change* what would be? Were they set?

Then the spring was just a spring again.

There were stone steps leading down into the pool the spring formed. A stream flowed away. The Apfelwein tapped this water for the hot baths, and for heating the rooms. The centaur hospitality might have made the inn famous, but it was the hot spring that gave it a reason for being there in the first place.

Wulf did not feel any urge to get into the water. That wasn't what the dragon wanted.

No. Just a connection.

He knew what to do.

He drew his dagger and lay on his stomach by the edge on a stone patio. He dangled his head just over the edge. His arm with the dagger in it extended over the water.

The night air was very chilly, but the stone was warm from the spring, and comfortable. If he hadn't been buzzing from the dragon-vision, he might easily have fallen asleep here considering the day he'd had.

He dipped the tip of the dagger into the water. It did not go in easily. Instead, the water felt like a thick syrup, almost solid. He had to use both hands and apply pressure to get it further in. Suddenly the water gave way and the dagger went in to the hilt.

And stuck there. Wulf didn't let go, but he felt that, if he did, the dagger would stand upright in the steaming water.

Then the vision kicked in. Wulf *spread* through his land.

It wasn't that he went here and there, even instantly. No, he was *everywhere at once*. He experienced all things about the land in one grand vision.

But it *was* a dream. Because the dragon was an unborn baby. An embryo waiting to hatch in an egg that was the world. The dragon was sleeping, becoming what it would be, gathering its thoughts over thousands and thousands of years.

There was only one tiny point of consciousness in all the dragon's vast mind. This was Wulf himself. He wouldn't be able to remember even a small portion of what he experienced, be aware of it all, of the people, *all* the people. The rivers and streams. Every fallen leaf. Every flitting sparrow.

But he would remember the dream of the land. He would remember how the story of the world told itself day and night, never stopping. In the eastern marches, where

Sandhaven and the mark met, villagers in their houses, their cottages, their barns, their shepherd camps, sleeping, getting ready for the day of labor ahead of them tomorrow.

Some up already.

Here a goatherd looking for a lost kid, following its bleating into a thicket, cutting through thorns to get it free before wolves or something worse came to take it.

There a sentry in a border post watching the dark plains of Sandhaven, ready to light a signal fire if soldiers came, if the mark was going to be invaded again.

And in the west, Barangath, the centaur village that Ahorn came from. The astronomers working till dawn, observing stars. Trying to look *through* the starlight and gain knowledge of the Never and Forever beyond the veil of night.

And down in the valley, buffalo people tending their herds.

Farther south, to fields of tobacco and cotton stubble. It was past harvest, and he could feel the earth itself sighing, resting, the cover crops of clover and barley holding the soil as the chopped remains of summer decayed to compost and a new life in the spring.

And he was at the Apfelwein also, feeling the tired muscles of his soldiers. The nervousness of the horses in the barns and corrals, the quiet resolve of the donkeys staked out in a pasture to do absolutely nothing more—or less— than they had to.

Further south, he neared the edges of the dragon's dream. The deep and ancient forest of the Greensmoke Mountains. Secret caves beneath them that no man or Tier had ever seen, or probably ever would.

Up through the capillaries of water, though the roots of trees.

Surfacing to find—

Something running through those woods.

Moving north. Moving desperately.

Someone.

Someone who didn't belong.

Someone being *chased* from the land beyond the dragon's awareness.

Headed toward Tjark.

This person had a dark cloud behind him. Roiling, boiling, behind him.

It's the *cloud* that's chasing that . . . whoever it is, Wulf thought. His contemplation of this fact was only a tiny moment, a small piece of a melody, in the vibrating, resonating sleeping mind of the dragon of Shenandoah. But it was that small piece of consciousness, that one awake mind, that the dragon built on to make sense of its dream.

This was why the dragon called. This was the reason for the dragon vision.

The dragon needed him. As a fire needs a spark.

The running person was getting closer. Toward Shenandoah. Toward Wulf.

Then Wulf was a young man sticking a dagger into sulfurous hot water. He pulled his hands, and the dagger, out. He rolled over on his back, catching his breath. He gazed up into the muscadine vine covering the edges of the roof. A few clumps of wild grapes still clung to the vegetation.

There wasn't any doubt that the vision was true. Something, or someone, was *seeking* him.

"Blood and bones," Wulf said in rough whisper to himself. "How am I going to get Saeunn to Eounnbard *now*?"

"You're not," answered a faint, familiar voice from nearby.

Wulf sat up quickly, gazed around.

Saeunn Amberstone was a half pace from him. She stood in the light of the half-moon. She wore only her white linen sleeping shift. A faint breeze lifted it slightly and wafted the fabric about her legs. Her feet were bare. The dark stone on the chain around her neck caught the wan light from above and shone with a faint purple glow.

She sat down beside him. "I've missed the moonlight."

"You should be inside," Wulf said.

"I've been inside long enough," Saeunn replied. "I don't have much time, and I want to spend it under the stars."

"We're going to get you to help." Wulf caught himself fiddling with his dagger. He carefully slid it back under his belt.

"I'm beyond help now, my love."

"Don't say that," Wulf replied. There was anguish in his voice. "We can save you. We *will*."

Saeunn shook her head. She leaned toward him and gently kissed him.

"Saeunn, I will not give up, I will not—"

She put a finger over his lips. "This might be our last night together, my love. Let's make it count."

Wulf sat silent and gazed at her for a long time. Enough moonlight made it under the shelter to illuminate her hair, and the glowing stone put sparkle in her blue-gray eyes.

She was beguiling. Everything he wanted. Everything he had ever wanted for as long as he could remember.

Wulf brushed a wisp of hair from her cheek. He ran his hand under her blonde locks and touched her neck. Saeunn smiled. He pulled her gently toward him.

"All right," he said.

He kissed her, hard and for a long time. She returned the kiss hungrily. Finally Saeunn turned her head and whispered in Wulf's ear.

"I did love being a star," she said. "But I love being a woman, too."

They kissed again, lying down together on the warm stone beside the spring.

"And you," she said. "And you."

CHAPTER TWENTY-FIVE:
THE DARK ANGEL PRINCESS

Marguerite saw Windy one more time after the priest in the black coat and red collar had come through, looking for the queen's crown.

The next morning the shadow thing came out just as Marguerite was going to bring in the bucket of milk that her sister Evangeline had milked from the cow earlier that morning.

There was Windy standing beside the barn door.

"I have to go," it said. "To find the Dark Angel Princess and her brother, the Pale-Haired One. It's all becoming clearer. I have to take the crown to them."

"Well, I wish you the best travel," Marguerite said brightly. She was going to miss Windy the fulgin, even though she could hardly say she knew it very well. "What will you do after that task? Can you come back here and play?"

"No, Marguerite. After I have done that, I will die. It is the way I *want* to go. I will have done what I was born to do. And I can rest. It is really hard to be moving all the time like this. I would like a good long rest that lasts forever after I get this one thing done."

"I will never forget you," said Marguerite. "The shadow that saved me from the pigs. Windy the magnificent! That's you."

The shadow had no face, but it seemed to vibrate a little bit, as if it were momentarily happy. Then it disappeared, this time for good.

When Marguerite went to get the eggs for the day she looked under every chicken and there was no crown.

That was too bad. She would have liked to have seen it. But it was better that she didn't have it in her mind if the Romans and the red-collared priest came back.

Over the next days, Marguerite continued her tasks. She still daydreamed about being a handmaiden of Princess Ravenelle, but she knew that the truth was she was going to be a field worker like everyone else on the plantation when she got to be ten. But that couldn't keep her imagination from taking her places she would never see in real life. She just had to be careful to keep such things out of her surface thoughts.

Her master had recovered from his own treatment at the hands of the Romans. This hadn't made him any easier. If anything, it had hardened him, taken away the kindness he'd sometimes shown.

He would notice if he caught her daydreaming. He might beat her for getting above herself. But now she was six and she was already good at hiding what she was thinking. Very good indeed.

The fulgin creature, calling itself Windy now, had almost run out of strength. The soldiers and the red-collared priest had been pursuing it across the land for days and days. During that time it had steadily worked its way north, always aware of where Ravenelle Archambeault was located. It could feel her like a compass felt north.

On its last night traveling, it had to risk a charge right up the main road into the village of Tjark.

The Romans were out in force to search for it. It knew that if it took a circular route to get to the princess it would take too long.

The fulgin was growing weak.

It might run out of strength and never make it with the crown. And since that was the creature's reason for existence, it had to take the chance of a final direct run.

The red-collared man was smelling, sniffing. Getting closer and closer. And his army had gotten bigger and bigger as more soldiers arrived.

They had sent a large force to catch it. Yet the fulgin had managed to sneak its way north as the Dark Angel Queen had wished. It felt a sense of pride, or at least fulfillment. It wouldn't do to get caught here at the end. There *must* be a way through.

The Romans had moved to cut it off in front. Now it had to find a way under, over, or around them.

That was when it remembered the little slave girl Marguerite. It remembered what it had done to save her from the nasty snorting-snout animals.

My name, thought the fulgin. The answer is in my name.

Yes, there was a way through. She had named it Windy.

If it had been able to laugh, it might have done so as it whirled by. It whipped the tent flaps of the camping Roman soldiers. And if the red-collared priest had not had his windows closed in the plantation house he was sleeping in that night, he might have sniffed the amber crown as it passed him by.

The night was pleasant. It was a good thing to be outside, and not stuck in a house like the red-collared man.

The Dark Angel Queen would understand. She liked to ride the land, *her* kingdom. She liked to go to the mountain tops and look from the peaks and take it all in. The fulgin had this memory from her, one of several small tokens that it cherished.

Then the whirlwind set down just outside of Tjark.

The little princess was very close now. It could sense it. For the first time, it felt a pang of regret that it had to cease soon.

But it was content. It had met the little girl. It had made a friend.

It had a name.

And it was going to accomplish its great task.

If a thing like the fulgin could be happy at all, Windy was. And it was the happiness more than anything that had shielded it from the sniffing, sensitive nose of the red-collared man.

It was late in the night when the fulgin shadow thing crossed the border from Vall l'Obac to Shenandoah. Soon the Romans would be on its trail again. But there was time to deliver the amber crown.

There was *supposed* to be.

But try as it might when it got to the town, it could not sniff out the Dark Angel Princess. She was in one of the buildings, but there were so many people. It was confusing to follow her scent.

Finally it did sniff *something*. The princess? Maybe. With a sigh of relief it followed the trail.

But when it got there, there was only a little spring of water. It was a smelly spring, too. Some kind of fire-like odor bubbled up with the water. Maybe that was what it had detected.

The fulgin was full of disappointment. Would it ever find the Dark Angel Princess?

Beside the spring, something moved, some *one*. The

fulgin saw that there were two people lying by the spring. They seemed to be tangled together.

Were they sleeping here?

Then one of the people by the spring, a girl with the palest blue eyes imaginable, had looked up from where she lay.

She *saw* it. She saw the fulgin!

How had she done that? No one could see it at night.

Even little Marguerite had not been able to see it except in sunlight when she could pick it out from the regular shadows. But somehow this one *could* see.

There was moonlight this night. Maybe that was why. Maybe some people could see better in the moonlight than in the day? It didn't know. There was so much it didn't know and never would.

"What is it that you are looking for, little thing?" asked the woman with the pale, pale eyes.

"The dark princess who needs a crown," the fulgin answered in its whistle-voice. "I cannot find her anywhere."

The woman with the pale, pale eyes gazed at the fulgin for a long time. It thought about running away, but it felt safe in the woman's presence.

Finally, she spoke. "I know where to find the princess you are looking for, little thing," she said. "I will go and get her. Then you can tell us about your journey."

This filled the fulgin with contentment. It wanted to tell the Dark Angel Princess everything. All the things that it had seen. And it especially wanted to tell her about little Marguerite. The one who had named it. The one who had saved the Couronne de Huit Tours from the Romans.

I have had an exciting life, the fulgin thought.

And then it saw the Dark Angel Princess approaching. So beautiful.

It had done everything it had been told to do. It was very, very happy. It knew how to be happy now.

"There is so, so much to tell you," the fulgin said to Ravenelle Archambeault. It felt positively *filled* with words, with impressions it wanted to share. "But first I have a crown to give you. It is from your mother, the Dark Angel Queen. She says to tell you that she loves you. She says to say she loves you no matter what."

The fulgin unburdened its heart to the Dark Angel Princess, and died.

CHAPTER TWENTY-SIX:
THE HEIR

Ravenelle was amazed and incredibly sad at the same time. This was undoubtedly the royal crown of Vall l'Obac. Her mother's crown. She didn't know what this strange creature *was* that her mother had conjured up. But the fact that the crown was real was enough to make her frightened that something horrible had happened to Queen Valentine.

They were inside the mead hall by the giant fireplace of the Apfelwein now.

They sat in rockers. Ravenelle held the Couronne de Huit Tours on her lap.

It was warm. She was surrounded by her foster-family. Her best friends.

She felt terrified.

"I was so worried that I hadn't heard from Mother for

over a year," Ravenelle said. "But it was so selfish. I didn't think that it might be because she *couldn't* send any message to me."

"What *did* you think?" Saeunn asked.

Ravenelle looked down, abashed. "I had pretty much convinced myself that she didn't want me anymore."

"We've all met your mother," said Wulf. "She's a hard woman to like, you know. Always acting superior around us barbarians and all. But there was never any doubt how much she loves you, Ravenelle."

Ravenelle felt a blood tear forming in her eye. She wiped it away. "I guess there isn't. I get so confused because I can't even remember home. I've never even *met* my real father."

"If what that thing said before it disappeared is true," Wulf said, "then the Romans are right behind it. Rainer should be back pretty soon with Jager's scouts."

As if in answer to a summons, Rainer appeared. He swung his cloak behind him. He warmed himself close to the fire coals for a bit, then sat down in the rocker they'd saved for him.

"So?" Wulf asked.

"So, there *is* a Roman legion out there. About a league south into Vall l'Obac on the Montserrat Road.

"You crossed the border?"

"Had to. We saw fires in the woods. Hundreds of them. Got trouble all right."

Ravenelle held up the amber crown in her hands. It

glowed warmly in the light from the fire. "This is my fault," she said. "It's because *I'm* here that *they're* here. I can ride off with this thing and they will follow me. Probably. This is what they're after."

"I don't think they are going to let any of us go now," Wulf said. "We'll have to fight to break out of here. And besides, we won't let you leave us, not now. Rainer would kill me, for one thing."

Rainer nodded. "Have to get ready soon, m'lord," he said to Wulf. "I started talking with Jager about what to do. He's coming up with a plan to present to you."

Wulf nodded. "Listen, I want him to talk with the centaurs. Tell Ahorn to get over this silly feud with his cousin. Bring the town leaders in on the plans we make. They can help." Wulf considered for a moment. "And they will have to evacuate. The whole town. There's no choice now, if there are as many Romans as you think there are."

"Oh, they're out there, all right," Rainer replied.

"Maybe while we fight them, we can get Saeunn out," Wulf said, almost mumbling to himself. Ravenelle glanced at Rainer. The obsession had returned, if it had ever gone anywhere. There didn't seem to be anything that could dampen Wulf's determination to take Saeunn to Eounnbard and . . . what? He wasn't even sure the Mist Elves had a cure for her condition.

After all, her condition was death.

"I won't abandon my family and my friends," Saeunn said

softly. "You have to see that this is more important than getting me to Eounnbard, Wulf. These people are invading *your* land. You are sworn to defend it."

Wulf shook his head. "No. I'm not going to choose between the land and you. The dragon isn't making me do that. Why should anyone else?" He stopped rocking and stared into the fire. "What we are *going* to do is face the Romans. We're going to fight to allow the town people to get to safety. Saeunn, Ravenelle, and the other women will head west. Then we will rendezvous and keep going south to Eounnbard. There's no reason why we can't. Everybody is trying to stop me from doing something that my heart tells me is the right thing to do."

Ravenelle set the crown back on her lap and reached over to take Rainer's hand gently in her own. "Wulf is crazy as a bat flapping around a tower with no windows," she said, loud enough so Wulf could hear her.

"Yeah," Rainer replied after a moment. "He is. But he's also right."

Ravenelle sighed. "Then I guess we have to get ready for the Romans. What am I going to do with this crown?"

"Get it out of here," Rainer answered. "Then . . . anything you want. You don't need a crown to be a queen." He squeezed her hand and stood to go. "You never did, Princess."

CHAPTER TWENTY-SEVEN:
THE FLOOD

The Roman Imperials lined up at dawn in rough squares of a hundred. Romans attacked in staggered checkerboard rectangles as much as possible. They moved through the woods and the Tjark village outskirts, so there was no real "battlefield" to spread out on. But these were seasoned troops and it didn't matter. They had fought the Nubian rebels of southern Aegypt. Many of them were veterans of campaigns deep into the Afrique jungles or the deserts of Araby. Their commanders knew how to position themselves for the best effect in all kinds of terrain.

It was part of the Roman marching training to learn how to flow around obstacles while not breaking ranks. On either wing of the troops rode the Roman cavalry. They were ready to swoop in and soften up a target before the infantry hit.

They could also crash into the ends of an enemy's lines and attack from the side while the troops fought head on. Most deadly of all was when the cavalry broke into the rear of an enemy and attacked the supplies and reserve forces, or the enemy itself from behind.

Wulf knew how the Romans fought. He had studied it for years under his old weapons master, Marshal Elgar Koterbaum. And as a scholar, he'd read about it many times in the sagas. A battle of Kaltemen against Romans was described in detail in several of them, especially two called *Hlafling's Folly* and *Rugga's Saga*. These were part of a group known as the Battle Sagas. Wulf had spent a year working through them with the best and toughest teacher of all, Albrec Tolas. Tolas also happened to be a master scholar at Raukenrose University.

I still can't believe Tolas made me memorize sagas by playing mumblety-peg with a *real, sharp* knife poking between my fingers, Wulf thought. But it sure was effective.

In most of these stories it was a *very* bad idea to fight Romans head-to-head. They worked together like swarming ants and overwhelmed even very strong foes. No, the best way to take on the Romans was with raids, surprise attacks, and running battles.

This was where Kaltemen were at their finest anyway. It was how they had kept the Roman colonies from taking over the north for many centuries.

In the north, in the Kalte kingdoms, the gentry learned

how to fight in small groups, and battles were usually hardly anything more than a bunch of small bands of men loyal to a certain leader coming together without a lot of coordination between them. It wasn't a perfect system. They could make a savage attack, but they could also get distracted. Each band of warriors had its own separate goals which might or might not be the same as the others.

Wulf had learned how to fight a different way while taking back his own city of Raukenrose from invading Sandhaveners. It was the way his father and his right-hand man, Earl Keiler, had discovered worked best when they fought Vall l'Obac during the Little War. The great thing that the Mark of Shenandoah had going for it was that its troops were a mixture of humans, Tier, and other-folk. In the case of Jager's company, they were a mixture of every warrior type from buffalo men with their war pikes to bear men with longbows. These were longbows that most human archers, no matter how muscled, couldn't draw. And there were centaurs and quick human soldiers who were deadly at swordplay.

Jager was an instinctive tactician. He knew how to use them together. He'd proved that during the bloody Battle of Raukenrose Meadow.

Wulf had killed his first man in battle there. He had almost been gutted himself. Sometimes he saw the dying man's surprised eyes in his dreams—always *just* the eyes—and woke up tense and shaking.

Wulf and Jager arranged their one hundred men not to

win against the Romans, but to slow them down long enough for the villagers, the supply wagons, and, most of all, for Saeunn and Ravenelle, to get away.

Ravenelle carried the crown. She'd wrapped it in linen and put it carefully into one of the saddlebags of her horse.

Then the company would fall back and try to slip away itself. They hoped to sting the Romans badly enough to throw themoff pursuit. The Romans might then burn the town down in frustration. But the people would live and could rebuild.

Wulf didn't like that the plan included retreat.

It helped that Rainer, who was always practical when it came to fighting, completely approved. "Every other way of doing this will get us all killed," Rainer said. Wulf hadn't had to say anything for Rainer to read his mood and his doubt.

"You're not going to like *this* decision I've made," Wulf said. He paused for a moment, took a breath, then blurted out, "I want *you* to go with the girls."

Rainer shook his head strong enough to rattle his chainmail hood. "Blood and bones! Don't ask me to do that. I want to fight Romans!"

"You know I'm asking you because you're the best."

Rainer didn't bother denying it. "Curse it to cold hell," he grumbled.

"Will you?"

"Yes, all right," Rainer finally said. "Makes sense."

The Imperials came.

The cavalry attacked first, trying to sweep into the town from the southeast. Scouts reported they were arriving from down a road that led to the central valley. Jager sent his best archers to meet them. The Romans on horses met a line of bear men longbows in the woods. They also encountered trees felled on the one-cart roadway to block their way. Two bear men with axes could take down a good-sized tree in moments.

When the cavalry showed up, the archers knew to aim for the horses and then fight the cavaliers on the ground. The horses were armored in front, but less so behind. So the archers let them pass by and then shot the horses in their sides.

There were over a hundred Roman cavalry troops versus twenty bear men, though. The Romans on horses had almost broken through.

It had taken killing ten horses and twenty or thirty Roman soldiers to stop the cavalry raid. Finally the cavalry rode away, bloody and full of arrows. A bear longbowman's pull could penetrate an oak plank at twenty paces. Most of the dead and wounded Romans had gone down thinking to the last moment that they were safe behind their shields— only to get a rude and deadly surprise when an iron-tipped arrow burst through and sunk into an eye or throat.

But the eastern cavalry attack was just an opening stunt. The Romans marched in along the main road from the south to Tjark.

The real fight was about to begin.

Chapter Twenty-Eight:
The Invasion

"Those blood-eaters have to come soon," said Captain Jager. He stared down the road and waited for the approach of the Romans.

But it took a while for the blood-eaters to show up. Wulf could hear them long before he could see them. Their scale armor clanked. Their coronets, the battle horns used by the legions, blared. Then the eagle standard appeared down the road. The first one hundred square was marching toward them.

The Imperials carried a bronze eagle on a pole with the legion's name and number. Wulf couldn't make it out from this far away. When they grew closer though, he saw it was the IX Legion. A big one.

Which meant there could be up to five thousand soldiers descending upon them.

The town people were streaming out to the north as quickly as they could. Many of the human elderly and children rode on the backs of centaurs. Normally this was forbidden, but the centaurs made a sensible decision to let themselves be used as transport in this instance. So the Romans were descending on a mostly vacated town.

But.

The Roman army at a quick march could soon overtake anyone on foot. And their cavalry could range far ahead and attack whoever they came across. They had to be held here if the townpeople were going to make an escape.

"Would you look at that!" Jager said. "See that flag hung from the crossbar on a pole, m'lord?" He climbed nimbly on to the back of one of his master sergeants who was a buffalo man. Jager pointed. "There, about two ranks back?"

"No. . . . Oh yes, I see it now," Wulf replied. It was a blood-red streamer hanging from a short stick nailed to a pole held upright. The bottom of the banner had jagged edges cut into it. "It's a flame gonfalon."

"Does it mean what I think it means?" Jager asked.

Wulf continued to watch a bit longer, then his mouth felt dry and he swallowed. He looked at Jager. "It means 'give no quarter,'" he said. "They plan to either kill us or make us slaves. No prisoners of war."

"That makes things pretty clear," Jager growled. He turned to face Ahorn, who was nearby. "Are they ready with the water ram?"

Ahorn nodded. "Yes, Captain."

"All right, Lord Ahorn, bring on the flood," Jager said. There was something wild and menacing in his catlike smile.

Ahorn saluted with a bump to his chest. He charged off, carrying Jager's orders.

Wulf waited. The Roman boots pounded like distant thunder. The dust cloud they kicked up grew closer and closer.

In front of the dust cloud raised by the approaching Romans, water came pouring out. It poured from either side of the forest. Two big torrents of water. It covered the Montserrat Road. It ran in streams down the wagon tracks. It flowed from the road and filled the ditches and grassy shoulders lining the road.

It turned the ground to muck.

Chapter Twenty-Nine:
The Raiders

"Hold a moment," Rainer said.

His group of refugees came to a rattling stop of horses, mules, Tier, and people.

Ravenelle rode up beside him. "What is it, Stope?" she asked.

He held up a hand. "Quiet, please."

Ravenelle would usually get indignant at being treated in such a way, or at least pretend to Rainer that she was, but now she was just too *tired*.

After a moment, he lowered his hand. "It's not thunder," he said. "I thought it was."

"Well, that's good then," said Ravenelle. "No rain."

Rainer shook his head. "It's *not* good, m'lady," he replied. "Because if it's not thunder, it's probably boots and horses."

"Our men coming to meet up with us?"

"I wish. No. They are going to retreat northeast and draw the Romans away. Then they will cut over to us in the west. We shouldn't see them until tomorrow."

"So who is it?"

"Roman cavalry, probably. A raiding party sent behind the lines."

"And they've found us," Ravenelle said.

Rainer shrugged. "Maybe. Bad luck if they have."

"So do we turn and fight? What do you recommend, Mr. Stope?"

"We should run," Rainer answered grimly. "We have faster horses."

Ravenelle motioned toward the villagers who were traveling along the forest trail with them. "We can't just leave these people behind," she said. "They'll be slaughtered."

Rainer nodded. "I guess we shouldn't."

From the trees, the little owl Nagel swooped down and circled around them. Rainer seemed startled and he reached for his sword. Ravenelle leaned over and put a hand on his arm.

"It's Wulf's owl, Stope," she said. She patted her shoulder. "Come!" she called to it.

The owl landed harder than she'd expected. The owl's breath whistling quickly in and out of its beak nostrils sounded like a knife on a whetstone. She could feel the heat coming off Nagel, and the rhythm of the owl's heartbeat fluffed her breast feathers up and down.

"You are tired, Nagel," Ravenelle said. She turned to Rainer. "Stope, can you get her some water?"

Rainer untied his water sack and handed it to Ravenelle.

"Be all right," the little owl rasped.

"Hop down to my saddle horn."

Nagel did so. Then she accepted a long drink as Ravenelle squirted a stream of water in her mouth.

"Good," the owl finally said. "I have news."

"Did you see any Romans?" she asked. "Imperials headed in our direction?"

"No," Nagel said. "Doesn't mean they're not. Had to circle north for the currents."

"Curse it," Ravenelle said.

"Did see something," the owl continued.

"What?"

"People. In the woods. Heading this way. The Keiler girl. And some others. I know her red hair."

"Bear men?" Ravenelle felt hope rising. A crew of bear men might make them a match for Roman cavalry. Maybe. She'd have to ask Rainer.

"Just men. Strange men, too. Feathers in their hair."

"How many."

"Fewer than your fingers, more than mine," the owl said. "Rest now."

"How far?"

"Can't answer . . . have to rest now. Dark girl. Blood girl. Keep me safe."

Then the little owl tucked her head under her wing and fell asleep perched on Ravenelle's saddle.

Ravenelle stroked the owl's feathers and thought about what to do.

The crown. Saeunn. She was supposed to keep them *all* safe. And now it would be for nothing because of some chance encounter with a raiding party.

She did what she usually did when she needed to decide. She imagined how bad things could get if she made *no* choice.

And this *would* be bad. Saeunn and herself used by the Romans. Saeunn dead from the strain. Rainer killed. Herself dragged away in chains.

Her mother's crown lost forever.

We will defend you, Mistress. We will die before any of that happens to you.

She'd let her thoughts leak out to her bloodservants again, the warrior brothers Harrald and Alvis Torsson. This was the blind Harrald answering her.

We're very good at our jobs, you know, said Alvis, the youngest of the brothers. *And we depend on you. Harrald for your eyes. Me for the way you keep me from . . . my spirit illness inside. So it's self-preservation for us, too.*

I appreciate you both, Ravenelle thought-spoke to them. *I'm sorry I got you into this situation.*

Truth is, we were getting a little bored, Mistress, Alvis replied. *A man likes to apply his skills.*

All right, Ravenelle thought. *We fight.*

We fight, the brothers answered in union.

"What do you think, Stope?" she asked Rainer.

Rainer nodded toward the nearby forest. Even she could hear the "thunder" now.

"They're here," Rainer said, drawing his sword.

Rossofore smelled the amber. It was part of his abilities as a newly forming mandrake.

He had tracked the crown for days. It had taken him a while to realize what had happened. The marchioness had cast a spell from deep in her Aegyptian heritage. Somewhere in Vall l'Obac, probably in the castle, there *had* to be a forbidden book of Aegyptian magic, the Heka. Valentine or someone close to her had conjured with it to create a *sheut*, a shadow being. This particular type was known as a "fulgin" for its utter blackness of form.

The sheut was real enough to carry something the size and weight of the Couronne de Huit Tours. It had fled north with the crown, traveling through fields, forests, and plantations. Rossofore had questioned dozens of colonials along the way.

He'd discovered something disturbing. Even though he controlled the more powerful adder cake, most of the colonials were still dominates of Valentine. He could not easily yank their wills to his own control. He'd broken minds and driven several people to madness trying to do it until he learned that physical pain worked just as well. So he'd switch to using torture to be sure they told him all they knew.

His discovery also meant that he couldn't burn the queen. Not yet.

When he drew closer to an amber source, his transforming body *reacted*. His skin grew more scales. He could do more with a mere thought. He'd learned to squeeze a man's heart until it burst, for instance.

It was fascinating.

Exhilarating, too.

When he realized the sheut had reached the princess and delivered the crown, he knew he had to move quickly. He sent the bulk of the army to crash through the town and cut a way north. Meanwhile, he joined a raiding party of Roman cavalry that crossed far to the west. They'd left early in the morning, and he'd instructed the main force to wait until they got well away.

By the time the legion struck Tjark, Rossofore and his raiders were deep into Shenandoah. He had picked up the movement of the Couronne de Huit Tours and was homing in on it like a pigeon to its roost.

He would have the crown soon, and he would punish Valentine mightily for what she had done calling up a sheut.

He would capture the daughter along with the crown.

The daughter she gave up to barbarians, to use as they wished.

The daughter she never came for.

Like the son she never came for.

Why did you leave me in that place, Mother?

Rossofore instantly crushed the thought. Or tried to.

Marchioness Valentine Archambeault was *not* his mother, real or imaginary.

The amber must be affecting my mind, he thought. But I am too strong for it to overwhelm.

No one is my mother. I am like nothing else. Without compare. The first mandrake of the New World.

He would fulfill his vows.

He would capture the heretic daughter.

He would make Valentine watch as he consumed the crown.

Then he would make her watch as he burned her daughter alive with his own living fire.

Not long now and he would have her and the crown.

He could smell it.

It was a group of about fifteen Romans, about half on horses, that attacked them.

One of the riders was not a soldier, but dressed in what looked like the black cassock of a priest. He wore a bright-red priest's clerical collar.

Rainer didn't have time to try to figure out who this was. He rode forward to meet the first of the attackers.

They were in the trees and Rainer headed for a young

oak with a trunk about as big around as his thigh. He could have urged his horse faster, but he wanted to time it. A charging Roman cavalryman tore past the oak, just as Rainer passed it traveling in the opposite direction. Rainer swung his sword backward. It went under the Roman's helmet skirt and caught its edge on the back of the Imperial's neck, sawing in.

The Roman screamed, grasped his neck as his head flopped forward, the muscles severed. Then his horse lurched and he tumbled off to die in the leaves.

Rainer moved on to the next horseman. Meanwhile, the five men-at-arms he'd brought along with him fought well. He'd chosen them for their ability for close work. But they were outnumbered. He saw a horse go down and Romans pounce on Corporal Bara, two poking with short swords, one swinging a battle ax.

Bara was skewered and quartered.

Another Roman was on Rainer. He ducked a blow, then got in one of his own. It glanced off the Roman's scale armor chest plate. And this opened Rainer up for a butt from the Roman's sword hilt.

A gauntleted hand smashed into Rainer's face and he tumbled from his horse. He managed to hold onto his sword. As he went down, he twisted in air and took a swipe at the legs of the horse the cavalryman was riding. The sword bit into the horse's foreleg. The beast screamed in terror and jerked away. This threw the horseman to the ground as well.

Rainer walked up to him, kicked him onto his back, and jammed the tip of his sword into the man's face.

He split it just below the bridge of the Imperial's nose. Dead center.

The man feebly tried to grab the sword, but died in midreach. His arms fell to his side. Rainer jerked the sword out. He turned, looking about wildly to make sure that Ravenelle had led Saeunn and the other women away from the fighting. He didn't spot her.

Back to the Romans.

An unhorsed man approached him on foot. Rainer stepped over the man he'd just killed. The other had to glance down to clear the body. That was when Rainer lunged forward. His sword caught the Imperial below his metal jacket and sliced into the groin.

Blood spurted from a severed artery. The Roman didn't seem to notice, but surged forward. He was armed with a mace and not the Iberian sword. It had a longer reach than Rainer's weapon. Rainer backed up more as the man swung his mace in a deadly arc in front of himself.

He must have incredible strength, thought Rainer. The Roman lifted the spiked mace again—Rainer knew how heavy they could be—and this time swung vertically.

Rainer stepped back and the blow landed in the dirt in front of his feet. Then Rainer thrust in with his sword. But it was the man's turn to dodge. He stepped sideways as Rainer's sword came through.

Then he grabbed Rainer's arm.

With a roar from his throat and a grinding wrench, he pulled Rainer off his feet. He slammed Rainer to the ground.

The Roman stood over Rainer.

This is *it*, Rainer thought. This is how I'll die. Smashed into a mess of brains and blood in the forest leaves.

The Roman was about to bring down the coup de grace when his groin wound caught up with him.

The spurting blood had stopped. Rainer had sliced through an artery. There was no blood left in the man's body. The Roman's last look was of surprise as the strength left his arms. He dropped the mace.

Then he fell dead from the dreadful blood loss, right on top of Rainer.

Rainer kicked him off. He sat up and looked around.

There by an oak were a couple of his own men, dressed in the von Dunstig and Shenandoah livery, and *there* near a cedar tree was a centaur, fighting hard against the Romans. Men were off their horses now. Romans were poking with lances and javelins when they could. One of Rainer's men had dropped his sword and picked up a mace. He was using it to smash against two Romans who faced him.

We're outnumbered, Rainer thought. We're good, but it's only a matter of time until they overwhelm us.

Then he looked back over his shoulder and saw something that filled his heart with terror.

The figure in the black robe and red collar had ridden past. Rainer could see a ways ahead in the woods.

The red-collared man had caught up with Ravenelle.

She'd swung her horse around to face him.

Rainer could clearly see the burlap bag with the amber crown jolting against the back of Ravenelle's saddle.

Ravenelle's bodyguards, the Torsson brothers, seemed to be off to the side, struggling. He couldn't believe it.

They were fighting *each other.*

One swung a sword that crashed into the other's upraised sword. Then the other kicked his brother in the gut and the brother stumbled backward. Both took up their swords again.

Rainer couldn't tell which was which at this distance, but clearly the two brothers were battling to the death.

The black-clad man held out a clenched fist. Although he was several paces away, Ravenelle jerked as if she'd been punched.

She reached for the bag with the crown in it, as if compelled.

What was going on?

But he had no more time to think. An angry roar came from behind him. Rainer turned just in time to face yet another Roman bearing down upon him. There was murder in the man's eyes.

CHAPTER THIRTY:
THE MUD

The willow-wood pipes had muddied the road and the surrounding landscape. Now the team of centaurs and townsmen manning the pipes had moved them closer to the town and were opening them up again.

The pipes were hollowed-out tree trunks. They had been hammered together, with the smaller top end fitting into the base of one trunk. Do this over and over again and you get a pipe that can carry water. That pipe is also extremely heavy and hard to move quickly.

It took a team of over a hundred centaurs to move the willow-wood pipe they had made for even a few paces. But they tugged and pulled it until an area as long and wide as a field march in two directions had been turned to mud.

They'd been doing this all night. They'd spent an entire watch drenching the road until it could absorb no more water. They let it be for a half-watch while they got their baggage ready to run to join the fleeing townspeople. Or, for the ones who were staying, got their weapons sharpened if they were planning to hold off the Romans.

Before the flood pipes were opened, the road was already sopping. It might look dry, but the soil beneath was soaked.

It was no wonder that a flood of water instantly turned it to mud.

The water came from the stream that ran from the hot spring, the Therme, behind the Apfelwein. The pressure was created by using a water ram, a device Master Tolas had explained to Wulf once. He hadn't truly been able to picture it then. But he'd remembered the idea, and suggested it to Jager and the town militia commander.

Now that he saw this perfect example, the principle of how a water ram worked became obvious. If you collected water from a big stream and kept making the pipes leading away smaller and smaller, the pressure of all that water trying to get into the smaller and smaller pipes would let you send water uphill. Or to spray out at great force.

If you can move that pipe, you have a hose for diverting and squirting water wherever you could position it.

"That's going to irritate them, m'lord," Jager commented to Wulf.

"I hope it does more," said Wulf.

"Aye," Jager replied. Then he screamed out to his troops, "Positions!"

Jager had spread his line across the low south walls of the town and into the forest. On both left and right side were his longbowmen, archers, and a squad of crossbow-wielding badger men who had all joined the army together after the Raukenrose battle. They had come from Hyugel, a trading village along the North Fork of the Shenandoah River.

Beside each of the archers was a sharpened sapling stick that he'd cut in the woods. These were pounded into the ground leaning away from the archers. Their tips were sharp. An attacker on foot wouldn't have any trouble stepping around the stake to cut down an archer, but their horses were a different story. The sharp stakes drove horses crazy. The stakes were also hidden a pace back into the woods so that the horses wouldn't be able to see them easily.

Most of the archers had taken seven or eight arrows from their quivers and stuck them tip first into the ground. This was for quick grabs and rapid fire.

In the center with Wulf and Jager was the main body of his small force, about seventy-five troops. They were a mix of humans and Tier. Some of the humans were Sandhaven refugees, who had fled the eastern kingdom after the royal court had fallen to the Talaia priests. They hadn't wanted to be slaves to the mind control of the Talaia blood cake. The celestis had infiltrated the powerful Kalte capital of Krehennest and was spreading through Sandhaven. Wulf couldn't blame the refugees for getting out of their former country.

But the use of the new black-colored celestis wafer—*adder*

cake, it was nicknamed—was even worse. It was quickly displacing the old red cake in the empire. Adder cake was ten times as potent as the red cake used by Talaia followers like Ravenelle. For one thing, it made the Roman Imperials able to act as one unit—at the speed of thought.

Which Wulf hoped was about to get them in trouble.

For a moment, the approaching Imperials hesitated. The dust cloud they rose on the road settled a bit.

A *thump* on his shoulder. It was Nagel. She'd been out scouting.

"They aren't going to do it, are they?" Wulf said. "They'll pull up, find a way around the mud."

"Something's driving them," replied the raspy voice of the owl. "Like wind blowing leaves. They'll move and then comes the blood."

She was right. After that moment of delay, the entire front line seemed to galvanize like iron filings around a magnet. They straightened up, as if listening to a distant voice.

They're getting their orders delivered mentally, Wulf thought.

Then as one, the front line of the Romans marched directly into the mud.

The others followed.

Into the muck went men, centurions and commanders on horses, and all.

Chapter Thirty-One:
The Wheel of Fire

Harrald and Alvis laid into each other again. Harrald was the better fighter, but he didn't have Ravenelle's eyes. He was locked in thought with his brother and saw only what his brother could see. He was watching himself be attacked, feeling his brother's fury.

But it was enough to keep him alive and parrying Alvis's sword, at least for the moment.

Alvis fought with desperation. His new dark master was using his own hatred for himself and what he was doing and directing it at Harrald Torsson. A keening, wolflike call rose from his throat.

Ravenelle watched in horror. She couldn't do anything.

Soon one brother would get in a stroke and gut the other. Then, in despair, kill himself. Either way, it would all be over soon.

She knew who the man in the cassock was now, or at least *what* he was. A Talaia Grand Inquisitor. His will was built for complete dominance. He'd instantly invaded her mind. Taken by surprise, Ravenelle's defenses had crumbled. *Probably* she could have resisted him if she'd known he was coming and she'd prepared.

Not now. He'd broken into her thoughts. Expertly thrown her into a dream space that *he* controlled.

She was in the Inquisitor's power.

Know me, little princess. I know you.

Who?

My name is Magister Rossofore. I've come to save you from your own folly.

Rossofore turned from dealing with the men-at-arms to face Ravenelle.

She felt as if her gut were punched again by his outstretched fist, though he hadn't physically laid a glove on her.

The crown must return to its rightful owner.

My mother!

Your mother is a heretic. The crown belongs to the faith now. And I am the faith's holy representative. You will obey!

Ravenelle shook her head. "Never," she called out. *I haven't got it,* Ravenelle thought-spoke. *You don't know where it is.*

"It's there with you, lashed to your horse," the one named Rossofore shouted back at her. He laughed loudly. *I can smell it. I can smell the dasein within the amber. The power. The glory. The crown belongs to Rome. You are only a little lost princess.*

"Leave me alone!" Ravenelle screamed. She had lost sight of the regular world and was walking on a flat plain of short grass. There were no hills. No buildings.

No color.

Only flatness and gray grass stretching in every direction. Overhead was a cloudy gray sky. If there was a sun, it was invisible, hidden behind the clouds.

But I can't leave you alone, a voice boomed from the sky. *It is my duty to bring you back into the fold, daughter.*

I'm not your daughter! Ravenelle chose a direction—they were all the same—and began to run.

You're like a dumb sheep running blind.

Ahead of her, there was a flash in the sky like lightning. The flash played around a cloud, then its source descended.

So bright. So blindingly bright.

It was a circlet, a wheel. Made of fire.

At this distance, she couldn't tell how big it was. But it was moving toward her, because the intensity of the light increased.

It was red-orange. And as it got closer, she saw it was swirling.

It was a turning, burning wheel.

Ravenelle cried out, reversed direction, and began to run away.

She could feel its intense heat against her back, and its light cast a huge shadow in front of her as she ran.

Of course you are one of my flock, daughter. Like any other. You seek the blessed Emptiness and I will give you that. Just as I will give it to your mother.

Leave my mother alone!

Things must be set to rights in Montserrat. We burn heretics now.

Ravenelle stopped running. Panting, breathing in air, she gazed up into the flat gray sky. She raised a fist.

I'll kill you. I am a princess of Roman blood. I'll take your mind and leave you with a blank slate, then I'll run my fingernails over the slate until you cringe. You hurt my mother. I'll—

The light behind her grew brighter. She couldn't help it. She turned.

Calm down, Princess. It will all be over soon.

The burning, spinning sky wheel descended toward her. It flashed in dark oranges, giving way to streamers of red flame.

You are the heir now, Princess. The heir to all your mother's domain. It's time you got your inheritance.

The fire wheel was closer. She could feel it. Hot wind. Heat not like a fire, but the heat of a smith forge stoked by the bellows.

Heat that would melt her flesh.

It's time for you to take your crown, Princess.

The wheel whirled over her head. She felt her hair sizzle and burn away. She knew this was only in her mind-scape, but it felt so very real. Smelled so terribly real.

She knew what happened in the mind could kill her. She'd seen it happen to others. Even made it happen. She had almost killed Gunnar, the prince of Sandhaven who had toyed with her once.

She tried to shield herself, but her arms wouldn't move, were not allowed to move. The burning wheel descended on her head like a crown.

The pain was unbearable.

It cut into her thought. Into her soul. Every part of her was in agony.

Ask me for it, daughter.

"Let me die," Ravenelle gasped. "Kill me. Get it over with."

Beg me for forgiveness.

"Never." *Not even if I have to endure this for a thousand years. To cold hell with your mercy. Kill me now!*

All right, then, Princess. I will.

The pain increased. A white-hot wind rushed through her. The crown was closing, slicing into her mind.

Die, heretic! Die knowing that all you care about will be—

Suddenly the pain lessened. The wheel of fire around her seemed to grow unbalanced.

It wobbled.

Then it started to dissipate. It stopped sawing her thoughts in two.

No! No!

The priest was screaming, but not at her.

So close!

Then, like a furnace door slammed shut, the pain was gone.

Ravenelle snapped out of her nightmare. She quickly found Harrald and Alvis with her mind.

Alvis had his brother on the ground and had knocked his sword away. He was rising for a final strike.

Drop that sword, Alvis Torsson! Ravenelle commanded.

Alvis obeyed instantly. Only to be kicked in the stomach by Harrald. He fell back on his rump.

Ravenelle flowed back into Harrald's mind, took the reins.

See the world through me, Harrald Torsson!

She gave him back his sight through her eyes. He moved faster than his brother. He shot back up, helped Alvis to his feet, and recovered his sword. Both men ran to Ravenelle's side.

Just in time for both of them to gut a Roman soldier who was about to skewer Ravenelle from behind with a javelin tip.

The man dropped the javelin and fell dead. His bloody guts spilled into Ravenelle's path, and her horse had to make a quick sidestep to avoid stepping on them.

CHAPTER THIRTY-TWO:
THE CLUB

Wulf and Rainer had debated whether or not to bring plate armor on the trip. The idea of the journey had been a quick, light expedition to the Mist Mountains and the elves at Eounnbard. Still, that meant traveling through the outskirts of Roman lands.

Enemy ground.

They'd need enough strength to defend against an attack by a border patrol or group of bandits. Wulf guessed that fifty attackers would be the maximum.

"In that case," Rainer had argued, "we should have a two-to-one advantage if we really want to look out for the girls' safety. And don't forget you have to *feed* one hundred men on the quick march there *and* back."

Buffalo men were expert wranglers and could move a

herd along as fast as men could march. So they had brought along a small drove of beef cattle.

Jager's company was a strong force. But it wasn't an army, not by a long shot.

The last thing Wulf had expected was to have to face an entire Roman legion.

So they had decided against bringing full plate armor for everyone. Instead, many of the men and Tier wore a chainmail shirt, or hauberk. Others, including Wulf, wore a jack-of-plates. This was a felt vest with sewn-in metal pieces. Wulf usually wore it over only a linen shirt. But this morning he'd put a hauberk under it as well. On his head he wore the trusty riveted helmet that had seen him through the battle at Raukenrose Meadows. The chainmail of the hauberk hung down to about the middle of his thighs. Under that were wool leggings. On his forelegs he wore plate metal greaves— shin guards.

But there were weak points all over his body where a weapon could get in. Cut. And kill.

And so can *we*, Wulf thought.

He checked that his sword was snug across his back. Then he swung up onto his horse.

He stepped out of cover with his horse and turned his back on the Romans. "Listen!" Wulf shouted to his men. "We're going to stall them. We *have* to make them pay a hard price. We *have* to give our people, our women, our children, time to get out of harm's way. We have to let all of Rome know that when it sets foot in this land—our land—it is going to get stung. Are you with me?"

The men behind overturned wagon and hay-bale barriers rose up and cheered. Wulf didn't wait. He hurried over to his archers to give them the same message. Then he crossed the line to the woods on the other side.

Meanwhile, the Romans struggled through the mud.

Thwack!

An arrow smacked into the ground three paces away from him.

Thwack! Another slightly farther away.

They might be mired, but he was in bowshot of their best archers at about three hundred paces. And several arrows *did* rain down.

Am I going to get killed before I even get a chance at them? Wulf wondered. But he knew he had to be steady.

Don't start.

Don't speed up the horse.

Deliver the final call to battle to the archers on the left.

Which he did, with more arrows falling.

Finally done.

Wulf badly needed a drink of water. He headed his kalter back to the middle of his line and kicked it as fast as he could to get there.

The arrows were getting closer. The Romans were emerging from the mud.

Now Jager had mounted up along with ten of his men. They gathered around Wulf.

"We *walk* forward," Jager growled to his men. "We want to draw them blood-drinkers out, give the archers plenty of time to do their job." He turned to Wulf with an inquisitive look. A year ago, Earl Keiler had done the same. Wulf hadn't known what this meant at the time and had to be told by Keiler.

Now he did.

Wulf drew his sword and held it up. It flashed in the red light of dawn. He swallowed as much spit as he could squeeze out to get his voice ready for another shout. "Forward," he yelled. "For Shenandoah! For the mark!"

Jager's company walked toward the Romans.

Who had troubles of their own in the mud.

But the sight of approaching enemies made them struggle harder. The front line drew their short, spade-like Iberian swords. Two lines behind the front got ready to throw javelins. Wulf was impressed. They were still disciplined even under stress. Even in the mud.

Some in the front line had stepped out of their boots or sandals and were barefoot. Still they marched forward. Closer.

Closer.

Wulf felt . . . calm. Ready. So different from a year ago at his first battle.

At fifty paces, the Romans charged. Javelins flew.

Wulf raised his buckler as spears rained down. One

bounced off the oak of the small shield. He looked around and saw that none had hit a man. This time.

But one horse had taken a javelin to its hindquarters. Horse screams were always terrible. This horse's neigh of pain made Wulf grit his teeth.

The horse charged forward, kicking and bucking, trying to get the javelin out of its back. The rider, a bear man, couldn't stay in the saddle. He flipped off the horse backward and landed with his face on the ground. The horse charged toward the Romans, then veered off to its right. There, several Roman archers brought it down with arrows.

The Romans kept coming forward.

Almost there, Wulf thought. Almost in range.

Now a hundred of them were in the sweet spot.

Stuck.

The mud made them slow. And Jager's archers were ready.

A cloud of arrows flew from the left and right.

The Romans threw up their shields, and many collected arrows. But many arrows got through. Wulf saw the first Roman go down. An arrow had found a way under his breast plate at the neck and into his chest. Another shouted in pain when an arrow sliced through his forearm. With arrows flying from left and right, there was no way to shield from everything. Several arrows even caught Imperials in the back.

Then another volley.

The front lines faltered. A man in a centurion's helmet stepped out and screamed at them in Latin.

"Now you listen to me!" he shouted to his men. "The only way is forward, lads! Kill them! Kill the Kalte scum! Find that crown, and the magister will give us our weight in gold!"

Just as well most of *our* men don't understand, Wulf thought. But the centurion's challenge had its effect on his men. They lined up, formed a shield wall.

They started forward.

"Hoo, hoo, hoo." A guttural grunt with each coordinated step.

There was another square of foot soldiers lining up behind this one. More arrows, more falling Romans.

Almost there.

Fifty paces.

Twenty.

"Charge into 'em!" Jager shouted. Wulf supposed that to the Romans, his Kaltish might as well have been angry bobcat growls. Wulf and his line surged toward the Romans.

The fighting got brutal very quickly. Swords plunged and hacked. Maces swung. Axes fell. Javelins were thrust into bodies.

These Romans knew how to fight.

But so do we, Wulf thought.

He crashed his horse's front side into a Roman shield. The force of the blow caused the man to stumble back, leaving enough of an opening for Wulf to stab down from above. His sword cut through the Roman's shoulder and neck. Wulf used his horse's momentum to push harder. The sword clanked against the rear scale armor of the Roman. Wulf yanked the sword back. It came out in a shower of blood and gore.

The Roman cried out in agony and tried to take a swing at Wulf with his good arm. Wulf batted the sword away with his own.

The Roman soldier fell.

Wulf looked for another to fight, but his own men swarmed around him, forming a wedge and cutting into the second line of Romans.

Meanwhile, arrows kept falling into the ranks of Imperials behind the line.

There still wasn't *that* much return fire from the Romans. They were arrogant in that way. Their bowmen weren't strung up and ready. They had expected this to be an easy rout lead by the swordsmen.

Jager pushed up beside Wulf.

"We're bloodying them, m'lord," he said. "But look at the mess of 'em." He nodded toward the rear ranks they could see over the heads of those fighting. "There's so many."

They were like a field of wheat, stretching far back along the Montserrat Road and out of sight.

"They're going to push us back by sheer weight," Wulf replied.

"Aye."

"We'll draw them to the barricades. We can fight better there."

Jager looked at the Roman ranks again and growled. "We'll do some killing today, that's the truth," he said.

Slowly but surely, the Imperials pushed Wulf's men-at-arms backward toward the town.

Even while they retreated, his archers kept pouring arrows in from the woods. Several groups of Romans tried to move to the sides to take on the archers directly, but the mud held them tight and made them easy targets. The ground stakes speared their horses when they charged.

Then Wulf was behind an overturned wagon. He sheathed his sword and jumped down from his horse. He felt a tap on his shoulder. Wulf swung around and raised his fist, ready to smash someone in the face.

Until he saw it was his servant, Bleak. "May I hold the horse, m'lord?" the faun asked in his woeful voice. For once, Bleak's normal downcast tone seemed to fit the day.

Wulf handed him the reins, then turned back to the fight.

A javelin punched into the upturned wagon bed beside him. Its tip came out the other side.

Wow, those guys are strong, he thought. He glanced at the splinters. The wagon bed looked to be made of hickory planks, which was as dense and tough a wood as you could get.

In front of him was his own men's shield wall that was

giving way. It parted and another Roman burst through. Wulf leaped out from behind the wagon and stabbed the man in the face, going in just below his nose and coming out the side of his head.

The Roman was surprised and never had a chance to defend himself. It wasn't fair.

Too bad.

"That one would have done the same to you, man," whispered a voice in his ear. He realized that Nagel had found him. She was sitting on his shoulder again.

"How are the women?"

"Getting away. But there are others near them."

"Romans?"

"Maybe. Sneaky Roman cavalry. Came around from the west and picked up their trail," Nagel said. "I warned the dark girl, the one with the blood tears."

"Ravenelle."

"Yes, her," Nagel said. "But others, too are nearby. An archer. Red riding hood. Skraelings with her."

"Skraelings?" Wulf said. "Where in cold hell did *they* come from?"

"Don't know. But they might help fight Romans."

"We have our hands full keeping *these* Romans off her tail right now."

"You smell fierce."

"Thanks."

Then the owl started up from his shoulder.

"Watch it, man!" she rasped.

From his left, Wulf saw a Roman stepping forward, drawing back his sword to strike.

There was no time to bring up his buckler. The Roman brought the sword forward.

And Nagel was in the Imperial's face. She fluttered, batted him with her wings, squawked and clawed at his eyes.

The Roman stumbled back.

"Thanks, girl," Wulf shouted. "I didn't even see him coming and—"

Bam!

Something very hard hit him in the back of the helmet, sending it flying from his head.

Blurry colors. His vision unfocused.

Wulf staggered forward, then spun around to see who had done the hitting—

Only to swing right into another blow from a fast-moving club.

Now he was able to focus—when it was too late.

Somehow, although it was far too fast for him to move and defend himself, his eyes functioned more quickly. He picked out the grain of the wooden club as it approached his temple.

Cold hell, Wulf thought. *It's hickory.*

Then his head exploded and he fell into darkness.

PART TWO

CHAPTER THIRTY-THREE:
THE AFTERMATH

Thump!

The owl Nagel was back. She perched on Rainer's shoulder. He swatted at her reflexively. She was ready for it though, and fluttered momentarily away, then settled again.

"The man is alive," Nagel said. Her breath was coming fast, her words rasping. "Lord Wulf. Alive, but taken."

"*Taken*? What do you mean?" Rainer snapped.

"Taken by Romans. Taken in chains."

"Curse it to cold hell! And you saw this?"

"Yes."

"*Where* did they take him?"

"I know not," said the owl. "But aim to find out. Into Vall l'Obac, that I know. *Now* you fight, man, so you can help me *later*."

She flashed from the trees and dove into one of the

Romans attacking Rainer. The Roman screamed as the little owl caught one of his eyes with a hook of her claws. He swatted at Nagel, but she was an expert at avoiding human blows, and just as quickly flew away. She tore away the Roman's deflated eyeball in the process. When she flew away, it was stuck to her talon.

Rainer put the man out of his agony by stabbing him through the throat.

But the other Roman saw his opening and stepped forward to cut Rainer down.

An arrow punched through the soldier's scale armor and sank up to its fletching in the man's chest.

He stopped short and a blew a bubble of blood from his lips. Rainer punched forward with his sword, allowing the arrow shaft to guide its tip to the newly formed weak spot in the Roman's armor. The sword sliced through and into the flesh below.

The Roman fell off the sword and grasped at the arrow as he slid to the ground. He jerked several times, then stopped moving.

Rainer turned to see where the arrow had come from. This was one of the most *unexpected* sights he'd ever experienced.

Nagel had told him, but he hadn't believed. Now he saw for himself.

A band of *Skraelings* had emerged from the underbrush. At least Skraeling was what he thought they were from the clothes they wore. Leather jerkins. Leather leggings to the knees. Moccasins. But their hair and faces were the giveaway. Their hair was laced with feathers and cut in ways that made the locks stand up like the feathers of an angry jaybird. Some had metal or bone earrings—or more feathers dangling from their earlobes.

All had the bronze skin and high cheekbones of Algonquians.

Except one . . . did one have flaming *red* hair?

Then he recognized *who* he was looking at.

Ursel Keiler.

As he watched, she turned, aimed her bow, and put an arrow into the black-robed figure who had pursued Ravenelle.

Then, almost too fast for Rainer to follow, she pulled another from her quiver and shot it. And another. And a fourth.

He'd never seen an archer so fast and accurate.

Then a fifth shot.

But . . .

The figure had now stretched out his hand and balled his hand into a fist. The arrow came to an arm's length from his face . . . and *stopped*. Instead of striking, or moving forward at all, there was a flare of light.

The arrow seemed to richocet away. But not in a random direction. It turned over in *midair* and flew back along the *exact* path from which it had come.

Ursel tried to duck, bowing forward in an attempt to let the arrow pass over her head.

Rainer was perplexed and mesmerized by what he was seeing. He was startled when something hit his *own* shoulder from behind and glanced off his chainmail shirt.

He spun around to see a Roman with a bow who had gotten off a shot at him. Two arrows sank into the Imperial's neck and shoulder while Rainer was watching.

One of the Skraelings had shot him.

Then he heard a cry and a look of anguish on the Skraeling's face. At first Rainer thought he was looking at him, Rainer. Then he realized he was gazing over Rainer's shoulder.

Rainer turned around again.

The arrow flying back toward Ursel had struck her.

Deep.

Rainer ran toward Ursel to help. But when he got near, he saw that he was too late. The arrow had entered Ursel's shoulder and buried itself into her body. The entire length of the shaft was inside her, crossways in her torso and probably part of a leg.

Ugly.

Probably fatal.

Almost certainly.

This was *not* a wound you recovered from.

Rainer glanced over to see that the black-robed figure had fallen. He lay motionless, arrow-filled, in the leaves of the forest floor.

The other Skraelings made short work of the remaining Romans around them. The Skraeling who had cried out came and knelt next to Rainer. He was weeping. He held Ursel's face and stroked her hair.

"Didn't tell her," he muttered. "Not really."

"Didn't tell her what?" Rainer asked.

The Skraeling man seemed to notice Rainer for the first time. He shook his head. "It doesn't matter," he said. "She is . . . was . . . wild. Alive every moment."

Rainer leaned closer. He gently pushed the man's hands away, then put his ear to Ursel's mouth.

He heard the faintest breathing.

"*Is* alive," Rainer said. "Barely."

She probably wouldn't be for long. But she wasn't dead yet.

"Ursel," he whispered to her, hoping that she heard him. "We have the best healer in the mark with us. Hang in there. You're going to be all right."

Ursel's eyes were closed and she lay slack.

No use, Rainer thought. She's too far gone for even an elf healer and a buffalo wisewoman to save her.

No one comes back from a wound like that.

"Tretz, the Risen One, give her strength and healing," he prayed quietly.

"What did you say?" the Skraeling asked, suspicious. He was looking down at the aster tattoo on Rainer's forearm. It marked him as a Tretzian, follower of the Risen Dragon.

"I just prayed for her health, man," Rainer answered. "It can't harm her."

"To what god?"

"To *the* God," Rainer answered. He let the Skraeling hold Ursel's head, and stood up, looked around.

Where was—

There she was. He sighed heavily in relief. *Alive.*

Thank you, Tretz, for keeping her safe.

"Ravenelle," he called out. "Can you get your dainty princess butt off that horse and come help me?"

The arrows had come from nowhere. Four had sunk into Rossofore before he even realized what was happening. One was in to the fletching. It had cut through some organ inside him, because he could feel the weakness of massive blood loss wash over him.

No. I *can't* end like this. I *won't.*

He'd deflected the fifth arrow with all of the mandrake *dasein* power within him. It had been a very near thing, for the arrow was headed for his heart.

He then tried to run away. After a step, another arrow cut through the meat of his right calf muscle. He tripped over its shaft with his left foot, tearing it further through the muscle. He also lost his balance and fell onto the forest floor. He sniffed in the odor of wet, moldy leaves. It was a smell he had always disliked.

It went with hardship and poverty. Cheap wine and vomit. Like the rotten smell of the dock street at Ostia.

It ends like this. My nose sniffing filth. Like the day I was born.

But he heard a cry of surprise from the distance.

And the next, killing blow did not come.

He lay for a while, biting his lip against the pain. Pain like he'd never known.

Was this the kind of pain the heretics felt when they burned?

No, *worse*.

At least *they* were half drugged from the smoke before the flames got to them. Probably.

Pain, but Rossofore knew he could take it. If only he could find a way to live he would get his revenge and—

Slowly, with trembling hands, he reached for the satchel within his robes. He found it. The last of his amber beads from the Golden Rose of Lerocher. With what strength he had left in his body, he brought a bead of amber to his lips.

Stuck out a blood-covered tongue to take it.

And dropped the bead onto the filthy forest floor.

He took out another bit of amber, dropped *that one*.

No. Careful. Do this right, or die.

He slowly moved the final amber bead to his mouth. Pushed it in.

He swallowed the amber along with a mouthful of blood.

Within moments, he felt strength return.

He was still in agony. But he could move.

Could crawl.

He felt his hands clawing up again. His skin mottling to scales. His nails extending.

With these gnarled claws he began to pull his mangled body along. Arrows through his body caught on the ground, in the leaves, as he struggled.

If anyone had seen him, a single boot could have crushed the life from him.

Rossofore went unnoticed.

Leaving a trail of blood and gore, he pulled himself deeper and deeper into the woods. Found a rock to huddle next to as the amber slowly healed him.

Later that night a weasel, following his blood trail, slunk near. It had come to see if there were something dead to feed on.

Instead it found Rossofore. His claw-hand snaked out and snatched the weasel by the neck. He ignored the clawing, hissing animal. With a feral grunt, he dug his teeth into the weasel's belly. Ate.

For the next day he lay in the rock's shadow. He lapped the weasel blood, gnawed its meat and guts, and sucked the marrow from its bones.

That night he was able to stand up.

He pulled the arrows from his body. In the morning he could walk. Slowly. With a limp.

His hands had not changed back to human. They were still grotesque claws. So he hid them under his robe.

Rossofore began the long slog back to Montserrat, killing and eating innocent things along the way.

CHAPTER THIRTY-FOUR:
THE VANQUISHED

Blood and bones, it hurts!

Wulf awoke feeling as if his arm were being ripped off. A Roman soldier yanked him up. When he turned to swing a fist at the man's face, another soldier caught him.

Twisted the arm, spun Wulf around.

"Stupid barbarian," the Imperial said. He spit in Wulf's face, then head-butted him in the nose and upper lip. Wulf's teeth drove into his inner lip and a cut in his nose split open. Blood ran down his mouth and chin.

Still Wulf fought. The Romans threw him down and kicked him with booted feet. Wulf laughed wildly, lost in the exploding pain.

What was funny? Romans in the tapestries wore sandals. Not *these* guys. They had hobnail boots.

When they got tired of kicking him, one of the soldiers knelt on Wulf's back and tied his hands behind him with a length of hemp cord. Then two of them yanked him up and threw him against one of the Apfelwein barns with other prisoners. There were about ten or fifteen survivors. Some were buffalo men involved in the last stand. There were two bear-men archers and one of the beaver people, who had been the quartermaster for Jager's company and not much involved in actual fighting—until today. His right eyelid and one side of his face were swollen, and his fur was matted with still-wet blood from a dozen cuts.

There was also a centaur.

The Romans had Ahorn. His legs were hobbled together, with a rope around each ankle. He had a collar and chain around his neck. His hands were bound in front of him.

Ahorn looked miserable. One side of his face was bloody and there was a slash across the horse portion of his chest. It seeped blood.

There were more cuts all along the sides and back of his horse portion.

Wulf dragged himself to a sitting position and looked around.

The Apfelwein Inn was burning. They were close enough to feel the sheets of heat coming off it as it became engulfed. Some soldiers stood nearby, still holding the smoking brands they'd used to set the place on fire.

Wulf sat up. Somewhere a horse was screaming in

agony. He remembered how he hated the sound of horses in pain.

No, this was worse.

It was a centaur screaming, half of its lungs human, the other half equine. Wulf recognized the human portion of the cry as that of Syrinks, the innkeeper's daughter, and Ahorn's cousin. The sound was pure misery. It made you want to retch. Wulf swallowed hard to hold in his throwup.

He sat for quite a while trying to figure out if it was day or night. The fire of the burning inn was bright, but the sky seemed dim. He finally decided it was twilight, only because his vision seemed to be getting darker. Maybe he was passing out again. There was something wet and sticky drizzling down the back of his head and neck. He imagined that maybe he'd had the back of his skull carved off, like a slice of bread. But no, that couldn't happen and him still be alive.

Could it?

No. It couldn't. He was hurt, but not mortally wounded, or else he'd be dead by now. But there was always the green contagion to contend with afterwards. Gangrene got under the skin and ate the flesh until a whole arm or leg was still hanging on a body, but dead.

He did pass out for a while. Then he awoke with a start.

Something hit his head. Then his shoulder. A voice made of only scratching sounds, but somehow understandable.

"I'm here, man," said Nagel. "I can smell that you are alive."

Wulf mumbled something. He wasn't sure what he was

trying to say, other than to acknowledge that he'd heard the owl.

"There isn't much to do at the moment," Nagel continued. "You have to *not* die. I have to find help."

"No help," Wulf mumbled. "Tell them to run."

"Lady Saeunn, the dark one, other women. Escaped. Many warriors, too. The centaur children are safe in the caves. Many others lie still tonight. The bear girl does. Too bad. Liked her."

Bear girl?

"It's night?" Wulf asked groggily.

"Yes, night now," Nagel said. "Waited until it was before coming to talk."

"How long have I been here?"

"Three, maybe four, watches."

A horrible thought came to him. "Rainer?"

"Alive. Killed Romans. Lots."

Wulf felt some of his ability to speak in regular sentences returning.

"Yes, all right. You have to be safe, Nagel," he said.

"No safety now," she said. "We'll bring help. We'll *find* you."

"No. No rescue," he said. "Nobody dies because of me."

"And these others?"

Wulf looked around at the bound prisoners nearby.

The noble Ahorn.

And buffalo men. The two bear men. Some were stunned. Some were slumped over. Some lay in pools of blood or worse and were obviously dead now. A few were sensible and seemed terrified. He knew he was. Beyond his numbness was fright.

"Good point," he replied. "Yes, help us if you can. You have to go now, though. They'll swat you."

"Been swatted before."

"Stick you with a sword."

"Been stuck before," the owl replied. "But I'm going."

"Good."

"Stay strong, man."

"I'll do my best."

"You are . . . a *good* perch," Nagel said. "Not so many are a good perch."

This was as close to an expression of friendship as Nagel had ever uttered, at least around him.

Wulf tried to smile, but the caked blood on his face wouldn't let him. "I like you, too," he said.

"Mouse-pleading nonsense. Must go now."

"All right," he said. "Fly with the divine ones' blessings, my friend."

"Don't need. Don't want. Will return."

The little owl unfolded her wings and flapped away.

Wulf closed his eyes. He couldn't sleep. But he did black out.

Rattle of metal. Lots of it.

And it was morning.

A detail of Roman soldiers was hammering manacles on

the prisoners. The smell of smoke and the crackle of dying fire coals filled the air. His arms and legs were covered by a layer of gray ash from the burned Apfelwein, which was now a smoldering ruin. So was the gazebo. The cottonwoods along the stream had been cut down.

They must have done that just from malice, Wulf thought. Damn them.

The manacles were hinged and clasped together by rivets driven through two metal latch sleeves. Two soldiers grabbed him by the hands and legs and roughly stretched Wulf out in the dust. Knocked the breath from him.

Hands bound. Legs circled with two ankle bracelets connected by a chain. They stood him up. He tried to take a step. The chain was long enough for him to shuffle forward. He wouldn't be running anywhere with these things on his legs.

"What's happening?" Wulf asked the soldiers.

"Huh?" one of them said.

He switched over to Latin. "Where are you taking us?"

The other soldier laughed. "Hey, it speaks."

"Are you going to—" Wulf tried to think of the Latin word for "hang" or "behead." He finally settled for something more general. "Are you going to execute us?"

The laughter grew. The soldiers slapped Wulf on the shoulder. Hard. "Execute? That'd be too good for you, Northman scum."

"Then what?"

"You're a slave now, barbarian," the Roman said. "You've already been sold."

"To who?"

The soldier shrugged. "Some are lucky. They get sold to a plantation to work the fields. Not you."

The soldier pointed to a group of men who were approaching. They carried sticks and had swords at their sides, but wore only coarse wool tunics and no armor.

They slumped as they walked, looking completely different from the straight-backed Romans.

"No, you now belong to the foulest, most despicable creatures you can ever imagine," the soldier said. "Those are overseers. You're bound for the pits, Northman."

"What pits? Fighting pits?"

"The mines, you idiot. The amber pits of Montserrat." He grabbed Wulf by the sleeve of the tunic, pulled him close. "You're going to spend what's left of your life grubbing in the dirt for the Empire. You're going to *wish* we'd executed you, boy," he said with a low growl. Then he drew his sword and stuck its point against Wulf's lower back. He dug it in enough to draw blood. "Now get in line with those other animals, barbarian. Get ready to march."

Because of the sword at his back, Wulf had no choice. One day he swore he would get his revenge, but that day would *not* be today.

He shuffled toward the line of his fellow prisoners. Roman laughter echoed behind him.

Chapter Thirty-Five:
The Wound

"Curse this darkness," Saeunn said. "I can't see a thing."

"I'll get a torch going," Rainer replied. He went to a pack horse to get one.

Saeunn knelt next to Ursel where she lay in the forest leaves.

Soon Rainer returned with a lit torch. It formed a pool of flickering light around Ursel, who lay on the forest floor, and Saeunn, who knelt beside her.

Saeunn's white shift was stained with mud. There was a nasty scratch on her face where a branch had whipped across her path. Saeunn paid it no mind.

"The arrow looks as if it passed under her ribcage, then next to her heart. It may have nicked the lower part of her heart. I cannot tell yet. And it cut through her left lung. That's why she's wheezing and the wound is bubbling."

Saeunn looked at the Skraelings near Ursel's shoulders. "Please hold her tight. I need to find out if the tip has lodged in her hip bone."

The Skraeling leader, Wannas was his name, and another Skraeling took Ursel by the shoulders. Ursel moaned in her stupor and coughed several times, bringing up blood, which flowed down her chin.

Saeunn put the fingers of her right hand around the arrow shaft. She squeezed it firmly, but gently. "All right, I'm going to turn it in the wound."

She tried to roll the shaft with her fingers.

It didn't budge.

She twisted it harder, straining.

Still nothing.

She sat back and sighed. "It does not move, which means it *is* in bone. It musty be stuck tight in her hip. This will be hard to get out. Very difficult."

"What if we push it on through?"

"We can't push it through. It is lodged in bone. To force it would absolutely kill her. And I suppose you know better than to just try to yank an arrow from a deep wound?"

"If the head comes loose and stays in there, which it usually does, the wound goes putrid and never heals. Dead in a few days."

"So we have to work the arrow loose from the bone."

"I've never seen it done," Jager said. "And I've seen men

die of lesser strikes than this." He shook his head. "Lady
Saeunn, this kind of arrow wound means death."

Saeunn nodded. "We will have to try, Captain," she
replied tersely. "Unless you have a better idea?"

"No, I do not, m'lady."

"I need a bowstring. The strongest you can find."

"Buffalo gut," said Jager.

"Yes, that."

"Always got an extra."

The bobcat man reached under his tunic to a small
leather bag he wore strung from his neck. He pulled out
various items till he found the bowstring. It was yellowish
brown. Jager unwound it with some difficulty.

"I'd usually run it through my mouth, get spit on it to,
you know, kind of supple it."

"Do not do that," Saeunn replied.

"It's gonna be stiff."

Saeunn took the string, felt the stiffness. "We have to boil
some water. Quickly."

Jager smiled and laughed raggedly. It sounded as much
like a cat trying to cough up a hairball as a laugh. "I can
handle that myself. Nobody can get a fire going faster than
a former tanner's apprentice. I'd get beat if I didn't."

He proved true to his word, and not long after water was
boiling in a metal cup. Saeunn meanwhile called for a block
of soap and more water. She washed her hands as well as
possible.

"Take your knife tip and dip the string in the water," she said to Jager. He did so. She waited until the bowstring had been immersed in the boiling water for a time.

But not *too* long. She wanted it clean, but fairly stiff.

In the meantime, she instructed the Skraelings to cut away as much of the clothing around Ursel's wound as possible. She told Jager to pull the string out with the tip of his knife.

Saeunn grasped the string and unwound it. She found its middle and doubled it there to form a loop. Then she made a drawstring loop through the eye of *that* opening.

She paused for a moment. Then she spoke to all nearby, but it seemed she was going over her proposed procedure to herself as much as to them.

"What I will do is put the loop on the arrow shaft, keep it loose. I'll follow the shaft of the arrow down into the wound with my fingers as far as possible. Then I will push the string in farther. It is almost as stout as metal wire, so I believe it will not bend, but follow the arrow shaft to the bone. If it stops before that point, we will have to widen the wound so I can get my hand further in. Please boil the blade of your knife again to prepare for that, Captain Jager."

"What's all this boiling of things?" Jager said. "The arrow's already in. Don't see what difference a hot or cold blade'll make."

"I don't have time to explain," Saeunn said. "You'll have to trust me, Captain Jager."

"That I do, m'lady," the bobcat man replied.

"Then let's get going," Saeunn said. She looped the bowstring over the arrow shaft as close to the wound as possible. Then she pushed it downward on the shaft, plunging her index and middle finger on one hand into the wound to guide the string. She began to work the string down the shaft and into the body with the other hand.

Even though Ursel was unconscious from loss of blood and shock, the pain must have been so intense it pulled her briefly to awareness—at least awareness of the pain. She let out a low moan of unmistakable misery. More blood dripped from her lips.

"Skraeling man, turn her head sideways," Saeunn said to Wannas. "Be sure she does not choke on the blood."

Wannas did as instructed.

Saeunn pushed on the string with small movements. The doubled strand seemed to go smoothly down the shaft for a way, but then a thrust on the string didn't get any more of it into the wound.

Saeunn tried several times, then huffed in frustration. "I can't get it," she said. "Jager, you'll have to cut the wound open. You have to be careful to only cut through skin and the fat layer, and no deeper into the body. Can you do that?"

Jager chuckled. "M'lady, I was flaying skins from beasts since I was a five-year-old kit."

He took the knife and made four small slices radiating out from where the arrow entered Ursel. Each seemed calibrated to go as deep as possible, but only through skin and fat.

"Very good, Jager," Saeunn said. She pushed her fingers deeper into Ursel's body.

Past the knuckles.

Deeper.

Ursel let out another cry of pure anguish.

The red-haired girl might have jerked away, but Wannas held her tightly down on the blanket on which she lay.

Finally Saeunn was able to get the bowstring moving once more.

She worked the string with tiny thrusts until she arrived at another barrier.

"It's where the shaft enters bone," Saeunn said. "Let's hope you're right, and it's a bodkin, Captain Jager. Otherwise I'm going to have to widen the wound path more and use a stick beside the shaft to pull it out."

Jager nodded toward the arrow end. "Notched fletching," he replied. "It's a bodkin."

"All right," Saeunn said. "Here goes."

With movements so small the others could barely detect it, Saeunn worked the bowstring farther down. Her head got closer and closer to the oozing wound as she worked. Then her shoulders relaxed the slightest bit, and she sighed. "I've got it as close to the bone as I can get it. Now to tighten it."

With a quick yank, she pulled on the string as if she were

setting a hook in a fish. "That's it, then," she said. "Now the hard part."

"The *hard* part, m'lady?"

"You two must both hold her tight," Saeunn said. "Maybe even sit on her legs, Captain Jager."

The bobcat man did this. Saeunn wound each end of the bowstring around her hands. She glanced at Jager and Wannas. They nodded that they were ready.

Then with a hard pull, she yanked up on the doubled string.

Nothing happened.

Saeunn grunted from the effort. She yanked again. And again.

Ursel's body moved, but the arrow didn't come loose.

It was still stuck tight in the bone.

CHAPTER THIRTY-SIX:
THE AMBER ARROW

With each yank, more blood poured from Ursel's turned head. A bloody bubble emerged from one nostril, as well.

She can't take much more of this, Saeunn thought. It's now or never. Need more leverage.

"Hold her," Saeunn said. She straddled Ursel, and put a knee to Ursel's surcoat.

Even *more*, she thought.

She lay on her back on the ground above Ursel's head. She put her feet on Ursel's shoulders. She moved down, and her legs hunched beneath her. Then Saeunn push all the way up, yanking the arrow as she did, putting her leg muscles into the pull.

This time the arrow came out.

It emerged with a bloody, sucking sound.

Ursel's cry of pain came out as a bloody gurgle.

Saeunn lost her balance and would have fallen over backward had not Wannas gotten up to break her fall.

Ravenelle approached. In her hand was a clay cup.

"All right," Ravenelle said. "I hacked a piece off and melted it. Now I have the Couronne de *Sept* Tours."

"I've already taught you much of the elves' *Thrimthriayur* healing method. You know that amber is the only chance to save her, Ravenelle."

"I hope you can," Ravenelle replied. "I just mutilated my mother's crown to do it."

"And it melted all right?"

"Like butter," Ravenelle said. "Beautiful butter. You were right. All I had to do was hold it in my hand and squeeze. It was like it *knew* what I wanted it to do. Flowed right into the cup."

"You are the heir. The crown knows this," Saeunn replied.

"I hope that's true," Ravenelle said.

Ravenelle handed Saeunn the cup with golden-brown melted material bubbling in it.

It was dragon amber. Of the purest kind.

Saeunn took the clay cup.

"Oh my," she said. "And so much."

Saeunn quickly straddled Ursel again. She knelt down and tipped the cup over the arrow wound.

The amber trickled out.

Saeunn used her other hand to work as much of the dragon amber into the wound as possible.

"What are you doing, Lady Saeunn?" Wannas asked urgently. "Is this how your kind prepare the dead?"

"No," Saeunn gasped. "This is life."

She continued dripping.

Pushing.

Kneading.

Until she had worked every possible drop of the amber into the wound.

It seemed to *want* to go down, to pour itself inside Ursel.

That is as it should be, Saeunn thought. Life seeks life. Soul seeks soul.

"The amber cleanses, and heals."

Saeunn could still hear the words of Tante Esmerl, the aunt who had taught Saeunn the *Thrimthriayur*, the Greater Path of Healing, during her stay in the Old Countries across the sea.

"The amber knows life, for it is life. It knows dasein, *for it is* dasein. *The amber cannot bring a soul back from the final death, but can call a human soul from the Shadowland without Stars. The odes of men speak of it, if they but understood: 'The souls of men are the souls of dragons.'"*

"How can that be, Tante?"

"That is what humans are, *Evinthir," said Tante Esmerl. Her voice was as soft, and hard, as moss velvet on a stone. "The scattered dasein of the land-dragons. The bits and pieces of the dragon mind that have awakened early."*

"But why have *they awakened early, Tante?"*

"*The elves know not. The stars know not. But because of this, no matter how limited an individual man might be—and they can be very limited—each human, each thinking being, is sacred, as the dragons are sacred, for they are made of the same dasein. So are Tier and otherfolk. All are part of the dragons.*"

"*But elves are not?*"

"*We are star-stuff. Thou knowest this,*" said Tante Esmerl. "*When the dragons hatch, our work is done. We may live for eons, but we will, one day, wink out. The souls of men live forever. If they but understood this, much evil could be avoided.*"

"*So dragon amber is sacred, too?*" Saeunn asked.

"*Yes. But it can be used. It wants to be used. Life seeks life. Dasein seeks dasein.*"

"*How can we use it?*"

"*Ah, Evinthir, that is what I will teach you. That is the* Thrimthriayur."

Saeunn held her hands over Ursel's wound as the last of the amber entered. When she withdrew them, the wound began to bubble blood mixed with golden liquid amber. Then less blood. Then only golden amber. It spattered, but each droplet flowed back to the wound, back into Ursel's body. The dragon amber was expelling trapped air and, Saeunn knew, the tiny, unseen, poisonous things that were carried on the head and arrow shaft.

First the cleansing, then the quickening, as Tante Esmerl had explained.

Ursel's body began to tremble, then to shake. Then it

glowed. Not brightly, not so you could see the glow under her clothing. But her freckled face, her exposed torso, shone. Her bow-muscled arms gleamed.

There was a surge of power, a crackling in the air.

Wannas and Jager were both thrown onto their backsides.

"What have you done to her, Lady Saeunn?" Wannas asked as he picked himself up. "What's happening to Ursel?"

"Dragon amber is happening. It is *being* returning to her. Dasein."

"I don't get it."

"The lifeblood of the land-dragons, born in the cauldron of their hearts," Saeunn said, wonder in her voice. "I've never seen so much in my life as Ravenelle has distilled from her crown."

"So these dragons . . . they're *real*? I always thought they were the fantasies of our primitive ancestors."

"Of *course* they're real," Saeunn said with a chuckle. "Do you believe those ancestors you say you revere, those who came before you, were, truthfully, not as *smart* as you? Not as wise?"

"I don't. It's just—"

"Just that living men usually believe that they're somehow cleverer than the dead. That they have *advanced*."

"We *have*," Wannas answered defensively. "Potomak is an example. We've found *better* ways to do politics than all this monarchy and feudalist nonsense."

"But *not* better people," Saeunn said.

Wannas looked down at Ursel. Her body was still trembling, still glowing. He nodded. "No, people are the same as always, I suppose."

"The bad, and the good—and so many *kinds*," Saeunn said. "I think all of you are very, very *interesting*." She was about to say more, but then held her thought, and pointed to Ursel. "She's waking up."

Ursel blinked once, twice. Then her eyes opened.

"What's . . . am I dying?" she said, her voice soft, but not weak.

"No, dear," Saeunn answered. "You're not."

"Then . . . Lady Saeunn? Is that you?"

"Yes."

"I was shot . . . I remember—"

Ursel's hands came up. They were still glowing, although Saeunn noticed that the glow was beginning to fade. The amber was finishing its work.

Ursel reached for the wound in her shoulder. Her fingers skated over the tiny pool of amber that had covered the wound entrance. It was still semiliquid, but getting solid now.

"What *is* this?" she mumbled.

Ursel clawed under the edges of the congealed amber with her nails. She pressed inward, and the edge flare of the amber came away from her skin. Ursel worked the tips of her fingers under this edge. Worked in her two thumbs.

And pulled.

The amber came out from her body. It came out as a straight shaft.

"What's happening to me?" Ursel whispered. "That is *inside* me."

"Nothing bad, Ursel Keiler," said Saeunn. "Only good."

"The last thing I remember is dreaming—" Ursel pulled harder.

More amber was exposed.

"What the—"

It *was* a shaft.

"Blood and bones!"

The length of the shaft of amber was perfectly straight. In thickness, it was about the diameter of the arrow that went in before. In fact, it seemed to *exactly* match the path the regular arrow had taken into Ursel's body.

She worked her hands down the shaft, pulled it completely from her body cavity.

Then there it was in her hands.

An arrow made of amber.

Ursel, still lying on the ground on her back, raised this amber arrow above her eyes. She gazed at its golden glow.

Slowly, the inner light of the arrow, and of Ursel's skin, faded. But the deep yellow-gold of the material remained.

Not only was it molded to the wound of the arrow that had penetrated Ursel's chest, it was even pointed like a bodkin.

Ursel tried to bend the shaft. It gave the slightest bit, but did not break. She released the tension, and it popped back to straightness.

"It's an arrow," Ursel gasped in amazement. "From inside me."

"Yes. An arrow made of dragon amber, forged in the body of an archer," Saeunn said. "Pure dasein. Full of magic. It must be—"

Saeunn was still kneeling. She straightened up, perfectly erect for a moment. She took a deep breath.

Then she collapsed into the leaves.

"No, Saeunn!" said Rainer. He bent to pull her up.

She was completely limp.

"She's . . ." He felt her neck for a heartbeat.

There was nothing.

Rainer looked up at Ravenelle. Tears were in his eyes.

"This may have taken all she had," he said.

Ravenelle knelt beside Saeunn. She took the elf woman's hand and tried to shake her, pinch her, wake her. Nothing. It was limp.

Lifeless.

"Is she . . ."

Rainer nodded. "Yes," he said.

"No," said a quiet voice from nearby. It was Ursel Keiler. She was still sitting up, holding the amber arrow.

"We can save her. I *know* what we're supposed to do," Ursel said. "It's my dream. That cursed dream I've been having over and over. Me dead, then alive. Saeunn dead. It's a dragon-vision. The dragon has been speaking. To *me*."

Ursel stood.

She set her jaw with determination.

"I *know* what to do," she said again. "I know how to give Saeunn back a star."

Chapter Thirty-Seven:
The Birth

The answer was in the dream. *Her* dream while traveling through the Shwartzwald to find Wulf.

The dream of stars singing to the dragons.

The missing star. The missing note in the lullaby.

The single word that was the key to it all.

Eberethen.

Amber.

Stone.

Amberstone.

Saeunn.

She was the missing note, the missing star. Amber, dasein, the magic that formed the world from the Never and Forever, was needed. Amber could save her.

Ursel had dreamed it even while she was dying.

Then lightning crackled across the sky and struck—

Inside Ursel's body.

It flowed through her. Formed within her.

Lightning.

Life.

She knew how to make a star.

Ursel woke from the dream.

Knowing.

"The dragon. *Our* land-dragon. It showed me. Many times. In the dream, I was part of Shenandoah, part of the dream that makes the land. The star-song. I heard it. I *saw* it."

Abendar was the first to recover enough from the fact that Ursel was talking at all to ask her a question.

"*What* did you see? Answer carefully," Abendar said. "Dragon dreams have to be interpreted cautiously. Dragons are *not* awake, not conscious, and a dragon dream usually doesn't make strict sense in the waking world."

"I saw the stars singing to the dragons," Ursel said. "I know what they are doing. A lullaby. A broken lullaby."

"This is so," said Abendar.

"I know what to do."

"Well, *what* then?" Ravenelle said, desperation in her voice.

"This arrow." She cradled the arrow in her hands. "It's dasein. Dasein connected to me, melded in me, mixed with my blood. It will go wherever I want it to go. It won't stop until it finds the target *I* want."

"What does that have to do with anything?" said Ravenelle. "Even if it *is* true. Which seems pretty doubtful since that would mean it can fly around corners and through walls and things like that."

Ursel smiled. "What if the target is the sky?" she said.

"What do you mean?" Ravenelle asked.

"What if my target is *behind* the sky? Beyond it. No obstacles there."

Abendar nodded. "I think I understand," he said. "The stars. They are holes in the sky's vault. They are openings into the Never and Forever. This is where the souls of my kind come from." He scratched his chin. "Do you really think you can do this, Ursel Keiler?"

"Whatever it is, do it *now*!" Ravenelle shouted. Then she sobbed. "Try anything."

"I can make a new star," said Ursel. She hardly believed it herself.

"Yes," said Abendar.

Ursel stood up all the way up. "I've never felt so strong in my life. Did I really almost die?"

"We thought you *were* dead," said Ravenelle. "All of us but Rainer."

"Maybe I was," Ursel replied.

She put the amber arrow in her quiver. Then she picked up her bow from the ground. It was still strung tight. She felt it over to make sure that it was in working order. Then she once again took out the arrow. With a thumbnail, she scratched a nock into the end of it. The amber seemed to give just where her finger wanted it to.

"I believe I understand what you plan to do," Abendar said. "I want you to consider carefully, though."

"But—"

"Ursel Keiler, this is powerful magic. It could be used in many important ways." Abendar gazed at the glowing arrow. "I believe this artifact could destroy a great evil in the world. Maybe *that* is what it's intended for." He looked up, caught Ursel's eyes. "I know this sounds callous, but it doesn't make a difference in the great matters of the world whether one elf lives or dies. I want you to consider *not* using the arrow trying to save her."

"I would do what you say," Ursel said. "But there's one thing *you're* not taking into account."

"What is that?"

"I'm doing it because I'm *selfish*."

Rainer had been mostly silent since Ursel had fallen. He had watched carefully, and he was gazing now at Ursel. "For Wulf?" he asked.

"Yes," Ursel replied. "He can't lose Saeunn. She completes him."

"You love him?"

Ursel looked troubled for an instant. "He's alive, isn't he?"

"Yes. He is taken prisoner by the Romans. We have to find him. That's my next task."

Ursel nodded. "The thought of Saeunn alive will keep

him going. I know it will. We have to make sure it's a true thought."

"That's so," Rainer put in. "It has before."

"So that's my choice, Lord Elf."

Abendar nodded. He said nothing more.

Ursel carefully nocked the amber arrow to her bowstring.

Then she leaned back as far as she could and aimed for the sky. For the highest point in the sky.

No one made a sound.

Then Ursel broke the silence by speaking to the arrow itself.

"Arrow, my target is the Never and Forever," she said. "Go. And make a star."

She released.

The amber arrow flew up into the night sky. Behind it trailed a golden glow.

Ursel's eyes followed it until it became only a bright dot.

Then disappeared.

Long moments passed.

Then something in the sky changed. Something small. A new glint.

A new star winked into existence.

Not spectacular.

It was just that there was nothing in a patch of the night sky—and then there was something.

A star was born.

Saeunn moaned on the ground.

She did not open her eyes.

Ursel looked over at her. "But I was sure—"

"Saeunn Eberethen is alive," said Abendar, wonder in his voice. "A new star is born. I can hear her sing! This is a shock to her body. She'll need another of her kind to help her connect. I will speak with my star and through him to the others."

"How long will *that* take?" Rainer asked.

"As far as I know, this has never happened before," said Abendar. "It could be a day. It could be a century. I have no way of guessing. But I have to remain with her until it is done."

"You need to be somewhere safe, then," Rainer replied.

"The safest place in Shenandoah is my father's hall," Ursel said. "You can take her there. I'll send a message with you to make sure you're welcome. You can stay for as long as you need."

Abendar nodded. "But where will *you* go?"

"I'm going with Ravenelle and Rainer to save Wulf, of course," Ursel replied.

Abendar smiled and nodded. "Of course," he said.

"We'll get Jager to send messages to his sister at Raukenrose," Rainer said. "She'll probably bring down an army. We have to get rid of these Romans."

"Agreed. The *Imperials* who have taken *my* kingdom. *They* have to go. But we need the rightful heir of Shenandoah to lead," Ravenelle said.

"Wulf is heir," Ursel replied.

"Yep. We have to bring Wulf back," Rainer said. "The levee should be led by the rightful heir. It's going to take everything Shenandoah has to beat the Romans. They are really good at what they do."

"Saeunn is alive. I'm all right. And we need Wulf," Ursel said. "So let's go get him."

CHAPTER THIRTY-EIGHT:
THE HEADS

Though it was noon, volcano smoke hung over the city of Rome, and the air smelled of sulfur. Even though Mount Vesuvius, the volcano, was fifty leagues southeast, the city had been covered in a twilight gloom for most of the year. An even thicker black cloud surrounded Vatican Hill and the Basilica of Saint Judas.

No crops grew near Rome. Wheat, maize, beans, rice, and wheat had to be imported from the southern empire and from Aegypt. The only plants still alive in the city were night-crawling vines. They could feed on the dreary light that managed to filter through the clouds. Many of the crumbling stone walls of the city had the hunter-green vines snaking up their sides like streaks of reverse lightning.

A dark being in the shape of a woman walked quickly

down the center of St. Cybile's Square and climbed the basilica steps. Slaves sweeping the constant fall of ashes from the stones hurried to get out of her way. She paid no attention to them. Even though she was thousands of years old, she hated to waste time—and talking to the bishops could be a *huge* waste of time.

The dark being's name was Geizul. From head to toe she was coal black and shiny, like a statue cut from obsidian glass. Her skin, her hair, and her eyes were black. Even her teeth were black. Her body was shaped like a tall, thin woman, an elf. That was what she had once been ages ago.

Not now.

Her face was stretched in weird ways, especially her nose and chin. This gave her the look of a half-human, half-jackal. The black teeth in her mouth were pointed.

Geizul wore a dress that was also completely black. Like all things that came in contact with Geizul for any length of time, within a day they turned from whatever color they might have been to black.

Geizul's hair was long, but gathered in a bun. It was held in place by sharp pins carved from human bones. She wore a circlet crown around her forehead of black metal that had once been golden. It was shaped like a snake biting its own tail.

Anyone who came near Geizul would have immediately noticed two other things about her.

She smelled of dead things.

She did not breathe.

It was cold in the basilica. It had been much colder since the smoke had settled over Rome, and there had been several weeks this winter of ash-filled snow, something that didn't happen in the days before the Vesuvius eruption. Since many of the stained-glass windows were broken, the air inside was no warmer than outside.

The Bishops of Rome didn't care about the temperature inside or out. After all, they were just heads.

Guards in black scale armor stood at the doors of the basilica, but the dark being stepped past them without a word.

As usual, the heads were chattering. Their voices echoed in the nave, the large central chamber.

There were five of them, and each spoke without paying any attention to what the others were saying.

Talking heads with no bodies.

They were planted by their necks into a raised block of yellow-brown crystal the size of a haystack.

This crystal was all that was left of the amber of the land-dragon of Tiber. Finding and taking it was what had caused the eruption of Vesuvius. That eruption was the Tiberian dragon's dying breath.

On the floor, growing out in every direction from this crystal block, was thick black mold. The dark being knelt in the spongy mold and gazed up at the heads rooted to the block of dragon amber.

"Holy ones," Geizul said. "I beg an audience."

After a moment, the heads stopped chattering and turned their gaze to the dark being. The center head, which had once belonged to a large, lean man with horselike features, was the first to speak.

"Draugar Geizul," it said. "Why do you interrupt our work?"

It was a fair question. Despite the chattering, it *was* important work. The bishops were digesting the remains of a dead land-dragon—the crystal was its heart amber—and it was crucial that they convert that dragon amber into the mold that covered the basilica floor. This was their purpose in being.

Geizul fingered the star-stone ring on her left forefinger. Like everything else about her, it was black. Touching it usually settled her uneasiness.

"Holy ones, I come with a message from the New World, from my slave, the one called Rossofore," said the dark being.

Another of the heads, this one a woman's, fixed the dark being with a hawklike glare. "And what news does that miserable fool have to tell *us*?" the head asked. Its voice was as hawklike as its appearance, and would have made a normal person grind his teeth in irritation. It had no effect on the dark being.

"Rossofore sends word that the south is ready to do as

we wish. Our colonial opposition has been either eliminated or subdued. He says he will personally burn the heretic Marchioness Valentine Archambeault at the stake."

"The plan goes forward?" asked a third head. The head had been a man, a patriarch of Constantinople, in fact. When it had been a person, one eye had clouded over with a thick cataract. That eye was still milky white.

"It does," answered the dark being. "My sister Graus closes in on Potomak. With it we will control the Chesapeake Bay, and the lower Kaltelands."

"The New World must belong to the master."

At the mention of the one whose slave she was, the dark being bent and touched her forehead to the mold-soft floor. When she rose, some of the mold—*adder*, it was called— had attached itself to her skin. The adder hung for a moment, trying to find a way to root its way into her skull and her brain. But nothing living, however evil, could gain hold on Geizul for long. The strands quickly shriveled, died, and fell away.

"Uzel's will is my will," she said after she'd risen from the floor. "My will is his."

"Of *course* it is," said another of the heads. "We are all his servants to do with as he wishes. Never forget."

This head had once been a very stately looking man. The dark being had known him then. Geizul had been alive since before humanity had crawled from the mud, after all.

The stately looking head had been an emperor of Rome

once. He had converted the Empire's religion to Talaia and thrown Tretzians to the lions. He had burned Constantinople and Rome to rid the cities of their stinking presence.

The dark being remembered that the emperor had played the lyre while watching from this very hilltop as Rome went up in flames.

She had harvested his head herself.

The Nero head had outlasted many other heads. She suspected he had even found ways to eliminate some of the others.

"I never forget anything, holy one," answered the dark being. "Especially him that I serve."

"The Tiberian dragon amber is dwindling. We *have* to be transplanted soon," said the hawklike woman's head. She had once been the mistress of the ruling family in a city-state of northern Italy. Lucretia had been her name. She had become infamous for kidnapping the children of her enemies and torturing them if their parents didn't do her will. Then, when the parents *did* obey her, she poisoned the children out of spite.

I took my time harvesting Lucretia, the dark being remembered, and made her die slowly.

Of course, she'd made sure the woman's head didn't remember any of *that*.

"I hear and obey, holy one," the dark being replied.

The Nero head fixed Geizul in his gaze. "Draugar Geizul," he said. "*You* must go to Freiland."

"*Me*, holy one?" She hadn't counted on this. She *hated* leaving Rome.

"We have considered the matter," the Lucretia head put in. "The amber dwindles. Our existence is threatened. That cannot be."

"No, it cannot," Geizul replied.

"So you must go," the Nero head said. "*Personally*. Take the reins of the slave Rossofore. Ensure that the conquest goes according to schedule."

Geizul knew it was useless to argue with the bishop heads. Without them there would be no celestis. And without celestis, the Empire would fall.

"I hear and I obey, holy ones," Geizul said.

"Very well," the Nero head replied. "Remember he who we all serve."

"Always."

The heads returned to the chattering they'd been doing when she had first come into the basilica.

It was meaningless talk, Geizul knew. What they spoke were hopelessly mixed-up snatches of memories, brief chunks of some long-ago conversation, or just the broken shards of impressions and feelings. It was waste material from the digestion of the souls of people.

That was what the heads were *doing* when they spoke: destroying souls.

Souls were what dragon amber ultimately was made of.

Now those souls were nothing but stink from the rotting

corpse of the Tiberian dragon. All of their hopes, dreams, memories, and loves . . . gone. Gone forever.

The dark being stood up.

"I am the hand of power for all you decree, holy ones," she said.

Perhaps this wouldn't be so bad after all. It had been *ages* since she'd last visited Freiland. That time, she'd crushed the Skraelings of Tenochtitlan and converted them to good Romans.

Now the ultimate goal was finally in sight.

The dragons of Freiland would die.

They would be sacrificed to the emptiness. To her master's never-ending hunger for every living thing.

To the void.

To Uzel.

Praise him.

CHAPTER THIRTY-NINE:
THE PIT

The pit went straight down.

And down.

A hole in the earth.

A gaping maw leading to blackness.

The Vall l'Obac slaver guards lowered Ahorn into the amber mine with the same block and tackle they had used on the donkeys.

One man held the chain around the centaur's neck and pulled his torso down. Meanwhile, three others hitched him up to a horse sling. With the guards pushing, he was swung over the opening of the pit.

Ahorn kicked for a moment, even though he was still groggy from being hit in the head by a cudgel while they'd forced him into position.

As his friend was cranked down into the amber mine's

blackness, Wulf gazed after him until he disappeared. There was a look of absolute anguish on Ahorn's face. The centaur lived for studying the stars. Now he would never see them again if he couldn't get out of the pit.

That prospect seemed pretty dim at the moment.

Wulf felt a sharp prod in his back between the shoulders. The line of slaves moved forward. He himself would *not* be lowered. Men were expected to walk down. Then he saw what the path was. There was a spiral staircase that circled around the perimeter of the pit. The stairs were about four hands in length.

No wider than the north tower spiral turret in Raukenrose Castle.

The only difference was, the stairs in the turret had a handrail.

These stairs did not.

They were not cut evenly into the wall either. Some needed a bigger step down than others.

Behind him he heard an overseer say, "Going down is the hardest part, you scum. Since you are all chained together, you better hold each other or else you'll all get pulled in together if one of you falls."

The overseer gave the line of chained slaves a playful yank. Everyone swayed backward. It was only by leaning against the wall as hard as he could that Wulf kept from toppling over and into the blackness of the pit. He climbed down a long time on the slippery stone staircase.

The pit was very, very deep.

But the descending slaves were not the only ones on the stairs. A line of workers was winding its way *up*. Each carried a huge basket filled with black and yellowish rock.

Amber ore, Wulf figured.

Wulf had no idea how these men and women—they were practically skin and bones—could shoulder such obviously massive weight.

I may be about to find out, Wulf thought grimly.

The haulers took the outside on the stairs. But every time one passed, there was a shuffling dance to make sure there was room for downward and upward traffic. He was amazed at how close to the edge the climbers could get without falling. Even leaning hard against the rock wall as he descended, Wulf constantly felt like he was one step away from toppling over the edge and into the darkness.

As Wulf would come to know well, the stairs had been chiseled out of the side of the pit sometime in ages past, and spiraled downward. The pit was over a thousand hands deep. The edges of the stairs were rounded from generations of bare feet plodding over them. They were also worn smooth and slippery. A trip down the stairs to the lowest level of active mining could take a complete watch. A trip back up could take half a day—that is, if you were carrying a basket of stone on your shoulders.

Wulf tried to count the steps on his descent. He'd gotten to a thousand when he stumbled and was yanked back by the slaves on either side of him. He lost count then and never regained it.

Down they went. One weary step followed another. Always plodding onward and downward. Always taking the jolt of the next step until his knees felt as if they were made of tree sap. They paused several times along the way to allow the guards to sit and rest. No rest for the slaves. They were forced to stand and wait until the guards were ready once more.

To go down.

Down.

Down.

It seemed days had passed before they reached a spot that widened out.

This must be the bottom, Wulf thought. *Has* to be.

The cavern opened out into the rock wall. There were torches and fire pits deep within, stretching back as far as Wulf's eyes could see. Smoke filled the cavern.

But then they walked along the edge a little farther and then another set of stairs lead even *further* down. This was only level one.

By the end of another half-watch they reached the true bottom of the pit. There another cavern opened out, even bigger than the first. Wulf could only think that the pit had once extended down to the first cavern. Then when the amber played out, they kept digging farther.

Here at the very bottom Wulf saw that there was

practically a working village of mine slaves. There was a blacksmith. There was a stable. And in one of the stalls he saw Ahorn, still with an iron collar on his neck, but no longer shackled to anything. Ahorn looked utterly worn out.

"Lord Wulf!" he called when he saw Wulf. But when he did, a nearby guard reached over and hit him in the face with a long blunt-end stick. Ahorn reeled back, blood flowing from his nose and lips. The beating didn't stop there. Several others joined in. They smacked and poked his flanks until he collapsed in the stall.

"That'll teach you to keep your mouth shut, horse," one of the guards said in Latin. "Now get up!"

Ahorn didn't understand Latin, but he understood the prodding under his ribs. He wearily pulled himself to his feet again.

"Now the others are here. You'll get back in line, you Tier scum," the same guard said. He pushed Ahorn toward Wulf's line of slaves. One by one, another guard worked his way down the ranks. He unlocked each of their arm, leg, and neck shackles. When Wulf finally had the weight off him, he tried to stretch. But his body was so used to being contorted in confinement, his muscles wouldn't do what he wanted them to do.

He stumbled, hunched over, to Ahorn. "I'm glad to see you made it, my friend."

Ahorn shook his head. "Made it to cold hell and cursed

damnation forever and ever, it appears," he said. "Not to paint with *too* black a brush, m'lord."

For the first time in days, Wulf cracked a smile.

Wulf glanced up at the tiny dot of sky. The staircase spiraled upward around the sides.

There were five shafts cut into the side of the pit like spokes radiating outward into the stone. The entrances to the shafts were dark, but the distant sound of metal hitting rock echoed from them.

Wulf looked at the nearest guards. One was tall, the other short. Both were fat. They wore coarse wool shirts and wool pants tucked into heavy boots. There was a Vall l'Obac royal badge sewn onto each shirt. They were armed with cheap swords tucked into leather belts and what looked like leather batons or blackjacks. These were studded with nails.

The tall guard had a jagged scar across his face. Whatever had slashed him had also cut his nose in two, and the two sides had *not* grown back together right. The short guard had a greasy, drooping mustache. One of his eyes was evidently missing, and he wore a patch over it.

"Take a knee, all of you," Eyepatch said.

"No," Wulf said. The tall guard's hand shot out faster than Wulf had thought he could move. He had the leather baton in it, and he slapped the end of this, hard, into Wulf's temple.

White pain.

Wulf stumbled, caught himself.

Blood dripped over his left eyebrow. The slash-faced guard held up the baton to show Wulf what had hit him. Its end was embedded with small nails.

"That'll teach you," he growled. "And if it don't, there's more where that came from. Now do like he says and take a knee, you filthy barbarian."

Wulf dropped into a kneeling position. The tall guard turned to Ahorn and drew his arm back to strike.

"Kneel," the guard with the eyepatch growled, "or else Andros here will beat your head in and leave you a slobbering donkey. Don't need no brains to carry baskets. Just muscles and the whip at your back."

Ahorn stared at him with hatred, but also without comprehension.

Wulf suddenly understood what was happening.

The scum-sucker is speaking Latin. Ahorn doesn't speak it.

"Wait. I'll explain it to him," Wulf croaked out. "He can't understand your language."

"He'd better learn quick."

Wulf turned to Ahorn and spoke in Kaltish. "He wants you to go down on your knees. Can you do that?"

"Cold hell if I will," Ahorn answered.

"Ahorn, I think he'd as soon kill you as look at you. Let's do what he says for now."

Ahorn grumbled, but he folded his forelegs under and knelt before the guards.

"Now," said the short one, pulling on his mustache. "*Here's* how it's going to be, you filth."

Wulf kept up a low-voiced translation into Kaltish for Ahorn.

"You are here to dig and carry when we say." He pointed at Wulf and the others. "And you are here to haul when we say." He indicated Ahorn. "Get used to it, scum."

He pointed his stick at Ahorn. "You will never see the top again, donkey boy. There ain't no way for a donkey like you to make the climb on them stairs. You're down here for *good.*"

Wulf didn't bother translating this part.

"Dig. Haul. From now on, that's all any of you is *for*. That's all you'll *ever* be for again." He took his hand from his mustache and rested it on the hilt of his rusty sword. "Because, let me tell you scum something. *Nobody* leaves the pit. This is where you're going to live out the rest of your sorry lives. You dig. You haul. Then you die."

The tall guard stepped close to them. He smelled of dirt and sweat. He raised the leather baton. "Do you understand?"

"Yes," Wulf said.

"'*Yes, boss*' is what you say." He lowered the baton in front of Wulf's eyes. "Got it?"

"Yes, boss," Wulf choked out in Latin. *Facio, domine.*

"Now him." He pointed the baton at Ahorn. "Teach him how to say it right."

Wulf told Ahorn what sounds to make to approximate the Latin words. He didn't tell the centaur what they meant. Ahorn grunted it out.

The short guard drew his sword and came around behind Wulf. He kicked Wulf to the floor. He gave a whistle and another pair of guards moved in. They had hammers and chisels. They quickly took the shackles from Wulf's wrist and ankles.

Wulf tried to move. The tall guard laughed. This caused a snotty wheezing sound to come out of the hole in his nose. He put a hobnailed boot onto Wulf's back.

"In case you're wondering, there's plenty of Her Majesty's finest down here to make sure you scum work till you drop," he said. "So don't even think of trying to get out." He removed his foot. "Now get up, you piece of gutter filth."

Wulf stood. He rubbed his wrists. They were chafed and bleeding. There were also small but nasty cuts from the guard's dull sword.

Suddenly a woman's voice called out. It sounded like it came from one of the shafts. "We are coming out, boss."

A line of women emerged from a shaft. There were about ten of them at first. They each had a basket filled with rocks on their shoulders.

The woman in the front of the line approached the tall guard.

"Okay to go to the Up, boss?" she asked.

"Get moving," the guard growled. He reached over and

with a gleeful smile, pushed at the basket on the woman's back. She swayed to and fro trying to stay upright. Finally, she got back her balance without dropping the basket.

"Yes, boss, sorry, boss," she said, and headed for the stairs. The other women followed like a line of ants, each carrying what looked like an enormous weight on her shoulders.

And the ten women weren't all. More emerged. A line of men and women, with dirt-stained faces and wearing tattered rags, came. Each hauled a similar crushing load of rocks in rough baskets. There might have been fifty or more before the tunnel was clear.

The short guard motioned to Ahorn. "You, get over to that loading cart." He turned to Wulf. "And you—pick up a basket and get down that shaft." He pointed to a stack of the wood-slatted containers nearby. Wulf picked one up and turned to look at the guard.

"Eyes on the ground, scum!" the guard shouted. "Down the shaft. Now."

Wulf stumbled along in the dark, glad to be away from the blustering guards. The shaft was completely dark. He walked ahead not knowing where he was stepping. Finally the shaft turned a corner. Wulf almost ran into the wall at the turn, but he held up. However faint the light, he had *seen* the wall. There to the left, far away, was a faint circle of light. He headed toward it.

Sudden bodies pounded into him.

Bodies he could not make out in the darkness.

Wulf fell to the floor and was weighted down by someone or something gripping his arms and legs. He struggled, but there seemed to be many of them, and he couldn't break free.

"Get his shirt," a voice said. Another said, "Get his boots."

Wulf felt his boots being stripped off. Many pairs of hands jerked him up and started tugging at his shirt. He struggled mightily and pulled away for a moment. But whoever was attacking seemed to be able to see far more in the darkness than he could. He flailed out with a fist, but connected with nothing.

Then something hit him in the head, hard. He fell back, stunned. His shirt was stripped the rest of the way off, leaving him bare chested.

Wulf felt his wool leggings. The laces on one side were ripped loose, but they were still in place. At least he had pants.

Better get the basket.

He felt around and found the basket nearby. He picked it up and headed toward the light again, this time much more carefully and stopping at every sound he imagined might be attackers.

It was cold without a shirt. Wulf shivered until he warmed up a bit, then shivered again when the chill returned. The shaft bottom was not smooth or sandy, but was paved with gravel with sharp edges. Walking on bare feet hurt, and his toes grew cold and numb.

He heard a tapping sound. It grew louder as he trudged on. It became a banging, then was multiple bangs. Metal on stone. Cracking rock, crumbling stone. More banging.

The dot of light grew bigger. He saw that it was not a single circle of light, but a group of flickering candles. Some were set in wall crevices at the end of the shaft they were following. Some were held by filthy, ragamuffin children.

He kept going forward.

The end of the shaft was about ten paces across. Candles were spaced here and there, but there weren't enough to provide anything but a twilight-like illumination.

It was enough to see that there were diggers here. Then as he got even closer, he saw portions of the wall that were being worked. The rock here was veined with a faint golden glow, like a gossamer spider web somehow embedded in the stone.

Amber ore.

Wulf stumbled into the candlelight. No one looked up from his task. They were men. At least they appeared to be men. They were too straggly and dust-covered for Wulf to be sure. There were about thirty of them chipping away at the rock. Some had mallets they swung, others had pickaxes. But most of them had no tools at all.

The slaves dug with their fingers. Some were completely naked. Some had only tattered pants or a loincloth. A few had soot-covered shirts.

"Hey," Wulf called out. Several of the men hesitated, but

none turned around. "Hey, where do I put this basket?" he called louder.

One of the workers with an iron mallet turned to him then. He pointed to the side of the shaft. "Some over there," he said in Latin. There were four or five other baskets in a pile where he pointed. "Sent out a watch's haul. Women left with most of them." Wulf deposited his basket in the pile.

The man with the mallet looked him over critically while they did.

"Rats got to you, I see," he said.

"Yeah, I was attacked," Wulf said.

"Well, get used to it," the man replied gruffly. "You got to fight in the mine."

Wulf didn't reply. The man shook his head. "Soft you are," he said. "You'll harden or die. Likely die." He pointed the mallet's handle at a spot along the wall. "Best you get started."

"Started doing what?"

"Dig, boy. Dig."

"Dig?" Wulf asked. "With what?"

The man set down the mallet and gazed at Wulf for a long moment. He did something with his face that was maybe *supposed* to be a smile. It looked horrific on the man's soot-stained face.

The man raised his hands. They were black with soot and looked more like claws than hands. "With these, boy. With these."

"And what if I don't?" Wulf replied.

The man shook his head. "Don't work, don't eat. Rule of the mine. Don't make quota, nobody eats."

With that, he turned his back on them, picked up his mallet, and started swinging it against the rock once more.

Wulf shrugged. There was nothing else to do, at least for the moment.

He went to the spot the man had pointed to on the wall. Wulf turned to the withered man next to him. "Are we trying to find amber?" he asked.

The man didn't answer. Wulf reached over and shook him hard on the shoulder. "Hey," Wulf said. "What are we digging for?"

"Don't know about you, but I ain't digging for nothing," the man mumbled. "Not digging for nothing. Pulling out ore." He was so small and hunched he looked like a child—except in the face, which was that of an old man. "We dig. The women and old men carry. We all eat. We dig again."

Chapter Forty:
The Boy

Wulf pointed to the wall of the shaft. "Just dig with my hands?"

"What hands are for," the man next to him mumbled, then turned back to his work. Which was digging with his hands.

To Wulf it seemed like the man was merely pounding his fingers into stone with no effect. But then he saw the slave was working at small cracks with his fingertips, stabbing at crevices with his fingers and hands. A surprising amount of rock was coming away from the wall.

Wulf scratched his fingers along the wall. Nothing came away. He tried harder. All this did was scrape his fingers. He kept at it. Finally his fingernails found a flake. He pulled this away and a small crack opened up. He dug at the crack. It seemed like a whole watch had gone by before he got a small rock to come out of the wall. He tossed it behind him, as he'd seen the others do. Then he started working at another.

The digging went on and on. Wulf's hands started bleeding, first at the finger tips, then all over as he got more scrapes and bruises trying to take some pressure off his fingertips. His fingers began to seize up, to curl into unbending claws. His nails began to come off, too, and before long each one ripped away with excruciating pain.

He kept thinking that this *had* to stop.

A man could not endure it.

But he did.

At one point the line of women returned and picked up the stones the men had dug. They filled their baskets and left again for the surface.

There were no breaks. There was no water or food. They dug, for watch after watch.

Finally, from far up the shaft, came the shrill sound of a whistle. Almost as one, the men stopped digging. The women set down their baskets, whether full or half full. The children gathered the candles. They blew out all but one, the smallest. The man with the mallet took this one and headed up the shaft. The others followed as if drawn by the light, hungry for it. Wulf stumbled after. His feet were still too soft and aching to move as quickly as the other miners.

Don't lose the light, he thought over and over. Don't lose the light.

Though the gravel ground into his flesh and turned his foot soles into a bleeding mess, he kept the light in sight.

There was the faint smell of cooking up ahead. This hurried him up more than anything else could. He was starving.

He stumbled out of the shaft into the rounded main chamber of the pit.

This was where the smell of food was coming from. There were torches jammed into the walls. Several guards stood around, including Eyepatch and Scarface, the two who had brought Wulf and Ahorn down.

There was a huge kettle in the center of the circular chamber. It must have been five elbs across. The miners formed a spiraling line in front of the pot. They all tried to keep the kettle in sight, as if the mere sight of food was better than nothing. Two guards stood on either side of the head of the line. On a signal from a guard that was perhaps their captain, these two grabbed the first miner in line and shoved him toward the pot. A third guard stood beside him, watching. Wulf expected the miner to pick up a plate or a ladle or some sort of container to carry away his food.

Instead, the miner plunged his hands, soot and all, into the kettle. He raised them up cupped together to form a bowl. In the bowl was the soupy mix from the pot. The miner hungrily slurped it down, gasping to try to eat faster. He put his hands in again and ate a second helping of slop.

Then he tried to put his hands in yet a third time, but the guard by the pot slapped him away.

"*No third helping*," the guard said. "Quota was five stone low today."

The man tried again to get at the kettle, hunger in his eyes. This time the guard brought out his leather baton and struck the man across the face, knocking him backward.

Three other guards surrounded him and began to kick and pound with batons on the miner. They left him moaning, curled into a ball on the floor. Nobody moved to help the downed miner. All eyes were on the food.

Wulf moved toward the broken man to try to help him up, but a guard shook a baton at him.

"Get back in line, scum!"

Slowly the man pulled himself up and crawled away into the shadows of a side shaft.

"*No third helping!*"

The line moved forward. Wulf's stomach growled. It seemed to take forever, but finally he was next for the pot. The miner in front of him finished slurping his second handful and the line guards shoved Wulf forward.

He looked down into the kettle. He'd expected gruel. But this was *something else*.

Gray ooze.

In the ooze floated pieces of intestine and stomach. It looked like soup made from the leftovers of a slaughterhouse.

That's probably *exactly* what it is, Wulf thought.

He steeled himself and plunged in his hands.

The soup was barely lukewarm. He cupped his hands as he'd seen the others do and raised the slop to his mouth to slurp.

Disgusting.

Completely disgusting.

More awful than he'd even imagined. Slimy. Rotten. Chewy, but with bits of organ and intestines. No real meat.

With an involuntary reaction, Wulf spit out the slop. The rest of it ran from his hands.

The guard by the pot laughed. "Too good for you, is it? You'll soon think better."

Wulf shook his head to clear it. He *had* to get some food and liquid in himself. He plunged his hands in a second time and forced himself to eat, to slurp it in. He tried to get a second helping, but the guard took him by the back of the neck and yanked him away. The guard then shoved him toward the shaft where the other miners had gone when they'd eaten.

Wulf licked at the last drops of slop on his palms while he shuffled toward the shaft opening.

The other miners were walking down the shaft. There seemed to be light far away at the end. Wulf shuffled after them, his bare feet smarting whenever he stepped on sharp stones.

There were a *lot* of sharp stones.

The end of this shaft opened into a large room. There

were only a few candles in the room. But there was light. Wulf didn't see where the more general dim light was coming from at first.

Then a miner moved out of his line of sight and he glimpsed in the center of the room a single gigantic crystal rising out of the floor to meet the ceiling many elbs above. It had a twisting structure, like a frozen whirlpool. It was as big around as a tree trunk. It glowed with a blue-green hue. Not dragon amber, obviously, or it would not have been left in place. But maybe it *was* some other excretion of the Montserrat Dragon, the dragon that lay under Vall l'Obac.

On one side of the cavern, water dripped from crevices in the wall. It trickled down into a pool, a water hole. The pool was crowded by miners gathered around lying on their stomachs and drinking from it. Wulf went to join them. He waited dully for a while expecting a space to open. Thirst finally got the better of him. He pulled a struggling miner back and took his place.

He'd taken only a couple of swallows when someone tried to do the same to him. He kicked his assailant away. He drank more as fast as he could. Then a man and two women grabbed his legs and yanked him away in turn. One of them took his place at the pool.

He looked around. People were finding cracks and crevices to settle into. Portions of the wall were dug out and he saw what looked like whole families huddled inside them.

On the other side of the cavern from the pool, there was a pit. Wulf saw people squatting by it to empty their bowels and bladders, then kicking the feces over the side into the darkness.

That's a pretty effective natural outhouse, he thought.

Near the outhouse pit, Wulf noticed a fissure in the wall that looked empty.

He went to the crevice. It was too small to hunch over and get into, but squatting worked. He entered and made his way back into the dark rear of the opening.

At first he thought the rear wall had eyes. Then he saw it was a woman huddling with a group of many children. All were so filthy they blended in with the cave wall in the dim light.

"Hello," Wulf said in Latin. "I'm sorry for intruding. I won't hurt you. I just need a place to rest."

The woman said nothing. She hugged a very young child even closer.

Wulf wondered how the children ate. He hadn't seen any lined up at the slop pot earlier. But they must find a way, because here they were living down here. If you could call it that.

"I'll leave if you want me to," Wulf continued.

The woman still stared at him and said nothing.

"All right," he said in Kaltish. "I guess I'm staying here then."

Hearing this language, one of the children moved away

from the rear wall and approached him warily. It was impossible to tell through the soot, but it was probably a young boy. He was naked but for a ragged cloth tied around his waist. He seemed about the age of Wulf's youngest sister, Anya, which was ten.

"What does that choking and croaking sound do?" he asked.

"It's a way of talking," Wulf answered. "Another language."

"Doesn't sound like talking."

"Well it is."

The boy stared at him for a while, saying nothing. Wulf folded his legs out from his squat and looked around for the least rocky part of the crevice floor to lie down on.

"You come from the Up?" the boy finally said.

"You mean the surface? Yep."

"I never seen the Up," the boy said. "Is it right what Mater Om says about the light?"

"It would seem very bright to you, I guess," Wulf said. "In the . . . Up."

"Don't mean *that*," the boy pressed. "I mean about the big light, the Eyeburner, and the little one, the Silver Mirror. Is that stuff true? There are things like that?"

The woman in the back of the cave finally spoke. Her voice was surprisingly soft and musical. "Scando means the Sun and the Moon," she said. "He's never seen them."

Wulf nodded. "Yes, it's true, Scando."

"So bright you can't look at them?"

"The Moon, the Silver Mirror, you can look at all you want. But the Sun you can look at only for a moment."

"I would look at it longer. A long time."

"You would not be able to."

"You don't know *me*."

Wulf considered. "Maybe you could."

"I can do lots of things."

"I believe you."

"When I get bigger, I will carry a basket up. I will see the big light," Scando said.

"I hope you do," Wulf said. "Maybe you'll see it sooner."

There was a pause. "We took your boots, Pale Man," Scando said. "Serpo got them. And your shirt. Livia got that."

Wulf laughed. So this is what the miner meant when he said Wulf had been attacked by rats. Here was one of those rats.

But what could he do about it? Not a cursed thing.

"You get anything?"

"No. They're bigger."

"I understand," Wulf said. "Anyway, thanks for not taking my pants."

Scando laughed. It sounded a bit like two rocks scraping together. "We would have, but you were kicking too hard."

"Well, thanks anyway," Wulf said. "Please don't take them now, either. I want to sleep."

"Better *not* to sleep. There are spiders."

"I have to sleep. You have to sleep. Everyone does."

"Not me. Never sleep. Just nap a little. Back awake in the blink of the eye."

"Listen, Scando, if I sleep, will you leave my pants alone?"

The boy hesitated, then answered. "Yes. I will leave you be."

"How can I believe you?"

The boy smiled, and looked at the woman in the rear of the little cave. "Mater Om makes us tell the truth, that's how."

"How can I believe Mater Om?"

The boy laughed again, and this time it didn't sound so harsh. In fact, it sounded weirdly innocent coming from such a dirty, beat-up child. "Mater Om *always* tells the truth," he replied. "Everybody knows *that.*"

Wulf tried to keep his eyes open. But his body felt as if he'd been run over by a four-horse carriage. His fingers ached. His eyelids felt physically heavy. Too heavy to keep open.

Wulf slept.

When he awoke, there were spiders crawling on his chest. He could see them because they were *glowing.* They had a faint green phosphorescence. Wulf took in a gasping breath, but somehow managed to remain very still and not scream.

The boy named Scando was sitting next to him, thumping each spider off with a flick of his finger when it got too close to Wulf's face.

"*Caecus aranea angulis,*" Scando said. "*Venenosa.*"

It took a moment before Wulf's sleep-addled mind realized he was hearing Latin again.

Then the words came together and made sense.

Blind. Spider. Corner. Or maybe hiding place—

Scando repeated himself. He seemed very merry about it.

"Blind recluse spiders. Very poisonous," Scando said. "Like I said, Pale Man. Better not to sleep."

CHAPTER FORTY-ONE:
THE LASH

Days and nights blended together in the amber pit.

Wulf thought about Saeunn.

He thought about Shenandoah.

He tried to keep track of how long he'd been separated from them by scraping on the wall.

He slept in the cave of Scando and Mater Om each night. He'd settled into his own niche. That was where he made the scrapes.

He hadn't seen the sky in weeks. There was no way to know if it was day or night now. There was only work time, then the brief moment when he got to eat and drink, and then rest period. Then the guards came through and rousted everyone. They poked sticks into the corners and sometimes swords. It was best to crawl out when they gave the first call or else you might get stabbed or poked in the eye. Even if you were badly injured, you didn't get out of digging. In fact they seemed to make sick slaves dig even harder as examples.

Saeunn is alive. Nagel told me so.

With Scando's help, Wulf began to understand how the pit was organized. There were two large caverns that Wulf had seen when he'd climbed down. The lower cavern was by far the biggest. Here there was a large work area filled with mining tools, ore carts, and slag heaps. There was also a blacksmith shop, a carpenter's shop, a supply depot, and stables for the donkeys, horses, and centaur slaves. All the animals and centaurs were doomed to spend their life down in the dark.

Including Ahorn.

There were four or five centaurs who were given backbreaking labor. They had to haul iron-wheeled carts from the depths of the cavern to the main shaft.

For the first few weeks, all Wulf did was dig with his hands. Watch after watch, day after day. After he grew enough calluses, his fingers stopped bleeding. Scando and the other children were not forced to dig. They sorted the ore into different sizes, and held the few torches and greasy candles that gave diggers light to work by.

After a shift, which Wulf estimated must be at least three quarters of the day long, they were herded out and driven to the slop pot. Wulf had long since learned to force the nasty gruel down. He even tried to grab organ meat when he could get his hands on it. One piece of intestine or neck bone would last a while in his stomach. It would keep him from feeling hungry a little bit less than just the liquid. But he always felt somewhat hungry. He had lost nearly a stone of weight, he was sure. When he looked down at his arms and hands, he looked like a skeleton with just bits of dry flesh on the bones.

One interesting thing was that his beard grew in for the very first time. It felt like a dirty scruff, but it was definitely there. He supposed that with enough time it would grow down across his chest and even to his belly, like some of the beards of the older male slaves.

Other miners, most in fact, used sharp stones to hack off the ends of their beards. Somehow a notion of good grooming survived even in the death house of the mines. Wulf supposed he might do that himself one of these days, but his beard was still in no danger of getting long enough to warrant it.

Wulf wondered what Saeunn would think of his beard.

He saw Ahorn most work shifts, although they were forced to sleep in different areas. Sometimes when he had brought a load of rocks out to pour into the basket strapped to Ahorn's back, or the cart Ahorn was pulling, he could get in a few words.

Ahorn was bedraggled. He had bleeding gashes on his flanks, and there was a deep weariness to his eyes. They had started a game of Cup o' Blood cards in their minds. They played one card each time they met. Wulf found that keeping the arrangement of the cards of his hand in his thoughts distracted him enough to make it through days that would otherwise have been almost unbearable.

But a couple of months into their captivity, Ahorn stopped being able to remember his card hand. Wulf suggested they try an easier game. But Ahorn just shook his head.

"No, I'm afraid I might be done for," the centaur mumbled.

Then an overseer pushed Wulf away before he could ask any more questions.

Wulf found out from some of the other slaves what was going on with his old friend. One of the guards had taken a strong disliking to the centaur. Ahorn was being beaten mercilessly each day. He was also tortured in other ways, like having his head pushed into the water trough and held under until he passed out. He was only allowed to eat every other day, and any infraction the guard thought he saw meant no food and whiplash across the back or shoulders.

The slave pointed out the guard to Wulf.

It was Eyepatch.

Wulf could do nothing about it. Not yet. But he could look and he could remember.

And one day, there would be justice. Wulf swore it.

The thought of avenging his friend seemed a very feeble light in a very dark place, but Wulf nurtured it.

Because that was all he had.

And memories of Saeunn.

CHAPTER FORTY-TWO:
THE VENGEANCE

Finally the day came for Wulf to make his first trip to the surface. One of the women had fallen that morning, plunging to her death at the bottom of the pit. Now there was a space that needed filling in the hauling line.

The baskets that each hauler carried on his or her shoulders were just as heavy as Wulf imagined they would be. They were almost double the weight of the baskets that he and the other miners carried back from the dig site. He supposed this was to reduce the number of trips that must be made to the surface. He mumbled to one of the slaves wondering why the guards didn't just use a rope and sling to haul up the rock, in the same way they lowered new donkeys and horses.

"Ropes fray—and cost denarii," said the man. "Slave

backs hold out longer." He chuckled blackly. "And *we* can be beaten."

Wulf shouldered his load. He began the slog up the stairs. He had to go faster than he thought he should because the line behind him and the line in front moved at a steady pace that he had to match—or he would fall.

A guard moved up and down the line of slaves, always stepping to the inside of the staircase, and letting the slaves step to the outside, nearer the thousand-hand fall. When a guard saw someone slowing down he would give him a hard lash from a whip or a whack from a stick to get him back up to speed.

Or sometimes just because the guard felt like it.

After what seemed like a watch or longer of walking and climbing, Wulf began to see the dim glow of the night sky. He was so tired when he finally stumbled up and out of the entrance that he could barely force himself to look up. But he knew he had to if he didn't want his soul to die.

There she was. The Moon. The Silver Mirror, as Scando called it. Wulf got a guard's lash on his shoulder as a reward for standing still too long.

"Dump your load in the hopper and get back down there!" shouted the guard. Wulf took a deep breath of the night air. It wasn't smoky like the air in the cavern. Then he turned and began the long climb down again.

He went up and down two more times that shift. On the third climb, the moon had gone down and dawn was flickering on the horizon. He wished he could see the Sun, but there was a limit to how many trips anyone could make. He was at his.

When he was finished that day, he barely had the strength to fight for a handful of soup. Then he stumbled to Mater Om's cavern, found his crevice, scratched a mark, and fell instantly asleep. When he awoke he saw that Scando was sitting nearby flicking the recluse spiders away so that Wulf didn't have to wake up to do it himself.

"Thanks," Wulf said.

"No problem, Pale Man," the little boy said. He cocked his head. What seemed almost like a smile of sympathy came over his face. "The climb will get easier," he said. "At least that's what I have heard." Scando looked thoughtful. "I wish I could go up and see the Silver Mirror. Did you see it?"

"Yes," Wulf said.

"And what about the bright one, the Eyeburner?" asked the boy.

"It hadn't come up yet."

"They *move*?"

"Yes."

"Maybe you will see it today," said Scando. "If you do, you have to tell me all about it. And about how it moves."

Wulf shook his head. "We're moving into winter, so the days are getting shorter. Probably won't see it for a while." He pulled himself up and casually brushed a spider from his knee. "But if I do," he said, patting Scando gently on the shoulder, "I'll be sure to give you a full report."

Wulf hauled for the next few days. He was working at night, he discovered. It was growing colder and colder outside. Winter must be very near. Then one day there was snow on the ground when he emerged. There was a full Moon and it shone off the beautiful surface of the snow. The dark trees in the distance seemed to float on a clean surface of white.

Wulf stood and looked at this for a while, willingly risking a beating. He got one, too. But it was worth it. After the shift, he tried to describe the sight to Scando. It was hard to find anything that Scando knew that he could compare to a snowy landscape.

"I will just have to see it for myself when I get older," the boy finally said. Wulf was amazed at the way the tiny boy's optimistic nature never varied.

On the climbs up and back down, Wulf would often keep his mind from reeling by concentrating on the condition of the steps he walked. Some were crumbling. Some were chipped at the edge. Some were freshly carved.

He learned that it took several haulers falling to their deaths before the effort was made to recarve a faulty stair. Near the top, maybe a few hundred hands down, was one particularly bad stair. It had a flaking side that moved every time he stepped on it.

He remembered it was approaching and was careful to watch out for it on the way down that shift. He was being so careful that he didn't at first notice a guard coming up on the inside track of the stairs until the man was only a few steps down from him.

Eyepatch.

Something in Wulf's mind, something below his consciousness, seemed to harden. Was it possible that the guard would stop on the faulty stair and finally break it off?

No, that was too much to hope for.

But Wulf found himself begging of Sturmer and the divine beings for that to happen. He watched as the man's boot slid on the faulty stair. The chipped side gave a little, and the guard looked down. A surprise flash of fear came across his face. But the stair held. Eyepatch continued climbing upward.

About five stairs farther up, he got to Wulf.

The man growled, "Get out of the way scum!"

He leaned against the wall. He didn't make any effort to make room for Wulf. Wulf had to go as far to the edge of the stairs as possible to get around him.

Then a plan swept into Wulf's mind.

It *had* to be now.

The many days of resentment for his friend's sake bubbled up.

He *would* do this.

Without any more thought, Wulf took the empty basket he was carrying on his back and slammed it down over Eyepatch's head.

It was one of the big hauling baskets, and the guard's arms were held in place. Wulf spun Eyepatch around while the guard screamed bloody murder from under the basket.

But his screams were muffled by the heavy oak slats. Eyepatch struggled but Wulf had iron-hard muscles by this point. He'd been carrying a full stone of weight up thousands of stairs every day for months.

When Wulf had the man positioned on the outside of the stair, Wulf yanked the basket off Eyepatch's head.

The man stared at Wulf in surprise. He was too bewildered even to cry out.

Wulf snarled. "For the centaur," he said.

With a sudden snap, he pushed.

Hard.

The guard teetered for a moment, reaching out toward Wulf. Wulf moved his arms back. The guard's fingers touched the edge of Wulf's hand. A nail scraped skin. But not enough. The hand slid off.

Eyepatch fell.

The guard fell quietly at first, maybe in shock. But he began to scream part of the way down. It took a very, very long time before the scream stopped.

Wulf stood for a moment thinking about what he should do. From above on the staircase, there was an old woman who had been a slave for a long time eyeing him curiously. Farther down, another slave, a man, did not seem to have noticed what had happened above him. He'd heard the scream, but since the yelling had begun lower, the man was looking over the edge and *down* to see if he could see anything in the darkness of the pit.

Now was the time to make an alibi.

Wulf stepped to the weak stair. He brought his foot down on the edge. Hard. The broken edge cracked, but didn't fall.

Harder.

He stomped and again and again.

On the third try the stone crumbled off, and half the stair fell away.

It was all Wulf could do to keep himself from falling after it. But he leaned into the wall. Then a hand steadied him.

It was the old woman slave. She'd come down to help him.

She didn't say anything, but when she saw he was all right, she shouldered her basket and started down. Wulf stepped over the abyss he had created and kept going.

The entire pit lost meal privileges after the shift. There were extra beatings for days. But it didn't seem that the guards were trying to find out who had pushed Eyepatch. Maybe they knew it was hopeless.

Maybe they hated Eyepatch as much as the slaves did.

When Wulf saw Ahorn the next day, the centaur looked better.

"Amazing what not being beaten and drowned every day will do to lift the spirits," the centaur said.

"Did you hear what happened? To that one-eyed guard, I mean?"

Ahorn shrugged. "They sent a team up to fix a stair, I heard. Looks like one broke off and the demon guard fell into cold hell all on his own. Couldn't happen to a nicer demon."

"I agree," Wulf said with a smile. "Sometimes we get lucky like that."

"Of course, there's the alternate theory," Ahorn said. "Maybe he was *pushed*. But they don't know who to blame. They can't kill *everyone*. Do *you* know anything about that?"

"Not a thing," Wulf replied. "But like you said, it couldn't have happened to a nicer demon. Good riddance." Wulf reached out and put a hand on his friend's withers for moment. Fortunately no guard witnessed the small show of tenderness, or there would have been lashes.

"Take care my friend," Wulf said. "We *will* survive this. We *will* get out of here. I promise you that. I'm working on how to do it."

"You know I can't climb the stairs," Ahorn replied with a rueful look.

"Then we'll have to figure out another way," Wulf said. "Don't give up."

"What I'm saying is: don't *worry* about me. Get *yourself* out if you can."

"To cold hell with that. You're getting out too."

The centaur stretched and sighed. "Oh man, I haven't felt

this good in days!" he said. This time their laughter did cause
a guard's whip to lick both of their shoulders.

It's worth it, thought Wulf.

And he *was* going to get them both out of here.

There had to be a way.

Chapter Forty-Three:
The Senate

The guards might not know who had pushed Eyepatch over the side, but the slaves did. Wulf began to be treated with more respect after the incident. And then one rest period he was shown something he had never even suspected existed. He hadn't thought it *could* exist.

There were caves that stretched from the main cavern deep into the rock. He knew that. He figured they were digging shafts that had played out.

In the middle of the rest time one of the miners crawled into Wulf's lair. After carefully waking Wulf, the man motioned him to be silent. Wulf noticed that the man had a thumb that looked as if it had been broken and healed at a completely wrong angle.

For a moment Wulf was afraid he was going to be mugged again. Or worse.

Wulf followed the man. He noticed that Scando had stirred as well. He figured the boy was following behind at a careful distance, but he said nothing.

The broken-thumbed miner led Wulf past the watering pool and around the corner of the cavern. They came to a small opening. The man wriggled into the crack. Wulf followed.

By now Wulf was used to squirming through tight spaces. He followed behind the man without feeling a trace of fear at the close quarters. After a long belly-crawl, the crack became a cave. Then the cave opened up. Soon they were able to crawl on hands and knees. Then to stand up completely. The cave kept on and on.

Finally Wulf had to speak. "What is this? Where are we going?"

The man turned around and shushed him. "The Senate wants to talk to you," he whispered.

Wulf continued following along silently. There were several passages that led off from the way they were following, but the man knew where he was going. Soon the ceiling began to narrow down again. The sides closed in. They found themselves crawling, then squirming on their bellies. Finally the two squeezed from the cave entrance into a large cavern.

For a moment Wulf believed that they had gone in a circle and were back in the main resting cavern of the pit. But the shadows and rock shapes seemed a little different.

There were people, but no one that Wulf recognized. It dawned on him

We are in a *different* pit. There are *more* mines. They're connected.

They padded around the outside of the large cavern until they found a side room. Several slaves were there gathered around a low-burning candle that stank of rancid oil.

"Welcome to the Underground Senate," said an old and grizzled slave. "We heard what you did to the evil guard with one eye."

"Not sure I know what you're talking about," Wulf replied. "What do you want from me?"

"We want you to *join* us."

"Who is *us*?" Wulf asked.

"The guards rule the chambers, but they *don't* rule our minds. That's the great thing about being in the pits."

"If there is *any* great thing about being down here," Wulf said, "I don't see it."

The other chuckled. "You're from the north."

"You don't understand," said another of the figures standing around the candle. This was a woman. She had a dark complexion, and Wulf could barely make her out in the shadows. "They don't waste the red cake or the adder cake on us. They know they can beat us instead."

"What do you mean the red cake or the adder cake?" Wulf asked. But he had a sickening idea that he knew just what the woman was talking about.

"The celestis. The wafer that allows the royals and the gentry to hold our minds to their will, and make us do what they say."

"The wafer dipped in blood," Wulf said. "The Talaia mind-control herb."

The woman nodded. "At least down here in the pits we are allowed our own thoughts. It's a kind of freedom. More than the bloodservants in Vall l'Obac have, that's for certain."

"The freedom to work to death."

"And die free," said the old man. He seemed to be the leader. "We would like you to join the Senate. We feel that there is a lot we could learn from you about the north. Maybe it will be helpful when the day comes."

"What 'day' is that?"

"The day we all go to the Up and get out," the old man shrugged. "It's a prophecy. Only the Tretzians really believe it to be literally true. But we all live in hope. Maybe. Could be."

"What would it mean to belong to your group?" Wulf asked. "I don't know if I have the strength to make a lot of these meetings. It's a long way over here. They work me like an animal all day."

"We rotate where we hold it. There are five pits."

"Five? Blood and bones!"

"Yes. Some are even closer to your pit than this one. All are interconnected. There may be more that we don't know about. None of us has lived on the surface for years. That's one of the reasons we like to interrogate new slaves. But you have even more to tell us, I think. Such as who you are. Or were."

Wulf shook his head. "I'm not telling you anything until I trust you, which I don't yet."

"Understandable," said the man. "Our next meeting is five rest periods from now. If you want to come at that time, our man will escort you. Eventually you'll learn all the connecting caverns and can bring yourself."

"Do the others know about this?"

"Some do. Most don't," answer the man. "Obviously, we have to be very careful about who knows. If we're rooted out, we will be tortured and killed. That wouldn't be pleasant at all."

"My friend, the centaur Ahorn, should be part of this," Wulf said. "He's old and wise. A lot wiser than I am and in more ways."

"We will consider it," the man said. "There are passage-ways that a centaur could get through to some of the pits. But he and the centaurs are kept locked in a pen at night, as are the horses and donkeys. It would be hard to get him out."

"I'm still a little fuzzy on what it is you people *do*."

"We help each other. When someone is too sick to work, we try to find a way to replace him without being noticed. When a child is hungry, we try to see that he or she is fed, at least a little. It isn't much, but it's something. We also police. If one of our own hurts another, we sit in judgment.

We also apply punishment. Much worse than the whip and the club."

"What is that?"

"Shunning," said the other. "It is easy to go insane when you don't have anyone down here to talk to or depend on. But even in the worse cases, it is temporary."

Wulf nodded. Anything that brought some humanity to this piece of cold hell he was grateful for.

"And then of course . . . there is Tretz," said the woman in the shadows. "Sometimes he is in the mines. We try to aid him in his work."

"What are you talking about?" Wulf said. "Are you delusional?"

"Not at all. He is Tretz."

"Do you mean the dragon-god-thing named Tretz? The one the Tretzians worship?"

"The Dragon-*man*," the woman said. "The Risen Mandrake."

"Are you all *Tretzians* here? I'm not surprised. My best friend is a Tretzian. I know a little bit about your religion from him. It promises the powerless that they are still worth something. I can agree with that."

"We are not *all* Tretzians. That's not what I mean," said the woman. "But you will learn more in time—should you join us. Think about it."

"All right, I will," Wulf said. "Thank you."

And with that the meeting was over for him. His guide

led Wulf out of the room and back to the connecting tunnel. After the long walk, and crawl, he arrived at his resting crevice.

A few moments after Wulf settled down, he heard the scuffling of rocks and dirt and Scando crawled in.

"You followed us, didn't you?" Wulf said.

"Had to" Scando said. "That group is serious. Didn't know if they were going to ask you to join or kill you."

"It's nice to know that you care," Wulf said with a chuckle.

"Not just that," Scando replied. "Been collecting all the ways to the different pits. That was the last one I needed to know. Pit Four! Now I can go anywhere!"

Scando smiled broadly for a moment. His teeth were barely visible from the dim glow that came in from the exterior cavern. Then his teeth disappeared and his voice took on a sadder tone.

"Not true. Can't go *anywhere*. Can go anywhere *but* Up," he said. "Anywhere but Up."

CHAPTER FORTY-FOUR:
THE SICKNESS

Days blended together in the pit. There came a time after one shift when Wulf returned to his cave to find that, for the first time, Scando seemed upset. He hadn't believed the boy capable of anything but good humor. Now there were tears in the boy's eyes.

"What's wrong, Scando?"

"It's Mater Om," Scando said. "She's very sick. Do you know any medicine, Pale Man? Or can you call on some of your northern gods to help her?"

"Let's have a look and see what's the matter with her," Wulf said.

Saeunn would know what to do, Wulf thought. His own meager skill at healing was a very poor substitute.

He crawled back out of his sleeping crack and to the area

where the matron of the little crevice stayed with her brood of rescued orphans. The younger children were crying. The older ones were shaking her, trying to get her to move.

Wulf touched the woman's forehead. She was burning hot with fever. Her eyes were twitching under closed eyelids, and her body was trembling.

He turned her slightly to get a better view in the dim light from outside. That was when he saw it. Under her arms were patches that looked like hundreds of tiny ant bites.

"I need more light," Wulf said. "Find Broken-Thumb. Get me a candle."

Scando scampered out. Much more quickly that Wulf had supposed he would, the boy returned with a candle. He carefully cradled the flame to make sure that it did not go out.

He probably has no way to restart it if it does, Wulf thought.

Wulf took the candle and leaned close to observe Mater Om's arms. Red discolorations. Then he pulled open the sackcloth she wore as a dress. Her chest was covered with the same rash of red spots.

Measles.

He'd seen plenty enough cases to know.

This looked very advanced. Often the disease could be survived. Wulf had survived it in his own childhood. But for someone who already didn't get enough food and sunlight . . . who was worked to the collapsing point every day. . . measles would likely be fatal.

If only I had the buffalo wisewoman. Or Ravenelle.
Or Saeunn.

Saeunn and Puidenlehdet might even be able to cure it.

That Mater Om was infected was a shock to him. She had
come to seem like a force of nature. He'd depended on her
quiet, strong presence more than he could say.

More worrying, she took care of the orphan children of
all the interconnected pits.

All the children in the pits had been born in the depths.
Many of their parents had died. Some had been killed
outright. Some had been worked to death. Whatever had
happened, everyone knew that Mater Om would take the
orphans in. She would see that somehow they were cared for.

Mater Om worked in the mines just as anyone else did,
mostly carrying baskets up to the surface and back. But
people knew to give any extra food to her. Wulf didn't know
how she had started taking in orphans. Now she had enough
young children of about six or seven years old who could
take care of the infants while she was out working. Then
when Mater Om was done, she would tend to all the young.
As the children got older, like Scando, they helped out more
and more. Scando himself didn't know how old he was. After
a while the older kids knew that it was time for them to go
and make room for more children. Sooner or later, they
moved somewhere else in the cavern.

But no orphan ever forgot what Mater Om had done for
him.

The Underground Senate heard that she was sick before Wulf could even go out to mention it to his contacts.

It was Sophia, the pretty, dark woman from the first Underground Senate meeting who suggested that he seek out Tretz. She said Tretz was known to be in the pits right now. Wulf didn't know what to make of this. Sophia was not superstitious. She was very intelligent.

How could she believe in something so absurd as Tretz?

He'd gotten to know the woman better at Senate meetings. She had been the first to start calling him Pale Man after she heard Scando refer to Wulf that way. The name stuck.

Wulf didn't mind. He was pale skinned in comparison to almost all of the slaves. There were a few Kaltemen here, but most of the miners were Romans from the colonies.

"Tretz moves among us at times," Sophia said.

"I don't get it. What do you want to do?" Wulf asked. "Do you want to pray to this being for help or something?"

Sophia chuckled. "Praying might do some good, Pale Man, but that isn't what I mean. He is here."

"You mean this Tretz is *physically* down in this pit?"

"Yes. Sometimes. *Now.*"

"Really?"

"He's been seen in the Deep Pit. Pit Five, the guards call it. There is sickness there. He is tending to it. Tretz is a healer, after all. That's what all the testaments say."

"You actually mean Tretz, the dragon-man from the Tretzian codexes and sagas, is here? Or do you mean somebody who *claims* to be him is here, somebody who is playing on people's sympathies for who knows what reason?"

Sophia shrugged. "Does it matter? I have heard that it could be him. The Deep Pit has the most sickness, the most deaths. That is where he can usually be found."

"How do we get him here to help Mater Om?"

"You cannot just send for *Tretz*," Sophia said. "You have to *go*. That is part of it, his way. You have to ask. He won't do anything without being asked."

"So we have to take this very sick woman to the Deep Pit? She might die on the way."

Scando whimpered from the corner where he was watching. He was very clever in many ways, but he was still just a little boy in a very frightening world. He depended on Mater Om to always be there. And now she might not be.

"That is where we have to go with her. It's a broad tunnel from here to there. We can maybe drag her easily."

"No. We can't do that," Wulf said. "She's in bad condition." He scratched his chin and considered the candlelight for a moment.

Ahorn could carry her. But Ahorn was locked in a pen during rest periods.

"I have an idea," he said.

Getting Ahorn free was not as hard as he'd thought it would be. This was because the new stable guard who had replaced Eyepatch was new and very easy to distract. One of the other centaurs pretended to be sick and began to moan and shout. As the new guard was walking to check on the complaining centaur—and probably give him a beating—a small shadow passed him in the semidarkness.

It was Scando, who Wulf was not surprised to find was an excellent pickpocket. He took the keys to the stable lock from the dangling hook jangling against the guard's side.

Wulf unlocked the stable and Ahorn quickly followed him out. He handed the keys back to Scando, trusting him to get them back onto the guard.

Wulf carefully muffled Ahorn's hooves with some shreds of muslin from a slave shirt someone had sacrificed. Then he led the centaur into the large chamber. Several of the slaves already had gotten Mater Om ready to go. They quickly placed her over Ahorn's back. Then Sophia gently tied her on.

Wulf knew where the entrance to the passage to the Deep Pit was now. He led Ahorn there. The path was a long one and sloped down, sometimes very steeply.

Ahorn was not in the best shape of his life, of course. Such a long walk tested his stamina. For the past months, he had been putting his effort into carrying a heavy load of ore, but for only a short distance. He had not worked over an arrow's shot away from his pen for many weeks.

But he was Ahorn Krisselwisser, and he was able to bear up. They emerged into the Deep Pit central cavern, keeping to the shadows. There was no telling when a guard might decide to step in and hit someone with a stick—either for punishment for some infraction, or for no reason at all except fun.

He was met by a member of the Underground Senate, who knew he was coming. Word had been passed. There were ways to communicate between the pits with taps and small tunnels that Wulf didn't know much about, or *want* to know much about. The more people who had the direct knowledge, the more likely the secret could get out if someone were forced to confess during beating.

"We have heard why you've come," said the Underground Senate member. She was a young woman with matted, dirty hair, but a nice figure. Wulf was glad he still had enough strength of will to find a woman attractive even in these circumstances. "Lord Tretz is here. I can take you to him."

"And what is he supposed to *do*?" Wulf asked. "The closer I got to this place the more I doubted that it was a good idea to come here."

"He will help," the woman said. "You will see."

CHAPTER FORTY-FIVE:
THE FRACTURE

Wulf followed the pretty young slave as she led them around the edge of the cavern, the deepest part of the Deep Pit.

It was definitely warmer here than in Wulf's pit. Maybe we're closer to the Montserrat Dragon, Wulf thought. He'd seen in a vision once that dragons had molten rock in their hearts, and he believed it.

The slave quickly turned into an alcove in the rock. Wulf discovered that it was the entrance to a twisty cave. Ahorn had to contort his hindquarters so he could get through.

They emerged into a fair-sized cavern. Candles and a couple of torches lit the space with more brightness than Wulf was used to in the pit.

There were pallets of brown muslin cloth spread around the floor. Some were empty. Some had people lying on them. They were sick and hurt people. Some groaned, some coughed. Some had nasty wounds that oozed or were swollen and inflamed. All seemed to be in the last stages of life, weak from gangrene wounds, or some other horrible infection.

In the middle of these people a man in a brown tunic of broadweave wool cloth moved about.

In Raukenrose, he's be dressed like a pauper in the broadweave. Here the tunic made him seem like royalty.

The man was dark skinned. His hair was black. He turned to gaze at Wulf and Ahorn as they entered. For a moment Wulf was startled. In the man's eyes flashed a reddish sparkle like flickering fire.

The man in the tunic was standing over a younger man who was lying on the ground. This man was clutching his arm in what seemed like agony. The man in the tunic motioned for Wulf and Ahorn to come to him.

"You're just in time," he said. His voice was low and calm, but also conveyed authority. Wulf didn't for a moment consider *not* obeying. He and Ahorn went to the man.

The man in the tunic was about Wulf's height. He seemed an indeterminate age, not yet an old man—but certainly not a young man anymore.

He examined Mater Om on Ahorn's back. Then he turned to Wulf. "Help me get her resting on a pallet. Then we deal with this fellow with the break."

Wulf complied without any comment. He untied the soft rope that had bound Mater Om to Ahorn's back. With

Ahorn's help, they gently set Mater Om on a nearby empty groundcloth.

He turned back to the young man who was clutching his arm in pain.

"All right. Now we'll deal with *you*, my friend," the man in the tunic said. He turned to Wulf and Ahorn. "We're going to have to reset his upper arm bone. It's a simple break but he's gotten it far out of position."

"*We* are?" said Wulf.

The man smiled and nodded.

"All right, how do *we* do it? Where do you need us?"

"You hold onto his lower body," the man said. He turned to Ahorn. "You, lord centaur, grasp the broken arm by the wrist. On the count of three I would like you to back up, and pull the arm as you do it." Back to Wulf. "Meanwhile you, my friend,"—he nodded to Wulf—"you keep a hold and don't let his body move. Only let the arm be stretched out. When we have that done, I'll pop the bone back into place. Any questions?"

Wulf shook his head indicating he did not. Ahorn didn't say anything. He reached down and took the injured man's hand.

"Are you certain you want me to do this, sir?" the centaur asked the young man with the broken arm. "I'm not sure this healer knows what he's doing." The young man gritted his teeth and nodded yes. "All right then, I've got it."

"I've got him here." Wulf said. He laid his body across the

young man's torso to make sure he could not move. He had seen bones set before. Sometimes it took a great deal of stretching and pressure. It could all be ruined if the holders slipped and the pressure was suddenly released before the bone was back in place.

Ahorn stepped back, pulling the arm. The young man screamed.

Then tried to hold the scream in and grit his teeth.

Then couldn't, and screamed again.

Meanwhile the man in the tunic was running his fingers up and down the arm. He found the tips of the bone and worked them back into proper alignment. After he was certain he had them in the correct spot, he nodded toward Ahorn.

"All right, lord centaur, release the arm. Gently. Gently."

Ahorn did it, and the man with a broken arm lay back and gasped for breath. But he did not seem to be in nearly as much pain. The man in the tunic continued to run his hands across the area of the break. The longer he did this, the more the breathing of the young man settled.

And then Wulf saw it. The young man's skin was *glowing* with a reddish color. It was shimmering from within, from a source beneath the skin.

As if there's a light inside shining outward, Wulf thought.

Then the man took his hands away and the glow dimmed.

"Try to use it," the man in the tunic said to the hurt man. The other slowly sat up. He began to move his arm about.

When that didn't seem to hurt, he started to windmill it in a circle. He laughed.

"I can't believe it! I thought I was a dead man. There was no way I could work with an arm broken like that, not for many days. And you know they don't put up with that."

He turned to the man in the tunic. "Thank you, Lord," he said. "You saved me."

Wulf noticed that the man in the tunic didn't deny this. But he didn't seem to gloat about it either.

"How did you break the arm, my son?" asked the man in the tunic. He spoke gently but firmly. The other man looked down.

He seems embarrassed, Wulf thought.

Yet he calmly answered the man in the tunic's question.

"I got in a fight with my brother," he said. "It was over a woman. She didn't even *like* either one of us. But we *had* to fight. We always *have* to fight. Stupid."

"Do you *need* to fight?" the man in the tunic asked in a kindly tone. "Is that what you think?"

The man with the healed arm considered. Finally he spoke. "No, Lord. We've been practically at each other's throats since we were kids. It was a good thing at first. We helped each other get tougher. It's probably why we are both still alive. But do we need to do it *anymore*? I think we take it too far."

"Do you think he would agree with you?" the man in the tunic asked. "Your brother?"

"I don't know. Maybe," said the other. "But we do help each other as much as we fight. He doesn't want to lose my good arm any more than I do."

"Then go and tell him that," the man in the tunic said. "And forgive him for hurting you. You can either have your revenge on him—or keep a brother who has your back. Am I right?"

The other nodded. "You are. Thank you, Lord."

"Go and get some rest," the man replied. "But talk about this with your brother before you go to sleep."

"I will."

The man stood and walked away. He was still swinging his arm around. He seemed amazed that it worked so well now.

That healing wasn't a trick, Wulf thought. I *saw* the break. I saw how total it was.

Who is this man?

And what the cold hell is he doing at the bottom of a cursed *amber mine*?

As if in answer to Wulf's unstated question, the man turned to him and Ahorn.

"Hello Lord Wulf, Earl Ahorn," he said. "Pleased to meet you, although I feel I already know you both so well." He bowed slightly. "My name is Tretz. Just Tretz, nothing else. This woman you have brought is very sick. She does indeed have the measles, just as you thought, Lord Wulf. Do you want my help with this?"

Wulf was shocked. How did the man know? What kind of trick was this? It had to be one, didn't it?

But Wulf was not too shocked to forget what had happened to the man with the broken arm.

"Yes, all right," Wulf managed to stammer out. "Yes, please. She needs help."

Chapter Forty-Six:
The Mandrake

"Measles is a nasty disease," the man who called himself Tretz said. He was bent over Mater Om, examining the red patches along her arm. Then he looked at the even worse red splotches across her chest.

She was still unconscious. Tretz, or whoever this was, lifted up an eyelid. The normal white of the eye had turned a blackish red. Were even her *eyeballs* infested with measles?

"Can you help her?"

"Of course," Tretz replied. "She is a dear daughter of mine."

"She's your *daughter*?" Ahorn asked in surprise.

Tretz laughed. It sounded odd in this cavern filled with the sick and injured. Tretz didn't seem to care, though. He smiled good naturedly. "Oh yes. I have known Mater Om for a very long time. Since she was a babe in her mother's arms in the shantytown of East Montserrat."

"How could you have known her then?" Wulf asked. "She's . . . old."

"Not as old as you think," the man answered. "She has lived a hard, hard life. How old would you say she is?"

"I don't know," Wulf said. "Maybe fifty? Maybe even sixty?"

"She is *thirty-one years old*," Tretz replied.

"Blood and bones," Wulf murmured.

"Blood and bones," Tretz answered, nodding. "Yes, that's about all she has left." He leaned over her, examining the measles rash on her neck. "But it will be enough, I think."

"What are you going to do?"

"What do you *want* me to do?"

"Make her better, of course!"

"Do you believe I can?"

"You are obviously some kind of healer. That man's broken arm didn't fix itself."

"But you still think it might have been a trick."

"What does it matter? Can you help?"

"No," Tretz answered. "I cannot. If you can't believe, then I won't do it."

"What are you talking about? Heal her if you can!"

"Don't you think it might be better for her to die and get out of this place?"

"No, I . . ." Wulf started to answer. "Yes, it might be better for *her*. But not for the kids she tends to."

"You afraid it might be *you* who has to care for them if she doesn't make it?"

"No, I . . . I haven't thought about it. I don't think I'd do a very good job."

Tretz smiled. "Neither do I," he replied. "I'll ask you again: Do you believe I can help, Wulfgang von Dunstig? And what about you, Ahorn Krisselwisser?"

Both Wulf and Ahorn were too stunned to answer.

"How does this man know our names?" Ahorn asked.

Tretz turned away in what seemed to be frustration.

Or maybe it was disgust.

Then a small voice came from the entrance to the cave.

"*I* believe," Scando said. "I believe you can do it, Lord Tretz."

The man smiled. He looked up and gestured for Scando to join them.

"Take my hand, Scando, son of Vortrix and Ines," the man said. Scando slipped his small hand into that of Tretz. He nodded toward Mater Om. "Beatrice, the one you call Mater Om, is the only mother you've ever known, isn't she, my friend?"

"Yes," Scando said. "And she's *good*. She's so good to me. To us. You *have* to save her. I know you can."

"Yes," Tretz said. "She is very far gone, though. It will be difficult to call her back."

"I believe," Scando said.

"I believe, too," Wulf blurted out. "And if I don't, then help me to believe *better*. Do whatever you have to, just help that woman."

Tretz chuckled again. "Now *that's* an interesting request," he said. "I'll have to think on that one. 'Help me believe better.' In the meantime, let me see if I can call up a bit of fire to aid us."

"Fire, my Lord?" said Scando. "But she's already so hot."

"This is not regular fire, Scando," Tretz replied. "It needs somebody like you to light it up."

"Me?"

"Because you believe it can happen, Scando." Tretz loosened his tunic. "My dasein fire only works when there's a purpose. It's funny that way. Just a moment." He let the top portion fall away and bared his chest. "Don't want to ruin a perfectly good piece of cloth."

Tretz then closed his eyes and folded his arms across his chest. He seemed to tense, to grip himself tightly.

From the naked skin on his back, bumps began to grow. Mounds.

They the skin split.

Wulf was distracted by something else then. A red glow was playing under the skin of his face. Tretz's eyes were glowing crimson red. But his skin also was changing. Becoming mottled, scaly, like a dried mud flat.

Then there was a tearing sound, like a piece of leather

being ripped apart. The skin over the mounds on the man's back spread away and two . . . *wings* emerged. They unfolded as they came out of the skin. But these were no butterfly wings. They were huge. And scaly.

When they were all the way out, the wounds closed. The wings opened up. Each was at least five elbs from tip to tip.

Weird.

Magical.

Magnificent.

Scary.

Tretz breathed in. He breathed in for a very long time. Wulf couldn't believe a man's lungs could be that large.

But this wasn't a man.

Or at least, this wasn't *just* a man.

The man-dragon leaned over Mater Om. He opened his mouth and let out his breath. Only it wasn't breath now.

It was fire.

Glowing, *golden* fire.

Wulf started to move in between them, to save Mater Om from being engulfed.

"Stop!" shouted Tretz. "This will not hurt her."

Wulf pulled himself back. Whatever this . . . fire . . . was might kill Mater Om, but she was nearly dead already.

The golden flames washed over Mater Om's body. They licked under and around her.

Her body rose. Not far off the floor, no more than an elb. But it seemed to be suspended by the flames.

To float.

With nothing but the golden fire to support it.

The red patches in Mater Om's skin seemed to recede. Her body seemed to relax, loosen up. Wulf heard Mater Om take a deep breath.

Then the golden flame withdrew. Tretz began to breathe it back inside himself. As the flames retreated, they gently set Mater Om down on the pallet again.

With one big flap of the huge wings, Tretz turned his body to face Wulf and Ahorn.

"*That's* what the faith of a child can do," Tretz said.

Mater Om sat up on her pallet. "What's . . . where am I?" she said in a croaking voice.

She looked up at Tretz, but he didn't answer her. At that moment, his wings or whatever they were, withdrew themselves into his body. The scaliness of his skin faded. When he had the complete appearance of a man once more, he sighed contentedly, and smiled.

Then he closed his eyes and collapsed on the floor beside Mater Om.

It took them all a moment to see that his chest rose and fell. He wasn't dead.

Tretz was sleeping. And snoring.

Tretz didn't wake up for a quarter-watch or so. In the meantime, Mater Om stood up and went for a walk around the cavern. She began tending to the remaining sick people, offering a sip of water from a nearby dipper, or fixing a bandage, as if nothing had been bothering her just moments before.

Scando was hopping at her side, happy to be helping. Delighted that his mother was not going to die after all, but was all better.

"What do you think we just saw?" Wulf said to Ahorn.

"I'm not sure, m'lord," the centaur answered. He looked like he was blushing. But then Wulf saw that the centaur was *angry*. "What I am wondering—if this Tretz is a being of such power—and we saw that he *is*—then why doesn't he take these poor souls out of this hellish hole?"

"Is that *all* you wonder, lord centaur?" came the voice of Tretz. He sat up and rubbed his head. He had fully returned to being a man. "Why I don't lead a rebellion? A holy revolution?"

"Yes," Ahorn answered. "You can breathe . . . magic. That was pure dasein. I recognized it."

"You are right, my friend," Tretz answered. "It takes a lot out of me, let me tell you." He pulled his tunic back around his shoulders and cinched his rope belt while he spoke, but didn't yet stand up. "I *could* lead a revolution, free these slaves. Overthrow the kingdom. The entire empire. Would that suit you?"

"Yes! Why don't you?"

"All right," he said, and cinched a rope belt around his waist. "But, tell me, Lord Ahorn . . . do you think there might be more *important* things to do?"

"*More* important? Like *what*?"

"I might answer that one soul is worth more than a thousand Holy Roman Empires. Souls last forever, you know."

"We are in a terrible place in this pit. Children are suffering. Dying. You can talk about souls and spiritual things after you have saved *lives*."

Tretz nodded. He tried to stand, and took Wulf's offered hand to pull himself up.

"Yes," he said. "This *is* a terrible place. It is a blot on creation."

"So end it!"

Tretz shook his head sadly. "There are worse places than here. Many, many places in this world. I've seen them all. Just as bad or worse."

"Fix them! *If* you are the god of the Tretzians. They claim you are all powerful. Prove it. Fix the world!"

"Look around you," Tretz said. "What do you see, Ahorn? Do you see sick and dying people?"

"Yes."

"Rocks? Shadows? A few candles shedding light?"

"Yes, I suppose."

"I don't quite see it that way, myself."

"What do you mean?"

"All of these people here. You. Lord Wulf. The boy and his true-soul's mother over there. You are my candles. You are the light. Everything else is a shadow—and shadows don't really exist, you know. That is what the evil being responsible for this horrible place never wants us to understand. How completely full of nothing it is. How much of a void of nothingness *he* is."

Ahorn shook his head and stomped a hoof into the sandy ground. "*I* don't understand," he said.

Wulf had been studying his own feet, only half listening to the conversation. He was thinking.

Here is a dragon.

A dragon that's awake.

Ask it. Ask him.

"All right, you're a man-dragon," Wulf said. "A mandrake. I believe that much, at least." He looked up at Tretz. "Will it work? Taking Saeunn Amberstone to Eounnbard? Can they save her?"

Tretz shrugged. "Might," he said. "The only way to see the future is from the Never and Forever. It's the Always Now. You can stand back there, and take all of time in with one glance. You can turn your gaze here or there and find out what happened. But at the moment we're down here in the thick of things."

"So you *won't* answer me. Should have known. Okay, I'll ask you another question. What do your kind want *me* to do?" he said. "You can tell me. You can *talk*. You're a dragon."

Tretz nodded. "Yes. I am. And a man."

"My friend Rainer is one of your followers."

Tretz's expression softened to affection. "He is. Rainer

Stope is a good man. And the fact that he loves you like a brother says a lot about *you*, Wulf von Dunstig."

"He says you're the first to hatch. The first land-dragon to wake up. That's what Rainer claims."

"Yes."

"Since I was young, my own dragon has been in here, in my head. The Dragon Shenandoah. The dragon under the valley," Wulf tapped his forehead. "But it's been all dreams. Visions of centuries smashed together. Sometimes I think it's all nothing. Meaningless. What sense are you supposed to make out of an unborn baby's dreams? But *you* can tell me. You woke up. What do these visions mean? What am I supposed to do about them?"

Tretz smiled. "It's like you say. They're dreams. What does a mountain 'mean'?"

"Great. No answer." Wulf shook his head. "I'm probably going to die down here, so it doesn't matter anyway."

"You are asking the wrong question, Wulf."

"Blood and bones, what's the *right* question then?"

Tretz smiled broadly, baring his teeth. Wulf saw that his human appearance hadn't returned completely. The man's teeth were as pointed as an alligator's.

"You have grown up in stony places, Wulf. Castles. Forts."

"I suppose so. Sure."

"Let's say a man is in a building. A castle. *His* castle. And the castle is caving in all around him. Not just crumbling. Collapsing. It's old. The time has come. Timbers are cracking. Stones are falling. The man is doing all he can to shore up his castle, but it's no use. The castle is done for. If he stays there, he will be killed. He'll be dead and buried under the rubble."

"What about using the front gate?"

"Good idea. It's not closed. Somebody has opened it."

"So all he has to do is step through? Get out?"

"All he has to do is step through."

"So obviously, he should not stand there and die. He shouldn't waste time trying to prop up something that can't be fixed. He should save himself," Wulf said. He shrugged. "He can always build another castle."

"Yes, if he wants to," Tretz said. "Or build something else. Build somewhere else. Or make nothing at all. Just hit the road. See the world. It's not the castle that matters. It's the man."

"You're saying the whole world is a run-down castle?"

"I'm saying the world is what it is. What matters is *you*. People. What you choose to do in every moment. Be brave. Be smart. Be just. Be kind. Choose. It cuts a line through the Never and Forever. It makes you who you are. All of this—" Tretz turned his hand up, gestured at the cavern around them. "It's just *not* as important as who you are."

"I'd really like to get out of here, then. And to take my friends with me," Wulf said. "I wish you would help me be brave about *that*."

Tretz chuckled. He had a nice, quick laugh, Wulf thought.

For the first time in months, Wulf felt a spark of hope.

"Of course I'll help," Tretz said. "You only had to *ask*." The mandrake smiled. "Though it'll probably take me a month to sleep off what it'll do to me."

"What do you mean?"

"The use of dasein *always* has a price." Tretz snapped a finger as if he'd just remembered something. "Oh, that reminds me. There has been an owl person flittering around the pits, looking for you. I had a talk with her not long ago."

"What was her name?" Wulf asked quietly, hardly daring to hope.

"I know her by her true name, of course. You could never pronounce it."

"And what did this owl person say?" Wulf whispered.

"She said she didn't come alone," Tretz said. "That help is here." He smiled his jagged smile. "Maybe there's a reason you're down here after all. Or maybe it's absurd and meaningless. Either way, what are *you* going to *do*, Wulf von Dunstig?"

Chapter Forty-Seven:
The Kettle

Sergeant Crepin Benoit was worried about his dogs. He liked to keep a kennel for hunting on Saint's Days. He had seven dogs in all. Each of them was even *named* after a saint. Most dogs in the village near the mines got by on table scraps and squirrels and rabbits they could run down in the woods. But Crepin's hounds were special. Each week he carefully collected the best pieces of the butcher's slop that was shipped in from Montserrat.

It was all supposed to go to the slaves in the pits of course, but what good would it do *that* rabble? Much better for it to go to the upkeep of fine canines. The slaves could have whatever was left over. And if it seemed like they were a little short on meat during the week, he could always pick up some dead horse or cow from a farmer and throw that in the slave slop.

But lately almost all the barrels of slop from the big city had gotten thinner and thinner on the meat. They also gotten thicker and thicker on the grease in the renderings.

He wondered if folks were going hungry in Montserrat. They seemed to be eating pig intestines and cow tongues now.

If so, the pit master had not seen fit to inform his workers. Pit Master Theriot, who lived in the big house and never even visited the mines unless some functionaries showed up from the capital, seldom shared any news with his dominates like Crepin.

Crepin didn't really care. As long as he got his mental instructions every morning and carried them out as well as a fellow was able, he generally kept his master out of his mind. He could go about his own business in his own way.

But his dogs were beginning to get sickly, and that was a shame. Crepin held out as much of the organ meat as he could in the shipment. That made the slave gruel for today particularly thin, but no one but the slaves would notice.

Because of that, his dogs would get some much-needed hearts, gizzards, livers, and guts.

He attached the big wooden crane to the hook on the food kettle. With a grunt, he swung it out over the pit hole. Then, taking hold of the block and tackle crank, he lowered the kettle of lukewarm food down into the depths below.

He'd wait the allotted quarter of a watch and then pull it back up. He did this whether the slaves were finished eating or not. And if he short changed them a little on the time, he might get a few more choice pieces that the slaves missed in their rush to eat.

While he was waiting, Crepin went through the list of his dogs. Crepin loved his dogs, but he was very detached about their worth to him. He considered whether each was holding up his or her end of the bargain in hunts, or whether it was time to put one of *them* down. If so, he would add them to the slave kettle meal one day. He'd already done that with his old favorite, Boudin.

Poor mutt. Down the slave gullets he went.

There were other dogs that had gone into the soup. There was his bluetick hound, Laveau. There was old Sazerac, and young Tchoup, who both got bit by a cottonmouth and died a terrible death together. Crepin had cried over them.

There was the twin fitches, Marigny and Mignon, who got mauled by a bear. Yes, the slaves were lucky to have eaten such wonderful dogs.

Now that he thought about it, it really wasn't like he was stealing the meat from the slaves. They got it sooner or later. Why hadn't he thought of this before? They got the meat, even if it did go through the belly of a dog beforehand.

When it came down to it, the slaves were really eating better than they deserved.

Crepin felt a swelling of pride at the thought.

They were lucky to have him as their cook.

✛ ✛ ✛

Eusebi Guidry received the food kettle at the bottom of Pit Three and maneuvered it over to the middle of the main shaft so that the slaves could gather round on all sides and dip in hands for their daily meal. After he got the kettle placed, he usually sat back and watched the scum go at their gruel like the pigs they were.

But this evening, there was a commotion toward the village cave entrance. Good. Eusebi got out his club with the spikes in it. He was proud of how wicked the weapon looked and was happy to get a chance to use it. He went to see what the problem was.

Near the cavern entrance, two slaves were rolling on the floor in what looked like a choking match. Probably a fight over a piece of food or a woman or something. No matter.

Eusebi raised an arm and took to beating them until they let go of each other. He had to turn the back of one of the men into a bloody mess with the club to get him off the other. That had been satisfying.

When it was done, the two fighters scurried off, and Eusebi went back to the kettle to make sure nobody took too much. The slaves were selfish and didn't like to share one bit. When they got a nice chunk of something, they held onto it for dear life.

Selfish.

They were all scum. Animals.

Every one of them deserved to be here.

And there a man and woman were, tugging at both ends of a piece of . . . what was that? Eusebi couldn't quite identify what variety of meat it was they were fighting over. But he knew he had to put a stop to this nonsense. He moved between them and reached to snatch the meat from both their hands. But when he did, something strange happened.

From inside the kettle, a *human* arm reached out. The hand on the arm grabbed hold of his wrist—

"What the cold hell . . ." Eusebi muttered.

Before he knew it, Eusebi was being pulled into the soup. At first, he was so confused that he did nothing. But then when his head was almost under, he realized something bad was happening.

To him.

He tried to yank back. But that hand, the creepy, disembodied hand, was holding him steady. And something was weighing his back. He could not stand up.

His face went into the gruel. Into the slop.

He began to thrash about. He tried to reach his club but couldn't feel where he had stashed it in his belt.

What? Oh, that's right! I dropped it when I got yanked down. Maybe it's floating in the soup?

He reached around, scrambling to grasp it. His hands thrashed around. Nothing. Nothing to grab hold of, and he was being held down, pushed down.

When he knew he could stay down no longer without

breathing in some of the vile liquid, he put everything he had into thrusting himself up.

Eusebi was young and strong. He managed to do it for moment. He managed to clear his head above water long enough to catch a portion of a breath.

Unfortunately at that moment he also felt a tremendous crack in his head. He didn't actually feel any pain.

Just a ringing in his ears.

A tremendous pressure in his skull.

And then another crack.

The pressure was released.

Eusebi had two final thoughts then.

One was: Somebody found my club.

The second was:

At least I didn't drown in slop.

Cook Crepin Benoit cracked a smile as he worked the block and tackle to lift the kettle back out of the pit. It was quite heavy today. He supposed that rascal Eusebi had not let the slaves at it for very long. He was probably punishing them for something or another. That was his way.

Poor Eusebi. It had to be difficult being down there and controlling all those animals. You had to put them in their place once in a while—and come down hard. He didn't blame Eusebi, but, cold hell, it was a heavy kettle this time coming up.

The big metal pot cleared the lip of the pit. Crepin

brought it up another elb or two, and then swung it toward its resting stand in the cooking area. Crepin chuckled. Oh yes, the dogs would eat well tonight, thanks to Eusebi!

Crepin leaned over to see what delicacies he might find in the leftover gruel. There was *so much* slop left! He gazed down into the gray murk, looking for nice floating bits to strain out.

But then he saw something curious. One of those floating chunks of meat look like . . . well, it looked like a *human hand*.

He reached down and grabbed hold of it. Was this some kind of prank Eusebi was playing on him? If it was, it wasn't funny! Crepin pulled on the hand. It was attached to an arm. He pulled on that until the rest of a body surfaced.

Sacre bleu!

It was Eusebi!

What was going on?

Before Crepin could consider the question for long, the water next to Eusebi's body erupted. Another form, not dead at all, leapt out. He couldn't make out who it might be. But he could tell from the bedraggled clothing that it was a slave.

A slave, hiding in the soup!

Eusebi's club swung again. It connected with the side of Crepin's head. One of the spikes dug into his temple. This was like somebody dousing a complete fire with one bucket of water.

Crepin was dead before he hit the ground.

His dogs would go hungry tonight.

CHAPTER FORTY-EIGHT:
THE ROAR

There were ten guards milling around the pit entrance when the slaves came rushing out. They charged out of the pit with murder in their eyes.

The guards didn't panic.

This had happened before, and it had been easy enough to put down.

The way the staircase was made, only one person could come up at a time. So even if there were a hundred rebels, they still had to take on the pit guards one by one. In this way the slaves were always outnumbered. Not only that, there were two watchtowers with archers at the ready—or at least as ready as bored men could be, men who spent more time shooting rabbits than escaped prisoners.

Still, the guard towers would be expected to rain down a few arrows.

But this night there were no shots coming from the towers.

And when the guards on the ground charged forward, something began to hit them from behind. Two were immediately knocked over the edge of the pit. They fell screaming to their deaths. The guard at the pit entrance pulled out his sword and was swinging down when he was caught from behind by a strand of rope and pulled backward, choking. Whoever had a hold on him jerked the sword from his hand. While the guard was trying to deal with the rope around his neck, whoever had taken his sword then plunged it up and through his chest.

This left six more guards facing a whirling dervish at the pit entrance.

More slaves rose up from the pit. They were swarming out of the hole in the ground like a bunch of ants.

This was when the guards tried to run. But the dervish wouldn't let them. It caught up with them. They were fenced in by the very pen that kept slaves from leaving the area around the pit.

The dervish hunted three of them down. Each of the three tried to fight, but when they faced this dervish, this being, each realized they were up against something beyond their training. Their awkward strikes never did connect with flesh.

Perhaps the dervish had no flesh.

All the while, the dervish cut them to pieces. It did so

either quickly or with several slices that took off limbs or opened bellies.

It wasn't really a dervish, of course.

It was Wulf von Dunstig.

The guards just did not understand that they were facing a man who had trained most of his childhood to use a sword, a club—whatever weapon came to hand. Master Koterbaum had made sure of that.

These guards' own training was spotty at best, and mostly nonexistent.

As for the other three guards, the rioting slaves took care of them. Two slaves got life-ending wounds as a result, but that didn't stop the others. And since the slaves didn't have any edged weapons, they resorted to tearing the guards apart.

Just as they had the rocks in the pits.

With their bare hands.

The screams went on and on until all the guards lay dead.

"All right," shouted Wulf, who had ridden up in the kettle of slop. "Is everybody from the other pits lined up to come out of Pit Three?"

The Underground Senate leader who had coordinated the revolt with Wulf came beside him. He reported that yes, the rest of the slaves in all of the mine pits were concentrated in the Pit Three cavern. The guards had been taken care of at all levels now.

All they had to do was climb out.

"But the other pits have their own contingents of guards," said the senator. "I'm a little fuzzy about what you plan to do about them."

"Trust me. It's like I said. They will be taken care of," Wulf replied. "As soon as everyone has gathered into the main cavern of Pit Three, you are to close and seal off that interconnecting tunnel. Send word. Do it fast, like I asked you to."

"It's already done, Pale Man," said the senator. "There's no going back to the other pits that way now. We caused quite a cave-in."

"I hope it's enough to keep the fire out," Wulf said. He turned toward one of the watchtowers. Someone above had lit a torch. They were touching this torch to an arrow wound with pitch-soaked muslin. In the flicker of the fire, Wulf could see that the bowman had flowing red hair.

He knew who it was even if he couldn't quite make out the face.

Ursel Keiler was here.

Then she let go of the flaming arrow. It fired up into the sky. Up. Following an arc higher higher higher, then down down down.

The arrow was bright enough to be seen from all of the pit entrances.

This was the signal.

The roar started.

At first the sound was like thunder. The ground shook. A low rumble set the air quivering like jelly.

And then, in the distance, four pillars of golden light shot up into the night sky.

They flared at least a field-march high. Then a league. Many leagues perhaps. Huge fountains of golden light.

They climbed like spouts of color beyond the wisps of clouds in the night sky. Each of these pillars of flame was as big around as the entrance to a mine pit.

Gigantic chimney fires.

Only Pit Three did not have fire shooting from its bowels. This was the pit the slaves were all emerging from.

The flames shot into the sky for a long time.

The roar went on and on.

Tretz is really scouring the pits, Wulf thought. He must hate this place. He must hate it even worse than we do.

"It's Lord Tretz!" Wulf yelled to the growing crowd of liberated slaves. "That's his roar. He kept his promise. The guards are dead or running away!"

He climbed onto a table in the kitchen area and looked down at the assembling slaves. They were milling about the entrance stairway to the pit. They seemed stunned.

"My friends," he said to them. "You're free! You're free to do what you want! But those who want to . . . if you want to . . . you can go with me!" Wulf gestured with his hand toward the northern star in the heavens. "Follow me! There's a place where you can live in liberty! A place where the slavers will never find you again!"

He turned back to watch the flares. Slowly, steadily, they

died down. The roar became a rumble. The rumble became a murmur.

Then there was silence on the land.

Done, Wulf thought.

Right.

Not done.

Not done at all. Just started.

Wulf turned to a group of young men who had taken control of the pit's block and tackle. "Hey, you men! Help me finish this. Let's get everyone up here!" Wulf shouted. "Even the donkeys. Even the centaurs!"

That seemed to break a great tension in the crowd. There was a burst of laughter.

Wulf laughed along with the others.

Then he turned back to the men at the block and tackle. They were unhitching the kettle, getting it ready for other work.

"And whoever goes down to get them . . . tell my friend something. Tell little Scando, that, yes, he can ride on that centaur's back on the way up—if he holds on tightly and doesn't fool around." The men nodded and turned to the task, but Wulf shouted for them to hold for a moment. "Something else," he said. "Tell Scando that the Moon is out. The Silver Mirror. He can finally see her. Tell him he shouldn't be afraid. She's only a reflection."

The men said they would, and cranked the rope down into the pit with one man riding on its end.

Wulf laughed again. Somehow in that moment letting Scando see the Moon felt like reason enough to have lived his life to this point.

But even freedom below the sky wouldn't be that easy for his friend.

Not being afraid of the Moon was one thing. But there were more frightening things in the sky than her.

Soon, Scando was going to see the Sun.

Bam, something hit the top of Wulf's shoulder. Hard. Claws dug into skin.

"Ouch!"

"Hello, man," said Nagel in her raspy voice. "You look *terrible.*"

CHAPTER FORTY-NINE:
THE REUNION

"I guess Nagel's message got through," said Rainer. "We found out that you and Ahorn had been sold into the pits, but we didn't know if you were still alive, or if she could find you down there."

They were five leagues from the mines now. Rainer had offered Wulf a horse, but he'd preferred to walk with the slaves who wanted to follow him. He led several hundred to the plantation that Rainer, Ravenelle, and the others were using for a base.

Both house and plantation were called "Jacinthe des Bois."

The manor house belonged to a local landlord who had been terribly treated by the Imperials, it seemed. His mind was nearly gone, and it hadn't taken much for Ravenelle to dominate his will, even if he had wanted to resist. She had also helped him regain his sanity.

In return, the others in the family and the bloodservants fell in line quickly. The family had gone to visit a nearby plantation that had also given itself over, readily, to Ravenelle's authority.

It seemed there was a great deal of ill-feeling toward the Imperials in the countryside and insurrection was in the air.

For the time being, Jacinthe des Bois was theirs. They were gathered in the parlor of the manner house. The furniture was sumptuous, but Wulf found himself having to learn, very awkwardly, how to sit in an actual chair again.

One little bloodservant girl of about six or seven had glommed onto Ravenelle, it seemed. Even now, she was following every movement of her mistress, devotion in her eyes.

"Marguerite, can you get us all a glass of water, dear?" Ravenelle asked. The little girl skipped happily away to the spring house to do her mistress's bidding.

"Nagel did get a message to me." Wulf said with a grin. He put aside the blanket he'd thrown around his shoulders and pulled on a linen shirt that Rainer had liberated from the master's wardrobe.

Fine white linen.

The feel of home.

Nagel settled back on Wulf's shoulder. If he didn't know

better, he might think the little owl was happy to see him. "Well, she found *someone*. Someone who *told* me."

He felt his face cracking from the greasy soup that had dried on his skin. He found himself *longing* to take a bath. Soon.

"We were ready to act. We in the Senate had been planning an escape—"

"The Senate?" the Skraeling named Wannas said. "You had representative bodies down *there*?"

"Not exactly," Wulf replied. "The Underground Senate is a resistance group. Sort of. Anyway, I was most worried about reaching the archers in the watchtowers before they cut us down. I didn't think we could do it. That was always the sticking point in rebellions before. Plus, there is that chokepoint at the pit entrances. But we figured out a way around that."

"The soup kettle?"

"Yep, hiding me in the soup kettle."

"I took the ones on the north end out—at least the ones on the north end," said a woman's voice. The accent was from Bear Valley. Ursel Keiler entered the room. She'd been stowing her bow.

"Ursel's new friends—these Skraelings from Potomak who came down to see you—they got the others," Rainer put in.

"We have a lot to talk about," Wulf said.

But only one thing I really want to hear.

Wulf couldn't help it. He felt his spirit cringe inside, fearing the worse. "Tell me about Saeunn."

Rainer nodded toward Ursel. "That is Mistress Keiler's to tell," he said.

"Ursel, what does Rainer mean?"

"He means that Saeunn is alive, m'lord," Ursel replied. "She is resting at Bear Hall."

"That's not all. Ursel gave her life again," Rainer said. "I saw it."

"Saeunn is *cured* Wulf," Ravenelle said. "At least we think so."

Wulf turned to Ursel, tears forming in his eyes. "How?"

"It's a long story, m'lord," Ursel replied. "For now she sleeps deeply. But Abendar Anderolan thinks she will awaken and be Saeunn again."

Wulf wiped the wetness from his eyes with the dirty back of his palm. "If she had been dead . . ."

I would die, too. Right now. Even after fighting so hard for so long to stay alive.

"You know that's why I did it," Ursel said. "You don't even have to say it." Her voice was measured, but Wulf thought he could hear the hint of anguish behind it.

Ursel had saved Saeunn. Saved her rival.

"I'll never be able to repay you," Wulf said. "You have my friendship and loyalty forever, Ursel."

Ursel frowned. "I'm honored, m'lord," she said darkly. Then she shook her head as if to clear away bad thoughts.

She chuckled. "I'll always be there for you, Wulf. Until my dying breath. You can count on it."

Wulf nodded. "I know," he said.

"Right now we need to get the mine slaves spread out and hidden," Ravenelle said. "There are Romans soldiers within a league of here. They're heading this way."

"How did you—" Wulf began.

Ravenelle tapped her head. "You know how," she answered. "I hear their thoughts. Works within a league or so."

"Then how are we going to keep the miners safe? The Romans will just round them up and put them in the pits again."

"Ravenelle has control over this plantation and several others nearby," Rainer said. "Word is spreading that the Dark Angel Princess has returned."

Ravenelle shook her head. "If they think I'm really an angel with special powers, they're going to be very much disappointed," she said.

"We're going to spread them out," Rainer continued. "The good thing is that the miners *aren't* bloodservants. Their minds can't be detected or taken over with Talaia. They can hide practically in plain sight."

"A man once told me that there was one good thing about working in the mines," Wulf said with a chuckle. "I guess he was right."

The servant girl Marguerite returned with a silver tray.

On it were several goblets all filled with cold water from the manor-house spring. Helping her not to spill anything was a ragamuffin boy. He was grinning from ear to ear. They carefully set the tray on a side table in the parlor.

"Scando," Wulf said. "What have you been doing?"

"You were right, Pale Man," the boy said to Wulf. "I tried, but I *couldn't* look at the Eyeburner for very long. Maybe I'll get better at this, though. Or does its fire sometimes get weaker?"

"Never," Wulf said. "Have you heard from Mater Om?"

"The bloodservants have found a place for her and the children. They are in a barn basement near the servant quarters. It is a clean warm place. Also a good place for hiding. And there's *so much* food! Bread! Sticky sweet stuff!"

"Jelly? Honey?"

"I do not know, Pale Man."

"If you need to know what anything is, you come and ask me, Scando."

"Or *me*," said little Marguerite. She looked up at Scando as if he were some kind of hero. Whatever meager things the bloodservant girl possessed would seem like a fortune to Scando.

"I don't need you for a while, Marguerite," Ravenelle said. "Why don't you show this young man around some more."

Marguerite curtseyed. It was so delicate and sincere, the form didn't matter.

She turned to Scando. "I'll show you the pigs," she said.

"But you have to be *very* careful around them. And then I'll show you where the crown was hidden in the chicken house." Marguerite turned reverentially back to Ravenelle. "The Dark Angel Princess's crown. Want to see that?"

Scando was not used to such dedicated girlish attention. He hung his head and stammered. "Sure, I guess so."

Marguerite, who seemed totally fearless, took Scando by the hand and they ran out of the mansion parlor together.

Wulf's faun servant Bleak—who had survived the Roman attack, wandered with the remnant of survivors until he'd found Rainer, and who then accompanied the rescue party back south—took up the tray of water from where the excited children had left it and offered some to all.

Wulf took a sip. The spring water was so pure. So clean. So good.

"So the locals don't like the Romans?" he asked Ravenelle.

"They hate the Imperials. The leader, this horrible Roman inquisitor person, is threatening to take over and burn the queen."

"And your mother? Is she alive? Is she fighting back?"

Ravenelle nodded, but had to wipe away a stain of bloody wetness from her own eyes. "I don't know. We think she's a prisoner. The local folks tell me this inquisitor prelate has captured the castle, but he is keeping her alive for now."

"We have to do what we can to free her."

"We have to beat these Imperials and take back my

kingdom," Ravenelle said with resolve. "Which would *also* save your barbarian landholdings in the process." She cracked a smile.

Wulf nodded. "Yes. We are allies now. And we always will be, Ravenelle. You're my dear sister."

"I agree," Ravenelle replied.

Wulf was about to say more, but the realization had overcome him yet again.

. "Saeunn Amberstone is alive," Wulf said, just to hear himself speak the words.

"She is. And she has a new star, m'lord," Ursel replied.

"Saeunn's new star might have something of Ursel in it as well," Ravenelle said, a teasing look on her face. "Seeing as the amber arrow she used to make the star was born out of Ursel's *own* body."

Wulf shook his head. "I want to hear it all," he said. "But we have a lot to take care of now." Wulf took another long drink of water. He turned to Rainer. "There is something else. Some news I have for *you*."

"Me?"

"That's right, Rainer Stope," Wulf replied. "I happened to meet somebody you know in the mines. Somebody I think is an old friend of yours."

Rainer lifted an eyebrow. "Who would I know down *there?*"

"I'll tell you about it later," Wulf said. "All about it." He turned and gazed around at his rescuers. His friends. His family. "Right now, all I want to do is get the cold hell back to Shenandoah. Then we have to fight Romans."

"I'm with you," Rainer said. "But I expect Ulla might be waiting for us up north with a little surprise of her own."

"I'm in," Ravenelle said. "And I pledge my kingdom, as well. What little my family still retains."

"Even if we have to take down Rome herself and all the bishops?" Wulf asked.

"To save my mother? Even that."

"Good," Wulf said. "Because I met something in the mine. Some*one*. Or maybe he has been around all along and has just now shown himself to *me*. Not sure that it matters which. All I know is that what we're doing is not just about kingdoms and who rules anymore. We have to rid a great evil from the world."

"Either way is fine with me," Rainer said. A ferocious smile spread across his face. "I'll leave the philosophy to you, Wulf. I just want to fight Romans."

✟ END ✟